MW00630180

# THE IRON DOOR

*The Eighth Brian Sadler
Archaeological Thriller*

Bill Thompson

Published by
Ascendente Books
Dallas, Texas

This is a work of fiction. Where real people, events, businesses, organizations and locales appear, they are used fictitiously. All other elements of this novel are products of the author's imagination. The author has represented and warranted full ownership and/or legal rights to publish all the materials in this book.

The Iron Door
All Rights Reserved
Copyright © 2022
V.1.0

This book may not be reproduced, transmitted or stored in whole or in part by any means, including graphic, electronic or mechanical without the express written consent of the author except in the case of brief quotations embodied in critical articles and reviews.

Published by Ascendente Books
ISBN 978-17355661-7-7
Printed in the United States of America

## Books by Bill Thompson

Mysterious America Series
**SERPENT**

The Bayou Hauntings Series
**CALLIE**
**FORGOTTEN MEN**
**THE NURSERY**
**BILLY WHISTLER**
**THE EXPERIMENTS**
**DIE AGAIN**
**THE PROCTOR HALL HORROR**
**THE ATONEMENT**

Brian Sadler Archaeological Mystery Series
**THE BETHLEHEM SCROLL**
**ANCIENT: A SEARCH FOR THE LOST CITY**
**OF THE MAYAS**
**THE STRANGEST THING**
**THE BONES IN THE PIT**
**ORDER OF SUCCESSION**
**THE BLACK CROSS**
**TEMPLE**
**THE IRON DOOR**

Apocalyptic Fiction
**THE OUTCASTS**

The Crypt Trilogy
**THE RELIC OF THE KING**
**THE CRYPT OF THE ANCIENTS**
**GHOST TRAIN**

Middle Grade Fiction
**THE LEGEND OF GUNNERS COVE**

**THE LAST CHRISTMAS**

This book is dedicated to a small cadre of my readers who kept after me to finish the Brian Sadler series. None of those was more persistent than Wes Moore, and without the nudges from him and others, I likely wouldn't have gone back to my first protagonist and the series I greatly enjoyed writing.

Thanks to Steve Wilson and a plethora of other authors whose exciting stories that appeared in True Treasure and Treasure World magazines back in the seventies filled my mind with thoughts of adventure and buried treasure.

# Author's Note

I wrote seven archaeological mysteries featuring treasure hunter and antiquities dealer Brian Sadler, his lawyer girlfriend and wife, Nicole Farber, and his best friend, Harry Harrison. When I switched genres in 2019 and began the Bayou Hauntings series of ghost stories, many readers asked for an ending to Brian's saga. This book, the last Brian Sadler mystery, won't connect every thread, but I hope you'll consider it a satisfying conclusion. I spent a lot of time at archaeological sites and climbing ruins to get the meat for these novels, and they were my favorites to write.

Although this is a work of fiction, its theme is based on actual legends. If you do an internet search for "outlaw cave, Belle Starr's cave, or cave of the iron door," you'll find a lot of interesting material. Although many believe the treasure exists, so far no one's found it. Then again, it's on protected federal land, making it impossible to perform an intrusive search like the Lagina brothers are performing in the legendary Money Pit on Oak Island, Nova Scotia.

The article Harry Harrison mentions reading in the 1970s is real. It appeared in the March 1970 issue of *Treasure World* magazine and was called "The Door that Guards $11,000,000." Steve Wilson, the author, has written more Oklahoma treasure tales than anyone, and he graciously allowed me to use his name, cite the article, and take the substance of it for my book. Thanks, Steve, for that permission.

The Wichita Mountains are as rugged as I depict them. In the 1980s, my boys and I camped near Elk Mountain several times, having a fun weekend looking for the iron door. We never found it, but I have a hunch it still sits high up on a cliff overlooking a canyon.

Although train robberies occurred now and then in

Oklahoma Territory, the one depicted in this book is fictional. Belle Starr, the Younger brothers, and Jesse and Frank James robbed trains, and it's hardly a stretch to imagine them hijacking this one and carrying off the valuables to a secret hiding place in the Wichitas.

Oh, there's one last thing I should mention. Does the President's Book of Secrets exist? In a 2009 interview, President Obama said he'd seen it, but when the interviewer asked what it contained, he said, "I would tell you, but I'd have to kill you." How interesting!

I hope you enjoy reading *The Iron Door* as much as I enjoyed writing it. It's always fun spinning a yarn about a missing treasure.

# CHAPTER ONE

*My fellow presidents, can you decipher this puzzle?*
*Believe you can and you're halfway there.*

*Four four six one has frame and glass,*
*And something hid—a needed clue*
*To find the pass.*

*Inside the frame, wings in the air*
*Protect a secret I, six two,*
*Have hidden there.*

*The Cache is real, tho many doubt*
*Or laugh in scorn, and yet tis true*
*What it's about.*

*When Quanah Parker fought a war*
*He said he saw it, and could view*
*It from afar.*

*Pah-Che-Ka's face from Post Oak grave*
*Conceals a clue, and with it you*
*Might find a cave.*

*My numbers aren't as they appear.*
*To understand, read like a Jew*
*To make them clear.*

*Who wrote these words? a man might ask.*
*I'm Dutch Reformed, another clue*
*To ease your task.*

*To ye who follow in my stead*
*And puzzle deeply, ponder you*
*These words I said.*

*Undated and unsigned poem handwritten on page 87 of the*
*President's Book of Secrets.*

# CHAPTER TWO

*February, eleven months ago*

Brian Sadler and his wife, Nicole Farber, sat on a couch in the Treaty Room, the private sitting room in the president's residence. They'd been frequent visitors to the second floor of the White House since William Henry Harrison IV became America's leader. Harry joked Brian was here so often he should keep a change of clothes in the closet of the Lincoln bedroom.

Tonight's visit was a bittersweet reunion. Harry Harrison was immensely popular, and leaders of both parties had considered his reelection a sure thing. He'd been John Chapman's vice president, serving the remaining two years of Chapman's term after his untimely death. When he ran for a full term, he won by an unprecedented margin. This time he'd face no primary opponent, and victory in the general election was almost a certainty.

Three days ago, everything had changed when Harry dropped a bombshell on his party and the nation. In a two-minute prime-time broadcast, he announced he would not seek reelection. He took no questions, offered no explanation, and even his closest friend Brian Sadler had been caught by surprise. Minutes after the announcement, Harry called Brian and asked if he and Nicole could come spend the night as soon as possible. Brian, who was working in London, called his wife in Dallas, and they were in DC two days later. Tonight they sat across a coffee table from Brian's college roommate, the president of the United States, and his wife, Jennifer. Brian had been best man at their wedding, and Harry had reciprocated when Brian and Nicole were married in the White House just downstairs from where they sat tonight.

"I owe you an apology," Harry began, and Brian shushed him.

"You owed me an apology that time when you let me think you, Jennifer, and the girls were dead." That episode had terrified Nicole and him, and it had been weeks before they learned it wasn't true. "Your decision to leave the presidency is none of my business. I get it; in fact, the first thought I had was how tough your job is. Nicole and I have seen far more about what goes on here than the average American, since we've been privileged to be on the inside thanks to you all. I can't imagine the toll it takes on you and your family. That said, I'm sure your announcement shook your party leaders to the core."

"Yes, and that was the hardest part. I love this job, and I've enjoyed ninety-nine percent of what we've done in six years. The folks who run the Republican party helped me get elected, and I was blessed to get some things done that moved our country in the right direction. With a high approval rating like mine, it was completely unfair to pull the rug out from under them."

Nicole looked at him blankly. "Then why? Why leave?"

The president sighed. "Why. That's the question on everyone's mind. I can't tell you..." He paused, and Jennifer put her arm around his shoulders. "I can't tell you everything because we don't know everything ourselves." He drew in a deep breath and wiped a tear from his eye. "This is hard."

Brian had never seen Harry this emotional. He took Nicole's hand and said, "What is it, Harry? What's going on?"

Another tear rolled down Harry's cheek.

"It's my mother. She's been diagnosed with a rare brain disease. No cure, no hope. Always fatal. The only unknown is how much time she has. Months, perhaps a year, the doctors say. I don't have time to be president anymore. *She* doesn't have time for me to be president."

Nicole said, "Are they sure? Has she seen a specialist?"

"The best. It took a while to diagnose because it's so uncommon. She and Dad went to a neurological center in Houston. A specialist there wrote the book on this disease, and he's certain of it."

Nicole and Brian cried along with their friends. "I'm so sorry," she said. "What can we do?"

"Nothing," Jennifer said softly. "There's nothing anyone can do, not even Julia herself."

The president's parents were lifelong residents of Oklahoma. William Henry Harrison III had been a United States senator with Julia as his faithful sidekick, campaigning and politicking for decades until his retirement several years ago. In their mid-seventies now, the couple lived in the upscale Nichols Hills neighborhood of Oklahoma City but spent most of their time at their thousand-acre ranch an hour away.

Brian recalled how much Henry and Julia loved the ranch's rolling hills and verdant pastures. He paused when he realized how these memories distressed Harry and Jennifer.

"They're leaving the ranch, Brian. Jennifer and I went down there last week, and Dad told me he was putting it on the market. Mom's got moderate issues now involving using her hands and walking, but it's going to get worse fast, and they have to move to Oklahoma City, where she's close to the care she'll require."

Nicole's eyes widened. "Oh my gosh. They're selling the ranch?"

"That was the plan, but the minute I heard, I put a stop to it. Jennifer and I are buying it, and it'll stay in the family. We're going to live there. It was while we were in Oklahoma that I decided not to run again. As you can imagine, Mom was furious. She refused to let her issues interfere with mine, but deep inside, we all knew it had to happen this way.

"I'm their only child, and Kate and Lizzie their only grandchildren. I can't stay in DC fifteen hundred miles from them and try to focus on running the country when she faces a terminal prognosis. As soon as school's out for summer, Jennifer and the kids will move to the ranch. I'll come out when I can until the inauguration, and then I'll move too. You know the place; it's already set up for presidential security since it's been my western White House. Airstrip, Secret Service quarters, the whole nine yards. It's perfect for a former president's home."

Nicole voiced what was on both their minds. "The entire country is wondering why you decided not to run. Are you going to tell them?"

"I must, as much as I wish I could avoid it. I'll hold a press conference in the next few days. I hate to invade my parents' privacy at a time like this, but of all people, Dad and Mom know what it's like being in the spotlight every minute. He dealt with it for thirty years in the Senate, and now he has to deal with it again because of me."

Brian said, "Can I change the subject for a moment?"

Jennifer smiled. "Please do. That's why we asked you all to come. If anything can take our minds off all this, it's having you and Nicole here."

"You're forty-six years old, Harry. You've already been president, so what do you plan to do when you grow up?"

Everyone laughed easily for the first time tonight, and Harry chuckled the hardest. He and Brian shared a bond built upon decades of friendship. As leader of the free world, Harry could confide in only a handful of people with confidence that his thoughts would remain confidential. Brian was one of those.

"Until recent events transpired, I was bent on running again so I could spend four more years playing God for the American people. Now I'm forced to consider a future outside of politics. Everybody knows ex-presidents can never be 'normal' people. I can't join a startup company board, or open a law practice, or even volunteer with a charity. It's too big a hassle—the security alone is a burden no outsider should have to contend with. Jennifer and I will never really have time just for our family. The Secret Service will always be somewhere close by. I appreciate their help, and I understand why it has to be, but it makes things harder. To answer your question about what I'm doing next, I'm considering indulging my inner child by playing with trains."

Brian smiled. "Trains? Are you going to buy a railroad?" It was a tongue-in-cheek remark; the Harrison family had wealth, but nothing like that of some of their friends in Oklahoma City who'd become billionaires in the oil and gas industry.

"I'm thinking about writing a book. Seems like every former president has one, and it's a project that wouldn't interfere with my helping care for Mom. I don't want to write my autobiography—I'm too young to say I'm all finished. A political thriller like Bill Clinton wrote would be fun, but I'd like to write about something different that I enjoyed as a child. I loved my Lionel train set, I love Oklahoma history and reading about hidden treasure in the Wild West, and I'd love to write a book about trains and train robbers back when what's now our state was Oklahoma Territory and Indian Territory. Maybe a treasure novel."

A native Okie, the state's history had been drilled into Harry's head since the first grade, but Brian, who grew up in Longview, Texas, knew far less about the state that had been created from two territories in 1907.

"There were outlaws in Oklahoma?"

Harry said, "You bet. Names you'd recognize—Jesse James, the Younger gang, and the Daltons. Belle Starr. Bonnie and Clyde. Pretty Boy Floyd. All of them either lived in Oklahoma or pulled heists there. Others have written about them, but I'd like to give it a shot myself."

"An author? Well, it should suit you. You've always had the gift of gab, and you're a lawyer, so you should be able to spin a yarn people would enjoy. Being famous doesn't hurt either. I'm sure some publisher will give you a million or two for the rights."

"Coming from you, that's encouraging. You know a little about the media yourself." Harry laughed. As the owner of several high-end galleries specializing in some of the world's rarest antiquities, Brian had become a television celebrity, appearing often on cable news to discuss ancient relics. His archaeological documentaries on the History Channel had enthralled millions of armchair adventurers around the world, and along the way Brian had become a multimillionaire.

He also was familiar with security, although nothing approaching the level afforded the president. During the search for a horde of ancient treasure in Israel a few years ago, Brian had crossed the wrong people, and to this day his name remained on an ISIS hit list. The man who killed Brian Sadler would receive a million euros, and these days an armed bodyguard accompanied Brian whenever he traveled outside the United States.

Brian said, "The moment I heard you were leaving, I thought we should do something together. You're aware I'm wrapping up a job for the British Museum, but before long I'll be looking for another adventure. Now that I learned you're interested in outlaws and treasure, it'd be a blast working on it together."

Harry agreed but again pointed out the logistics would be a nightmare. "It's tempting," he added. "I've envied your adventures, even though I've had to get you out of trouble more than once."

Nicole jumped in. "That's because he doesn't understand the difference between caution and perilous risk. He's like a dog on the hunt. No matter how dangerous things get, he'll keep pushing ahead to see what's around the next corner or down the next hidden corridor in some temple somewhere."

With raised eyebrows Brian conceded she was right, saying her concern had made him more cautious over the years.

She rolled her eyes. "Seriously? I hadn't noticed. I

guess the subtle move in risk tolerance from crazy to semi-crazy is somehow supposed to be comforting." She squeezed his hand, a signal that this wasn't entirely a serious conversation. They all knew Brian's penchant for adventure. It had gotten him stranded in a cave in Guatemala with a dislocated shoulder; joining forces with a Mafia don to find a priceless scroll; and looking for treasure in Oak Island's Money Pit. Nicole had promised not to stand in his way, although every new adventure grated even more on her than the last. Now in their mid-forties, she wanted to settle down, while Brian was still searching for that next big thrill.

He said, "I'll keep you in the loop about my activities once you leave office. I know you'll have to stay close to your mother, but maybe we can work on something together that fits for you. Who knows? It's worth staying in touch, right?"

"Sure," Harry replied half-heartedly as a white-gloved steward entered the room with a fresh round of drinks. Once he left, Harry mused, "You'd better enjoy this while you can. After I'm out of here, don't expect a valet to fix your drinks when you come to the ranch. You'll be on your own."

They sat in silence, enjoying a time of somber reflection among four old friends, two of whom faced the heartbreaking inevitability of a parent's death. None could have imagined that a strange set of events would bring them together again in this very room.

# CHAPTER THREE

*Present Day*

Inauguration Day dawned crisp and clear, a monumental, quadrennial event that showed the American democratic process to the world. A duly elected president, applauded by many while disparaged by others, would take the oath of office at noon. The inauguration committee had worked for weeks to ensure it would come off without a hitch.

There was an air of anticipation as the final attendees were ushered to their seats. Outgoing president Harry Harrison paused to acknowledge Nicole and Brian as he and Jennifer descended the stairs to take their places. Behind them walked vice president-elect Archibald Perrin, holding hands with his wife Dee. They took their seats next to the Harrisons.

Only one seat remained, a front-row chair on the aisle reserved for Barbara Whittington. When she was seated, her inauguration as the first woman President of the United States would begin.

"She's playing this to the hilt, making everyone wait for her grand entrance," Brian whispered to Nicole as the assemblage chatted amiably and waited.

Nicole agreed. "This is her crowning glory, and she wouldn't miss the chance to bask in the limelight. She's just running late from the breakfast she hosted for her Florida delegation at the Carillon Tower Hotel." She looked over to a row of empty seats to her left. "Looks like none of them are back from breakfast yet. That doesn't seem right."

"But the vice president's here—"

"Because she snubbed him. He wasn't invited; so much for party unity. The Hill is buzzing about how she detests Senator Perrin, but he delivered those New York votes. Once she's president, he's no longer needed. The right-wing Republicans think she's a Socialist, and even the moderates in her party call her a RINO—Republican in name only. And don't even get me started on how much the Dems hate her."

At the top of the stairs behind them, the doors leading into the Capitol flew open with a bang. "Here we go," Brian muttered, uncrossing his legs so he could stand for the new president's grand entrance. But instead of Whittington, four Secret Service agents flew down the stairs to the front row. One leaned into the vice president-elect and whispered something, and at once Perrin and his wife stood and moved into the aisle. Two agents whisked them up the stairs as the other two led Harry and Jennifer out. There was a clear sense of urgency, and Harry glanced at Brian, raising his eyebrows as they passed. The dignitaries in the stands wondered among themselves what was going on.

Two minutes later when stone-faced agents ushered out the justices of the Supreme Court, everyone knew something had gone terribly wrong. A senator stood to confront a Capitol policeman, but he was ordered to take his seat.

The rows emptied one at a time as the dignitaries, accompanied by armed Capitol police officers, filed back into the Capitol. Down on the mall before them, more than a hundred thousand onlookers watched in disbelief. What was going on up there? Where was the president-elect?

The moment Nicole and Brian entered the building, a White House staffer took her arm and led her away. When Brian followed, the aide pointed to an open doorway and instructed him to wait there with everyone else. "I'll catch up with you when I can," Nicole called out over her shoulder as she was whisked down the hallway.

As Brian walked into a room filled with noise and confusion, an officer told him to turn off his cell phone. Over a hundred of Washington's power elite gathered in small groups, trying to make sense of the confusion. He looked in vain for Harry Harrison and his wife and noticed other notables missing. Vice President elect Perrin and Dee, the justices, and the majority and minority leaders all were somewhere else—a more secure location, Brian surmised. The place they'd taken Nicole.

Because his wife headed the outgoing president's transition team, Brian had met several of the senators and representatives in the room. He approached one, a senator from Brian's home state of Texas, and asked what was happening. He didn't know anything either, but just then a man in a dark suit entered the room and asked for everyone's attention. He introduced himself as Special Agent-in-Charge James Young of the FBI.

"I regret to inform you that President-elect Whittington was shot outside the Carillon Tower Hotel about twenty minutes ago. She had breakfast there and was walking from the building toward her limousine when a man breached a barricade and shot her four times before being killed by a Secret Service guard. The shooter is dead, and she is in surgery at Walter Reed Hospital."

Everyone began talking at once, and the agent shouted for quiet as he pressed his finger to a bud in his ear. He listened and then turned back to the crowd before him. "Quiet, please! Everyone, please be quiet! The president-elect is dead, ladies and gentlemen. Barbara Whittington passed away moments ago at 10:32 a.m."

Pandemonium erupted. Someone cried, "How the hell did it happen?" Another demanded to know where Archie Perrin and the justices were.

The agent assured them Perrin was safe and that Capitol police would escort them out of the building. As he walked to the door, Brian felt a tug at his sleeve. Nicole was back, and the White House credentials badge she'd removed for the ceremony hung around her neck. She handed him a guest pass on a lanyard.

"Come with me," she whispered, leading him into the hallway and through a maze of corridors to a door where Capitol police blocked a doorway. She presented her pass and Brian's, and after the guard made a quick call on his walkie-talkie, he opened the door and allowed them inside.

Brian's eyes opened wide; as he took in the scene, he realized he was about to witness something historic. Vice President elect Perrin and his wife stood beside Harry and Jennifer, talking quietly while the Chief Justice of the Supreme Court sat at a desk, writing on a legal pad.

"Is this...is he about to...?" She put a finger to her lips as the Chief Justice picked up a Bible and turned to Archie Perrin.

"Mr. Vice President-elect, we're ready to begin."

Brian and Nicole stood in surreal silence, two of twenty people who witnessed the swearing-in of Archibald Perrin as President of the United States of America. Those old enough to remember recalled the crowded cabin on *Air Force One* where Lyndon Johnson took the oath of office after Kennedy's assassination. It had happened since; just six years ago, Harry Harrison had become president when his predecessor died in office, and now Harry's own successor had been slain minutes before she was to become the nation's first female leader.

Despite clear rules for succession of power, it was a dark moment in time—another reminder of how different America had become in the years since 9/11.

# CHAPTER FOUR

Thirty minutes later, Brian and Nicole joined Harry, President Perrin and their wives in the Oval Office. Harry commented about how unusual it felt to see someone else sitting on what had been his side of the *Resolute* desk, and the new president shook his head.

"It certainly isn't where I expected to be when I woke up this morning. Everyone knows there was no love lost between Barbara Whittington and me, and I figured I'd be one of those do-nothing vice presidents who cuts ribbons in Guam or attends state funerals in Malawi. She was headstrong as hell, as you well know, and she would have done things her way."

He confessed that he was completely unprepared for any aspect of what faced him. "You know what this job entails," he told Harry. "You were thrust into it without warning when John Chapman died. How'd you handle it?"

"One step at a time, just like you will. There's a lot to learn, but there are a lot of people willing to teach you. That's the easy part; the hard part is figuring out who has your interests in mind and who doesn't."

Perrin nodded. "What about you? Would you be willing to stay for a few weeks in an advisory role?"

Everyone looked up in surprise. "Me?" Harry said. "I'm flattered, and frankly it might be helpful given the situation, but you've been in politics for a long time, Archie. You know that won't work. The people elected you, and even though I was blessed with a high approval rating, nobody wants a former president hanging around.

Your cronies, your constituents, and even our party deserve a fresh face. It won't be easy—trust me, I know—but you can do it."

"Look at it from my viewpoint," the new president argued. "I've just been thrust into the biggest job in the world. At least Barbara had ten weeks of transition, and she had an entire team in place. I've had what—an hour? And you know her; she kept me out of the loop on everything. I wasn't privy to one iota of information. Think about the good of the country, Harry. Please tell me you'll consider helping me out."

"Nobody on either side of the aisle would go for it. They'd crucify you. As you said, there's a transition team in place—*her* team. Let them guide you through the process."

Perrin snorted. "Seriously? You're not naive, Harry. Those people work—*worked*, I should say—for Whittington. Dead or alive, their loyalties lie with her, not me. Most of them hate me as much as she did. They treated me like the redheaded stepchild from election night until today. Now I'm taking the place of their heroine. Trust me, they'd rather see me fall than give me a hand. I need you." He stared at the flames dancing in the fireplace.

"The person you need is her."

Archie looked at him. "Who?"

Harry pointed to the couch across the room. "Her."

"What are you talking about?"

"You need Nicole Farber."

Nicole jumped to her feet. "Now, Harry, you wait just a minute—"

Harry's wife, Jennifer, interrupted. "Harry, what are you thinking? That would never work."

"For a number of reasons," Nicole agreed. "First of which is that I signed on to be *Harry's* transition leader, and as of today, my job is done. Like everyone present, I consider what happened to Barbara Whittington a national tragedy, but I'm not the person to lead a novice through the hoops. I'm barely out of the novice stage myself. What about your chief of staff, Harry? He's got the background;

he knows how everything works in the West Wing and where the bodies are buried. Politically speaking, of course." She smiled.

Harry spoke earnestly. "As far as I'm aware, no chief of staff has ever served two presidents. It wouldn't work, politically speaking, to use your phrase. But you're in a different place. People view you as apolitical. Yes, you and Brian are card-carrying members of the GOP, but you're not an insider. You picked up everything quickly, and you ran my transition flawlessly. President Perrin can create an innocuous title so you wouldn't be viewed as a threat by Archie's friends or his adversaries. And it wouldn't be for long—a few months should be plenty of time."

Nicole stood and walked across the room, considering how interesting it was to be here with the past and present leaders of the country, one trying to cajole her into serving the other. At last she spoke.

"I'm flattered, but I'm not interested. Harry, I agreed to help you because of our friendship. I wasn't qualified to run a transition team, but I did it. I dove into the middle of things, learned the ropes, and kept going. I know a lot more now than I did eight months ago, and I'm glad you agree everything went well, but my job here is finished. I'm going home."

Harry wouldn't let go. "The fact that everything went well is exactly the point. I needed someone I could trust, someone smart, savvy, and with a law degree to keep us out of places we shouldn't go. Archie—President Perrin—needs you now for exactly the same reasons. Brian's still working every week in London. It's quicker to fly back and forth from Heathrow to DC than Dallas. You can still see each other on weekends; it would just be here instead of in Texas."

"I'm all packed, and the apartment lease expires in ten days."

Harry smiled, knowing he'd conquered a tiny bit of resistance. "That's not an issue and you know it. You're grasping at straws." He took her hand and looked into her eyes—the eyes of a woman he cared very much for—his best friend Brian's wife. "Your country needs you."

"That reminds me of the Uncle Sam poster where he points a finger and says, 'I want you!' I don't know, Harry—"

President Perrin's secretary knocked, opened the door, and handed him a note. He read it and said, "I must let you all go now. It's time to step into the real world. Apparently people think they need to see me urgently. Imagine that. I have a million things to do. You know what I'm talking about, right, Harry?" As they stood, he said, "Think about it, Nicole. Take all the time you need. How about you give me your answer by ten tomorrow morning?" Everyone laughed, even Nicole.

The party broke up, and each returned to the real world after a short respite from the horrific assassination just hours ago. As Harry and Jennifer walked out, he almost collided with the Speaker of the House, a woman with whom he had butted heads frequently. Both caught by surprise, she gave him a curt nod and muttered, "Goodbye, Mr. President."

"She must be ecstatic," Harry whispered to Jennifer. He and Madam Speaker rarely agreed on anything. Now, with Harry out and a weak man sitting behind the *Resolute* desk, helpless and floundering, Harry was certain the Speaker would be more than willing to guide him where *she* wanted him to go.

Brian and Nicole followed the former president out into the hallway, where Harry asked them to ride along as Marine One took them to Joint Base Andrews for their trip back to Oklahoma. Typically the departure of an outgoing president would be televised, broadcasting his final wave as he boarded the plane, but after today's tragedy, Harry's ceremonial exit from the White House was lost in the melee. The nation's thoughts were reeling from an assassination and the prospect of a president who wasn't supposed to be there.

On the way to Andrews, Harry bombarded Nicole with reasons why she must help Archie Perrin in his first weeks as president. "The biggest issue was standing just outside his door when we left," he added. "The Speaker will become his puppeteer. He's seen as a weakling even in his own party, and there's no one he can turn to who's looking out for his best interests. It won't be that long, but for the sake of the country, you should help the man."

Every protest was met with another compelling reason, and when they reached the 747-200 that would take the former president home, she told Harry that for once she was glad to see him go. "You're our best friends, but I'm exhausted after listening to you badger me." She smiled to show she wasn't altogether serious, and he said he knew she'd make the right decision.

"What are you going to do?" Brian asked her as the limousine took them back to her apartment.

"At this moment, I don't know. I was looking forward to being back home, but I have to admit a part of me loves the action here in Washington. All the negotiating, strategy, dealmaking—I feel as if I'm finally realizing my potential. I was a great attorney, a star in the world of litigation, but nothing compares to the exhilaration of being in this arena. And if I'm simply President Perrin's advisor, I get to experience all the excitement without being in the public spotlight or being held accountable for my actions."

"Why didn't you just tell Archie you'd take the job and not leave him hanging?"

"Because I don't want Harry and him to think I'm a pushover." She smiled and took his arm. "A few more months in DC won't be so bad for us. Like Harry said, you're working in London most of the time anyway. Back when we were dating, there were times I didn't see you for weeks. We can make it work long enough for me to get President Perrin on his feet. It won't be that long."

Within days, Nicole Farber re-upped her apartment lease for thirty days and transitioned herself from one president to another, becoming a behind-the-scenes, untitled woman with top-secret clearance and the ear of the president any time she needed.

# CHAPTER FIVE

An old-fashioned bell tinkled as Brian stepped through the door into Bijan Rarities' gallery in London's Old Bond Street. He waved to Cory Spencer, who was positioning two large stelae in the showroom, and went straight to a massive vault door in the rear of the store, where he entered a passcode that would start a ten-minute timer to open the door. Most mornings Cory opened the vault, but when the boss was in town, Brian performed the ritual, opening the portal to tens of millions of dollars in relics and artifacts stored in the twenty-by-forty-foot room.

Cory went to the Keurig and brewed Brian a strong cup of coffee. Also an American, Cory had lived in London long enough that he'd switched to tea, and shortly he joined his boss at a conference table to discuss today's plans.

"Back to the museum this morning, I suppose," Cory said, and Brian nodded.

"This project might go on forever. The more progress I make, the more pieces they bring to me. Thank goodness I only signed up for eight weeks."

Brian's comment that the project was never-ending had merit. Iraq's capital had been in chaos in the weeks after the 2003 Battle of Baghdad. Terrorists and citizens alike had looted the National Museum, carting off priceless artifacts from Mesopotamian, Persian and Babylonian civilizations. The homes of wealthy citizens were looted too, and thousands of relics entered the black market, ultimately ending up in Istanbul and Amman, Lyon and Damascus, and a dozen European capitals. The ones bought by private collectors would never be seen in public again. Others were recovered thanks to the generosity of museums and philanthropists who paid the bandits and stored the relics until the chaos subsided.

Over the next twenty years, the British Museum became the gathering point for these recovered rarities. The museums and galleries that had protected the stolen goods shipped them to London, where they would be identified, studied, photographed and, if prudent, returned to their home countries. This was Brian's project—to determine where each one of hundreds of items originated, create a fact sheet with photographs, and recommend its disposition. Some would be displayed at the British Museum. Others would be returned, if the home country's politics and ruling regimes were stable enough to ensure the safety of the often-priceless relics. Ideally, someday each would be back in its rightful place, but thanks to politics and terrorism, some Middle Eastern countries would never get their artifacts back.

He wasn't the only expert working on this project, but he was the only layperson, a testimonial to his knowledge of antiquities and his reputation. For six weeks, he'd spent five hours of every workday in a windowless room off a dusty corridor in the British Museum's sub-basement. He sat at a table beside his laptop and lovingly beheld some of the most beautiful relics that existed, concentrating on each as if it were the only one. In that way he kept from being overwhelmed.

He donated the modest salary back to the museum; a millionaire many times over, Brian had no need for a stipend. This was a labor of love, and until Harry Harrison's revelation the other night in Washington, he had decided to stay on even longer to help the museum. Now he had more important things to do—personal matters involving his best friend—so these would be his last weeks in London for now.

# CHAPTER SIX

There was no man on earth more suited for his profession than Horace Wilmington Fleming. A bookish bachelor in his late sixties, his title was deputy curator of Presidential Archives. If one looked at an organization chart of the National Archives and Records Administration, Horace's name would appear far down the list, below a senior curator who—at least on paper—was Horace's immediate superior.

Other than being on the payroll of the Archives, the story was false. Horace Fleming hadn't attended a meeting, punched a time clock, endured a performance review or engaged with other employees at the Archives since his employment began in 1981. The senior curator who was ostensibly his boss had never met him; Horace didn't even have an office at the headquarters on Pennsylvania Avenue, rarely visiting that building when he wanted to research something stored in its massive underground vaults.

The visitor entrance to the Archives was on Constitution Avenue. As they stood on the sidewalk in front of the massive building, tourists had no idea that huge rooms with steel doors and time locks extended out under the pavement below their feet. When they queued to see the Declaration of Independence, they had no idea that a treasure trove of American history sat in vaults thirty feet below ground.

Whenever Horace went to Archives I, the informal name for the National Archives building, he used the employee entrance at the rear of the building on

Pennsylvania. He would pass through a security checkpoint and go on his way, and the guards would raise their eyebrows and wonder who he was. His face wasn't familiar, but his black-rimmed pass was extraordinary. Only one other Archives employee—the director himself—had a black pass. There wasn't a door in the building that the man couldn't pass through. There wasn't a room off-limits or a document he couldn't requisition. If he asked for the original of the Constitution, arrangements would have been made to remove it from its case and get it to him.

Guards sometimes looked for Horace in the employee database, but his name never appeared. He was a mystery man in a city where phantoms—CIA spooks, clandestine operatives and who knew what else—appeared on the payrolls and the org charts of one federal agency or another. Was he one of those? security guards would wonder. Given his meek appearance, he seemed anything but.

Having such power might have gone to another man's head, but not Horace's. An introvert, he was a man of few words and no friends. He went about his business without involving others. What he wanted to know, he found on the internet or among the millions of items in the Archives.

Horace's windowless office in the basement of the Eisenhower Executive Office Building—or EEOB—was his sanctuary. No one ever visited, and that suited Horace just fine. The twenty-foot-square room resembled the abode of a long-tenured university professor, complete with rolltop desk, an old-fashioned swivel chair and wooden tables stacked with books, articles and magazines. A pipestand on his desk held the briars he had smoked for years, and the scent that permeated everything enhanced the hideaway's eccentric charm. While his office appeared a disorganized mess, he knew the contents of every tottering pile.

All that research material had nothing to do with Horace's occupation. It merely gave him something to do during twenty-nine days of downtime every month. His unwritten job description could be summed up in one brief sentence—to protect, maintain and deliver the President's Book of Secrets. He was the man who broke the news to incoming presidents that such a book existed. And he was the courier who brought it to the Oval Office for one hour every month, for that was all the time a president was allowed to peruse it.

The repository of records in the National Archives kept Horace occupied during the one hundred and seventy-two work hours each month when he wasn't fulfilling his one-hour duty in the Oval Office. His predecessors must have done the same, because like him, they'd have gone bonkers if they hadn't come up with something meaningful to pass the time. He'd learned early on that the Archives were full of historical surprises, and his unlimited access privileges allowed him countless wonderful hours of exploration and discovery in the vaults.

Aptly, Horace's passion was United States history. Since he could requisition any document, any volume and any historical item the National Archives held, he took full advantage, writing lengthy research papers and manuscripts that no reader would ever see, on arcane subjects even the most learned historians didn't know.

The most fascinating thing that occupied Horace's time was the book itself. By default he was the foremost authority on it, because he wasn't subject to the presidential one-hour-a-month rule. He read and reread presidential entries, laughed at jokes, solved puzzles, learned astonishing, secret twists of history and their private lives. Sometimes he felt like a voyeur, peeking behind the presidential facade to unveil a chief executive's private thoughts and interests.

One item, a poem on page 87, challenged him and became his favorite. Learning the author's name on this one was child's play. Figuring out what it meant was a different story. There were oblique references that pointed to a particular southwestern state, but so far he hadn't cracked a number of clues that would allow him to decipher the puzzle.

## BILL THOMPSON

Page 87 caught the eye of some presidents who read the Book of Secrets. He watched with interest each time one of them studied the page, and he never breathed a word about what he knew. The President's Book of Secrets was for them, after all. He was merely the keeper, but if someone broke the code, he hoped they'd share it with him.

# CHAPTER SEVEN

*Six Years Ago*

Harry Harrison had been thrust into the presidency when his predecessor could no longer serve. He'd been vice president under John Chapman, who disappeared in an ancient Mayan tomb in Palenque, Mexico. Harry's best friend, Brian Sadler, had played a role in finding Chapman's body, while Harry had been thrust into the Oval Office with little preparation.

There had been issues of national security, governance, international relations, partisan politics, and a thousand other things that filled Harry Harrison's days and his mind in those crazy first weeks as president.

Once Harry had become comfortable with the routine, he began dealing with mundane things along with the critical items. One morning several weeks into his presidency, he noticed an unfamiliar name on the daily appointment schedule. Horace Wilmington Fleming was down for a thirty-minute slot, and Harry asked his personal assistant who Fleming was.

Cynthia Beal explained that Harry's chief of staff had scheduled the appointment and marked it top secret. "The man's title is deputy curator of Presidential Archives," she added. "I looked him up out of curiosity. He's in the org chart for the National Archives, so I called over to find out why he was coming, but nobody had ever heard of him. That can happen, lots of people work in buildings all over DC, but this was different. His name and number weren't even on their extension list, which is odd."

Harry asked his chief of staff about the odd appointment, and he said it was on the list of required meetings for new presidents. He had no idea who Fleming was or what he would tell Harry.

When she ushered Fleming in, Harry saw a bookish academic straight from the pages of a Dickens novel. A nerd perhaps, but he appeared more absentminded professor than geek. His tweed jacket was fraying a bit, and old-fashioned horn-rimmed glasses sat perched on his forehead. The stem of a pipe poked out of his jacket pocket, and Harry could smell the pleasant aroma of tobacco. Most people were awed by the Oval Office, but this sixty-something man took a seat and settled back in the chair, indifferent both to his surroundings and the man behind the desk. He introduced himself using both of his given names—Horace Wilmington Fleming—as though he were in Victorian England instead of twenty-first-century America.

He went straight to the point. "I'm here to tell you about a very special book, Mr. President, but first you must sign a promise never to reveal what you will hear. Every other president has done so." He removed a long cloth bag from his valise and took a yellowed, parchment-like scroll from it. After carefully unrolling the paper, he read a single sentence in a loud voice, reminding Harry of a town crier making a proclamation.

*As president of the United States of America, I promise never to reveal to another soul, excepting another president, the existence of the President's Book of Secrets or anything within its covers.*

Harry was intrigued. A volume known simply as the President's Book, the existence of which people had wondered about for centuries, was why the curator was here. When Horace stood and spread the parchment on the desk, Harry's eyes widened in amazement. The sentence Fleming just read, written in flourishing handwriting at the top, reminded Harry of the fancy scrollwork on the Constitution. Then, to his shock, he realized his fleeting thought of the famous document wasn't far off the mark.

Below the sentence Fleming just read were dozens of signatures, but the first was George Washington's. The father of our country had written that pledge and become its first signer. Every other president's signature was there too—in their familiar, unmistakable handwriting—and now William Henry Harrison IV was being asked to add his name to the list. And he did, removing a pen from his desk and signing it at the bottom.

"I'm floored," he muttered as he stared at the ancient parchment. "This document is priceless. This must be the only paper in existence where every single president's signature appears on one page."

"You're correct, Mr. President," Fleming replied casually. "I've been in my position since 1981. I've seen thousands of historical documents in my time, but nothing else like this." He leaned over Harry's desk, picked up the parchment, rolled it carefully, inserted it in the cloth bag and put it back in his case. Then he returned to his chair.

"What is your position, exactly?" the president asked. "My assistant said you were a deputy curator at the National Archives. Do you work in the Archives building?"

"No, sir. I suppose they had to add my name to an organizational chart to issue me a government paycheck. I work right next door to the White House, over in the EOB. I have a comfortable little office in the basement that I've dubbed the Museum of Antiquity." He put a finger to his lips, tapped his pipe and whispered conspiratorially, "Don't tell anyone, but I can smoke down there without anyone complaining!"

Harry laughed. The man was odd but not uncongenial. Awkward, certainly. Probably uncomfortable in social situations. Reserved and quiet. And he worked in the EEOB next door. How odd.

"Specifically what work do you do?"

"Deputy curator of Presidential Archives is my title, as you pointed out, Mr. President. I call myself something simpler. I'm the keeper of the book."

"Ah yes, the book. Why don't you explain to me

what I get for signing that pledge?"

As he listened, Harry wondered if during his tenure as president he would ever receive a more interesting, enigmatic and intriguing briefing. Fleming revealed that there was a book—a sort of scrapbook bound in vellum created by President Washington, who penned the first entry. Dozens of others had followed suit, until today the book had around two hundred entries. Some presidents inserted more than one thing, while others might not have participated at all. That was impossible to know, because many things included in the book had no attribution, nor were any of them necessarily inserted in chronological order. A few were signed, and one might guess the author by the subject matter and time frame of others, but for most entries, the chief executives who included them in the book did so anonymously.

Harry couldn't believe what he heard. "I guess it was the *National Treasure* movie that made the public think such a book might exist. But I never thought it was real. Does it really have the truth about things like JFK's assassination and Area 51?"

The man smiled. "It isn't exactly as Hollywood described it. Not every page contains a startling revelation, although there are enough that it's guaranteed to astound you. I find the mundane things equally fascinating. They allow a glimpse into what a particular president considered funny, interesting or significant. There are pen-and-ink drawings, musical scores, poems and comments about troubling events a leader faced. And there are governmental secrets, such as the ones you asked about. It's a hodgepodge of information written by your predecessors and intended for no other eyes but those of future presidents. That makes it singularly unique among the treasures of the world, I think you'd agree. Priceless, in fact.

"As president, you're a member of a very small group. But mine is even smaller. There have been only ten keepers of the book, beginning in 1792 when George Washington created the volume and penned the first entry.

I'm the tenth keeper, and I'm the only non-president alive who's seen it."

Fleming explained the process for viewing the book and for making an entry. The sitting president could requisition the volume from him. He would retrieve it from a secure repository in an undisclosed location. He'd walk from his office through the corridors that led into the White House and allow the president to view the book one time per month, and only for one hour. There could be no notes or photos taken, and per the signed pledge, nothing could be revealed. "I'll be in the room with you and the book at all times. Just you and me, sir, and no one else," he cautioned.

*One hour a month?* That wasn't nearly enough time. He asked Fleming, "What difference does it make how much time I take? You say there are around two hundred entries. I could never do anything more than skim them."

Horace agreed but said that George Washington himself created that rule. Maybe he didn't think there would ever be so many contributions. Maybe the short timeframe was to keep a president from studying a page long enough to memorize its content. Whatever it was about, that was the rule, and Fleming was the enforcer.

"Who was president when you took the job?" Harry asked.

"Ronald Reagan. I was a twenty-nine-year-old curator when the previous keeper retired. They tapped me for a top-secret position I never knew existed. It's been a fascinating thirty-seven years," he added with a broad smile. "I hope I have a lot more time remaining, as this has been the vocation of my dreams."

"When can I schedule my first viewing?"

"Whenever you wish, Mr. President. I'm not a betting man, but I'll wager your schedule is busier than mine. Just remember, it's for your eyes only. No spouses, no children, no colleagues or friends or Secret Service, ever. You can't even acknowledge its existence."

Harry smiled. "And what's the penalty for breaking

the pledge? How do you punish a president for such a horrific mistake?"

"With all respect, sir, it's not a laughing matter. This book has been a matter of national importance for two hundred and thirty-something years, and its secret has remained secure. The penalty for breaking the pledge is the knowledge, deep inside your heart, that you have betrayed the trust of the fine men who came before you, including the father of our country."

"Understood. I have one last question for you. Has there ever been a president who didn't want to see the book, or one that you book keepers decided wasn't worthy of seeing it?"

The corners of the man's mouth turned upward ever so slightly in what Harry believed to be the closest thing to a smirk he could manage.

"Twice in history a keeper thought it prudent not to mention the book to a sitting president for fear he wouldn't guard the secrets. Those names will never be revealed."

Harry smiled. "Was one in the twenty-first century?"

Without a response, the man stood, collected his valise, and handed over a card bearing a telephone number.

"I'll be awaiting your call, sir. Once a month I'm at your disposal. Call me, and I'll bring the book here."

As he left, Harry's mind raced. What a fascinating conversation, and what an incredible revelation. The fabled Book of Secrets was real!

# CHAPTER EIGHT

A president's schedule is filled with meetings, visits and social events. Having served as vice president, Harry knew the drill, but thrust into the office without notice, Harry had hours instead of weeks to transition. Thoughts of the enigmatic book were set aside in the frenzy of activity, and it was two months before he found the perfect opportunity to call the man who kept the book. Jennifer and the girls had gone to Oklahoma City to see Harry's mother and father, and for the first time there was nothing on the calendar for that evening. Excited as a teenager asking for a date, Harry dialed the number, and Fleming answered immediately.

"Good afternoon, Mr. President. When would you like to see the book?"

His response surprised Harry. The man must have been sitting beside the phone, waiting for the only person who had the number—the president—to call.

"How about five? It's after three now. Will that give you enough time?"

"I'll be at your assistant's desk promptly at five."

"I'll ask her to notify the Secret Service to clear you in."

There was a sting of chastisement. "Not a word, Mr. President, just as you agreed when you signed the pledge. There's no need to notify anyone; I'll be there at five. It's not my first trip to the White House, as you know."

At precisely 4:59 p.m. Cynthia asked the boss if he was expecting Horace Fleming. "He's not on the appointments list," she added, and Harry told her to bring him in. As she did, the scowl on her face did not go unnoticed by the president. Insistent upon keeping his schedule accurate, she was peeved when he went off on his own.

"How'd you manage to get through White House security?"

Fleming smiled. "You only have an hour, Mr. President, and it begins the moment I open this briefcase. I respectfully suggest you might want to concentrate on what you're about to see. There will be time for chitchat later."

It amused Harry how little this strange man cared for presidential protocol. He wasn't the least bit intimidated by the power of the building or the office or the man to whom he offered "respectful suggestions."

He took out a large volume—a scrapbook, he had called it—with a cover made of a smooth off-white material. Fleming said it was vellum, a calfskin binding used for fine books long ago. He handed it to Harry, who felt almost a reverence when he took it in his hands. In the lower right corner there were two initials stamped with gold leaf. *G.W.* The man who started the Book of Secrets. The first president of a new republic.

As Fleming watched, Harry opened the book. For this first look, he had decided to simply flip through the pages to get an overview. The first page was a handwritten note dated July 1789 from George Washington, explaining that he intended the tome to be a catchall for the random thoughts of many presidents to come. It was an uplifting, revealing missive, a clear sign that Washington believed the fledgling nation had a long, bright future ahead.

Horace had prepared him for some of what he found. There were cartoons, including a ribald one drawn and signed by Chet Arthur, a president who wasn't known for having a sense of humor. It was dated January 1882, a few months after he had ascended to the presidency after James Garfield's assassination. There was music—James Buchanan had drawn staffs and scales and created a little ditty about Miss Hetty, the bachelor president's faithful

36

housekeeper. He saw several other poems, some signed and others anonymous.

Many entries dealt with serious topics. Rambling thoughts penned by Abraham Lincoln revealed the depths of his despair over a country ravaged by civil war. Another item, this one unsigned and undated, was entitled "Area 51 in Nevada. The biggest cover-up this nation has ever seen." It consisted of two pages crammed with newspaper clippings and handwritten comments, and a glued-in pocket with a booklet marked "TOP SECRET." Harry made a mental note to read it later. There were thoughts about war and peace, politics and governance, sit-ins and segregation—things that occupied the minds of America's leaders over the decades since its beginning.

He glanced at the clock. The time had gone faster than he'd expected, and he hurriedly flipped pages to see which needed further time in the future. There were several that caught his attention; he'd just begun to read FDR's candid comments about Pearl Harbor when there came a ding from the stopwatch in Horace Fleming's hand.

"Time's up, Mr. President." He reached across the desk, closed the book, and put it in his case.

"They aren't in order," Harry said, wondering if he was allowed to talk about the book, and was pleased when Horace relaxed and replied.

"No. Some of the earliest entries are in the middle. Presidents chose where to make their marks, I suppose. It does make things more difficult, though. You may have noticed many of the pages bear no signature or date. Since they're out of order, it's impossible to know who created those entries, although handwriting, linguistic style and other factors can be giveaways. I'll admit I'm fascinated with the book—I have been since the day I first saw it— and I'm privileged to be exempt from the 'hour a month' viewing rule. I spend a lot of time examining the pages, and I believe I've deduced who wrote ninety percent of the anonymous ones."

"Which do you consider most interesting?"

The man stood. "That's not relevant, sir. The book

isn't for me, it's for you. What you learn is all that matters. I must go now. I've taken enough of your time."

Harry thanked him and promised to call soon to set their next appointment.

"I'll be waiting." Fleming laughed. "Every president who sees the book becomes drawn to it like a siren. You'll find yourself counting the days until you and I meet again." With a wave, he walked out.

Harry Harrison was a consummate politician and a capable, experienced leader. His mind was focused on the country's interests as he flew to Europe, spent a weekend at home in Oklahoma, and had innumerable meetings with congressional and business leaders. The days flew by in the early months of his presidency.

Only in the evenings, when he could kick off his shoes and relax for an hour before yet another obligatory dinner, did Harry have time to think about the book. How much could he learn from it? What secrets lay in those oversized pages? What revelations might he find in the writings of men who served a hundred years ago or longer? At last he could wait no more. It had been thirty days, and he punched in Horace Fleming's number. As before, the man answered at once.

"Ready for another viewing, Mr. President?"

Harry gave him a date and time, and after he hung up, he recalled something he had meant to check the last time. He pressed a button on the desk phone, and the head of his security detail entered the Oval Office.

"How may I help, sir?"

"Mike, check out something for me, please. A few weeks back, a curator from the National Archives named Horace Fleming came to my office. Can you tell me who authorized him to enter the building?"

The man was away only a few minutes. "Sir, according to the log, Mr. Fleming holds one of the highest security clearances in the government. He has access to the Capitol, the White House, Treasury—you name it. He offices next door in the EOB, but I presume you already knew that."

Harry nodded.

"He walked through the tunnel, entered the White House through the basement, cleared three security checkpoints without incident, and ended up at Ms. Beal's desk. Is there a problem? Something I should know about him?"

"No, not at all. It's just that he's an unusual man who doesn't reveal much about himself. He gave me some helpful transition information. He's been around since Reagan, and I wondered how he moves about, given all the security around here. That's all."

He dismissed the officer and went upstairs to dress for dinner.

# CHAPTER NINE

Handling the world's issues made a president's life daunting, but for Harry, learning that the President's Book existed was the most bewitching secret of all. Sometimes at night he woke from a dream about the mysterious things on its pages. He was addicted; he struggled to wait a month between viewings.

On the afternoon of the third time he saw the book, Harry turned pages and read a variety of entries. Some were whimsical—an entire page was filled with mind-bender puzzles created by Benjamin Harrison, a president about whom Harry knew almost nothing. Others were historic, and every one fascinated him.

He looked up now and then, unnerved to see Horace sitting silently, fingers laced on his stomach, staring at him. "May I offer you a brandy?" Harry asked the odd little man, who said yes, he'd like that very much. Harry reached for the buzzer to summon his valet, but Horace wagged his finger.

"No one else in the room, Mr. President."

"Okay, I'll fix you a drink if you'll turn off the timer. I won't be robbed of my time."

Fleming chuckled and stopped the watch while Harry went to the butler's pantry adjoining his office and returned with two snifters. "Louis XIII. Best in the world, in my opinion," Harry said, raising his glass in a toast.

With the timer ticking again, Harry returned to the book. Each month it seemed the time passed more quickly as he discovered more interesting entries. Tonight he discovered something new—an anonymous, undated poem on page 87. Thinking he'd ask Horace about it when the session was over, he reached for a pen, but as he started to write, Horace cleared his throat loudly. When Harry looked up, Horace shook his head.

*No notes. I knew that.* Harry smiled, put down the pen and studied the poem's enigmatic words. It consisted of an introduction and eight brief stanzas of three lines each. At that moment, Harry had a brainstorm. He'd memorize it in stages. Fleming hadn't said anything about committing it to memory.

"How much time do I have left?"

"Fourteen minutes."

For the rest of the session, Harry concentrated on the poem. Horace watched, knowing exactly what he was doing. President Harrison was committing part of the poem to memory. Other presidents had done the same thing with different entries. Since no notes were allowed, it might be considered a violation, but he wasn't taking notes. Horace had never reprimanded a president for memorizing, and he wasn't going to start now. He wasn't a babysitter. He was the keeper of the book, and he was careful not to overreach his authority.

When Fleming collected the book and left, Harry quickly wrote down the intro and two stanzas he had committed to memory.

*My fellow presidents, can you decipher this puzzle?*
*Believe you can and you're halfway there.*
*Four four six one has frame and glass,*
*And something hid—a needed clue*
*To find the pass.*
*Inside the frame, wings in the air*
*Protect a secret I, six two,*
*Have hidden there.*

For every monthly visit thereafter, Harry ensured there was a brandy on the table waiting for Horace, and the man thanked him for the gesture, saying no other president

42

had ever offered him a drink.

Harry would spend forty-five minutes thumbing through the book, reading articles and learning secrets. For the last quarter hour, he memorized two more stanzas. He wondered why the poem beckoned him like a siren. Perhaps it was the challenge, knowing that an anonymous predecessor wrote a cryptic rhyme in the President's Book for others to decipher. Had someone already solved it? There was no way to know. Was it a joke, created simply to baffle the reader? Could it be some type of clue? And who wrote it? Was it hundreds of years old or much more recent? The poem mentioned a cache and the Comanche warrior Quanah Parker.

The poem clearly referenced the American West, which was Harry's favorite subject. He enjoyed researching western legends, especially ones in his home state of Oklahoma. Quanah Parker had lived there, and he secretly hoped this poem held a clue to something even more exciting than being president.

Three months later he had memorized it all. Horace had watched Harry, knowing from where his fingers lay on the page that he was almost done. The timer dinged, and Harry pushed the book across the desk.

"Did you get it all, Mr. President?"

Harry grinned sheepishly. He knew the man kept an eye on him, but he hadn't realized Horace knew what he was up to. The impertinence of the question might have angered another chief executive, but not so for Harry. Instead he felt like a child caught stealing candy from a store.

"I can't memorize something? There was no mention about that."

"That's correct, sir. There's no restriction on memorizing, and you're not the first to do it. Just be careful what you do next. You swore never to reveal the existence of the book or anything it contains."

"Didn't Obama admit seeing it? I recall hearing something about that."

"Yes, in an interview with a talk show host during

his first year in office. But it came across as a joke. His words were 'I'd tell you, but I'd have to kill you.' His signature is on the pledge along with yours. It was a faux pas on his part, and I spoke with him about it afterward. He never mentioned it again, and I'm certain he never will."

Once the man departed, Harry opened a side drawer to his desk, rifled through a hanging file and brought out a legal pad. Six stanzas were written on it, and today he quickly added the last two, hoping he hadn't forgotten something during his chitchat with Horace Wilmington Fleming.

Now that he had the entire poem, the difficult part-- deciphering its meaning—was next. But now he didn't have to wait thirty days to see it again.

# CHAPTER TEN

*Present Day*

President Perrin was behind schedule, and it wasn't even ten o'clock. A National Security Council meeting about Ukraine ran late. A meet-and-greet with the recent Super Bowl champs in the Red Room ran over when every player wanted a selfie. As he returned to the Oval, his personal secretary advised him his nine o'clock appointment was inside, where he'd been cooling his heels for almost an hour.

Frances Anderson had been Perrin's personal assistant for nearly thirty years, by his side when he was mayor of New York City, governor of the state, and then a senator. She knew his penchant for sidestepping protocol when it suited him. He often set up his own appointments, sometimes inserting initials into the calendar so others wouldn't know who was coming or why. It had been frustrating before, but it was disruptive and irresponsible now that he was in the White House. Anyone meeting with the president had to be vetted, and visitor logs were retained indefinitely. Those were the rules, and when Archie followed them, it made her life much easier. But she'd given up asking. If he wanted to invite an old classmate or a friend or whomever—it was his prerogative, even though his staff and those assigned to protect the president resented him for breaking the rules and making their jobs more difficult.

She knew the man waiting for her boss. Frank

Innocente had been a significant donor since Archie's days as a senator, and he stopped by the office on occasion. When he came, he was treated with the respect a loyal constituent deserved.

Archie had penned Frank's name in for a nine o'clock, thirty-minute private appointment. She'd met him at the entrance, and as she escorted him to the West Wing, she briefly remembered the first time she met him. His rugged good looks and thick gray hair reminded her somehow of George Clooney, who'd been her secret heartthrob forever. This man was twenty years or so younger than she, but there was a presence—a confident vanity that could get the man what he wanted.

"Welcome, Frank," Archie said, coming around his desk to greet the man as Frances led him inside. "If you need anything, Mr. President..." she began, but he waved her away and offered his guest a seat on the sofa near the fireplace.

Per standing instructions, Frances stepped inside when his thirty minutes was up and said, "Your next appointment is waiting, sir." She found them both sitting on the couch, and the look on Archie's face caught her by surprise. He was deeply concerned, or afraid, or both.

"It'll be a few more minutes, Frances. Leave us now."

Twenty minutes later, he was seriously behind schedule. An American Red Cross delegation was in the Cabinet Room, the House Majority Leader was fuming in front of Frances's desk, and in fifteen minutes the boss had a lunch with Great Britain's ambassador to the USA.

"What the hell's going on in there?" the Majority Leader snapped, but Frances said nothing. She had no idea why he'd given Frank Innocente almost an hour, nor was it her business. But since it was her job to keep him on schedule, she had to do something. She stepped into the Oval again and saw Frank standing over the president, verbally berating him, his face a mask of rage. Archie looked terrified.

She caught part of the tirade. "When you needed

46

money, all you had to do was ask, and I donated. Over and over, Archie, and it's your turn now. You do what I want or..."

They noticed Frances at the same time. Seemingly relieved, Archie stood. "I'm sorry, but I can't give you any more time today. Frances will see you out. I'll be in touch."

It shocked her when he yelled, "Damn right you will. Call me this afternoon. You owe me." He marched across the Oval and slammed the door behind him. In all the years she'd worked for Archie, she'd never heard anyone talk to him in that tone. And now he was the president. The gall of that man! She ushered the Majority Leader in, turned back as she closed the door, and watched her boss sink into his chair as if the weight of the world was on his shoulders.

Thirty minutes later Frances received a bewildering call from the head of the Secret Service detail. "The boss has a guest coming tonight at seven thirty. Will you be at your desk? If not, should I ring the Oval direct to announce his arrival?"

"Who's coming? I don't have anything on the schedule that late."

"Frank Innocente. Looks like someone added it to the boss's schedule five minutes ago. He's the same guy we cleared for a meeting earlier today."

*The man demanded Archie call him this afternoon, but after the way Frank treated him, why would Archie invite him back to the Oval? None of my business.*

She told the agent to ring the president directly, since she hadn't been told to stick around.

During a brief afternoon break between appointments, she asked if he was okay. Although he never looked her in the eye, he said all was well, and she told herself to leave it. She'd been called Archie's mother hen more than once, and sometimes by the boss himself. He could handle things; he was president of the United States, after all.

# CHAPTER ELEVEN

Horace Wilmington Fleming arrived at the Oval Office promptly at eight, briefcase in hand and ready for another session with President Perrin. After a brief greeting, he sat, removed the book, and placed it before Perrin. Palming his stopwatch, he said, "Are you ready to begin, sir?"

"In a moment." Archie pressed a button on his desk, the one that summoned the valet from the butler's pantry. Across the room, the inconspicuous door opened, and a man walked in.

Stunned at the breach of protocol, Horace jumped up and reached for the book, but Archie pulled it away. By now the stranger stood next to the president. "Let's see it," the man snapped.

"Mr. President, you can't do this! It's strictly prohibited." Horace appeared about to cry as his pleas were ignored. He thought to himself, *What should I do? This has never happened before. I can't report it...there's no one who knows the book exists. Do I simply let the stranger look? What else can I do?* Defeated, Horace fell back into his chair and refused to watch what he considered sacrilegious defamation.

"I have to say I'm disappointed in you, Mr. President," he said, but the stranger told him to shut the hell up. The man studied the page intently, and to Horace's horror, he removed his phone and snapped a picture of it. Horace hadn't seen which page it was, but he knew without seeing.

At that moment the president yelled, "Enough is enough! I don't care what you do to me, but I won't allow any more of this! Now get out of here before I call the guards." The intruder grinned, pocketed his phone and walked out. With a mumbled apology, the president dismissed Horace too.

What happened was so bizarre, so unexpected and unprecedented and horrible that Horace felt violated, and in the washroom by his office he spent almost ten minutes rinsing his hands, as if that would somehow absolve the sins of another. He'd protected this book for many years, and tonight a president had broken the solemn oath in an awful way.

It would have surprised Horace to learn Archie Perrin felt worse about what happened than he did. He'd sold his soul one tiny slice at a time, beginning forty years back when he won his first race for New York state House of Representatives using illegal campaign contributions from people like Frank Innocente's father. As his career blossomed and he became mayor of New York City, requests for this favor or that became routine, and Archie Perrin was loyal to his supporters. Garbage contracts, street resurfacing jobs, sweetheart deals at the port—Mr. Mayor was on the side of the people who scratched his back.

His four years as governor led to a successful US Senate campaign, and suddenly both Archie and his backers were in Fat City. He never told his wife, Dee, where all the extra cash came from, nor did she ask. That was Archie's business, and his silent partners were ecstatic when he was picked to run with Barbara Whittington.

On Inauguration Day, a white male had stood outside a Washington hotel amid a crowd waiting for a glimpse of the president-elect. When she emerged, walking toward a waiting limousine, he fired four shots at her and one into his temple so quickly her protectors had no time to react. No motive would ever be established; the man had no history of violence, no social media presence, and no apparent reason to kill Barbara Whittington. People would classify him as a copycat killer aiming for his fifteen minutes of fame by committing one more senseless, violent act in a country seeing such acts committed almost weekly.

But her murder wasn't senseless at all. The result was that sixty-six-year-old Archibald Perrin, New York politician who'd been corrupted years ago, became president, because his friends wanted it that way.

Until the last couple of years, Archie had never heard of Frank Innocente. His contact was Frank's father, until that man was no longer in a position to wield power. For a time, others stepped in to demand favors and deliver bank-wrapped stacks of cash, but eventually Frank became the man assigned to manage Archie Perrin.

His father had planned Frank's life well, giving his son a new last name, ensuring he earned a university degree, and providing the money and connections to start a freight-hauling business in Dallas. Frank's new company was a success from day one, thanks to the families who controlled shipping contracts in New Orleans, Chicago, LA and the East Coast. Today the company's trucks hauled enough cargo to put Innocente Freight Lines in the top ten nationally.

Unlike those before him, Frank hadn't asked Archie for much; in fact, it was refreshing dealing with the son instead of his cruel, intimidating father. Archie and Frank became acquaintances and later friends, having occasional lunches in the Senate Dining Room when Frank happened to be in DC.

During one such meeting, Frank revealed his fascination with tales of hidden treasure and lost mines. He was a huge fan of Brian Sadler's archaeological adventures on TV, and he told Archie if he ever got into the White House, Frank wanted to know if the legendary President's Book of Secrets was real. "If it is," he added, "you're going have to tell me everything interesting you find out!"

They had both laughed at the farfetched idea. At the time, becoming the man in the Oval Office was beyond anything Archie could have imagined. He'd been in the Senate for years, and he expected to retire there. But, like other things in his life, his friends had different plans.

# BILL THOMPSON

After Archie became president, Frank's personality changed. Once cordial and outgoing, he became insistent and belligerent. When he came calling to learn about the book, he made demands, and Archie responded, like always. Breaking the sacred vow instituted by George Washington made Archie sick to his stomach, but he'd been breaking vows so long, he got over it quickly. He'd given Frank tidbits about page 87—the enigmatic poem that Horace Wilmington Fleming said was his personal favorite—and Frank demanded to see it.

Archie was in no position to say no to Frank Innocente, so Archie had called Horace Wilmington Fleming and committed the cardinal sin. Would he ever be allowed to see the book again? He doubted it, after his reckless indiscretion. Maybe that would be for the best, he thought.

# CHAPTER TWELVE

The ringing of his phone jarred Brian awake. Disoriented, he reached for it, noticing it was well after midnight in London. It was late for Nicole to be calling, even though in Washington it was still the dinner hour. He hoped nothing was wrong.

"Hey. Everything okay?" he mumbled.

"I know it's late, but this couldn't wait. President Perrin finally got around to ticking off a big agenda item today. Everyone's been wondering who he'd choose for vice president. It's been two months since he took office, and he spent an hour this afternoon interviewing the person he wants."

Brian was fully awake now because this was interesting news. The media had speculated on whom Perrin would select, tossing out names of politicians, large donors, beltway insiders, bankers and economists and corporate executives.

"Who'd he pick? Did the guy accept?"

He could hear the smile in her voice. "Does it have to be a guy, you sexist pig?"

He laughed. "Okay, did the candidate accept?"

"Not yet. She had to call her husband first."

"Call her husband? What are you talking about?"

She said nothing.

"*You?* He asked *you* to be vice president?"

She wasn't laughing now. "Can you try not to sound quite so astounded?"

"I'm sorry." He chuckled. "It's just…it's just…"

"It's just what? What's so damned funny? You don't think I could be vice president?"

He knew he was in dangerous waters. "That's not what I'm saying. You're just...well, for one thing, you're not an insider. You're not a politician, and as far as I know, every vice president in history has previously held public office."

"Are you trying to make a point? Because if you are, I'm not getting it."

He feinted. "So are you going to do it?"

"I wasn't completely sure before I called you," she snapped. "Now I'm thinking, 'Hell yes, I'd make a great vice president despite what my husband thinks.'"

"Hey, wait a minute. That's not fair."

"No, Brian. *You* wait a minute. I graduated top in my class at SMU Law, I was the youngest partner in one of the country's largest and most influential law firms, and the success rate on my cases was almost a hundred percent. I'm damned good, I'm damned smart, and I'll be damned if I wouldn't make a great vice president."

"Agreed. But have you thought about the fishbowl you're getting ready to climb into? The media will be all over everything we do."

She snorted. "The media? That's hilarious coming from you, mister TV personality. In case you haven't noticed, we already live in a fishbowl. Everywhere we go, people stop and stare at you, or ask for your autograph or want to shake your hand. You can't even go to the bathroom without a bodyguard. It's okay if people fawn over you, but not so much for me. Is that your point?"

*Man, this isn't going well.* "Come on. You're blowing everything out of proportion. What about Senate confirmation? The hearings and all that? Remember Kavanaugh? Are you up for that kind of hassle?"

"News flash. *Our* party controls the Senate. The president says my confirmation would sail through. Hassle? Sure, but I can take it. I'm obviously stronger than you think. Now I'm getting angry, and I'm sorry I called. I haven't made up my mind yet, but when I decide, you'll be among the first to know."

"Nicole, wait a minute. Let's talk through this—" He knew his wife, and he knew he'd crossed a line.

"I'm a big girl, and I can make my own decisions. Nighty-night." With a click, she was gone.

She was right, he considered as he tried to get back to sleep. She was the smartest, craftiest, and spunkiest woman he'd ever met, and she was strong enough to weather a bunch of senators nitpicking at her. She had survived a near-fatal crash when someone sabotaged her car in 2014. That was when she had left her stellar career at Randall and Carter, an enormous and powerful Dallas-based law firm. She'd opened a solo practice and had done well. And for almost a year, she'd been a huge asset to two presidents in DC.

When it came down to it, Brian didn't believe she'd do it. Not because of fear or misgivings, but because she cherished her privacy. They were enjoying life, and this decision would disrupt her life—and his—for at least the next four years.

# CHAPTER THIRTEEN

Sitting in his office at the Old Bond Street gallery in London, Brian received a notification on his phone. The president would hold a press conference at noon local time, just about an hour from now, to announce his choice for vice president.

Since inauguration day, when Perrin had been jarringly catapulted into the presidency, every media outlet wondered who he'd pick. Today that wait would be over.

Brian hadn't heard from Nicole since last night's sharp disconnect. He knew had she accepted, she would have called to run things by him, so as he watched on his iPad, he also wondered whom the president selected. Would his choice arrive with a wealth of political experience, allowing Nicole to leave her advisory position soon and return to Dallas? For both their sakes, he hoped so.

He watched ABC's live coverage showing an empty stage; then a group of twenty men and women who stood behind the lectern from which the president would address the nation. He knew the faces, although he'd met only three. There were members of Perrin's cabinet and several high-level staffers. Nicole was there too, poised and composed, her blond hair and scarlet dress a striking contrast to the others. Since she was working unofficially and without a title, it surprised him she was there.

He reflected a moment on her job, which they had agreed would last thirty days. She'd been there ten weeks so far, and instead of weaning her off, the president was adding more tasks and responsibilities. It wasn't something they talked about much; actually mostly everything was small talk these days, since they rarely saw each other except on the odd weekend. It was clear she loved what she was doing, and her presence on stage today signaled her job as a transition overseer had become much more important.

Perrin's press secretary introduced him, and he strode to the lectern. He seemed happy, relaxed and ready to reveal his nominee. He spoke soberly of the American people's horror when President-elect Whittington had been assassinated just minutes before she was to be sworn in. He acknowledged that the people had elected the first woman president in history, but instead they had gotten him. Today he repeated his promise to guide the nation, to keep it safe, and to act in America's best interests. He also promised that his vice president, once confirmed, would be involved in every major decision and high-level meeting.

The president continued, "Many times in the past, vice presidents have relegated to glad-handing and well-wishing, attending funerals and celebrations too unimportant for the president. As a nation, we recently learned once again that a vice president is a heartbeat away from the highest office. God forbid, I vow that should anything happen to me, I'll make sure my second-in-command will be prepared and ready."

He said that he had deliberated long and hard over the selection, considering people with decades of service to the government and others with no ties to Washington. He'd been open to any race or gender. He weighed the pros and cons and came to a decision.

"You'll learn everything about the person I've chosen," he said, "because I have faith in the press corps to do their jobs and give you absolutely every shred of information about this person's life since birth. I've selected a woman, in hopes that she and I will spend years working together and perhaps, someday, you'll have your female president after all. My fellow Americans, I present to you a woman who is capable, dedicated, willing to serve and ready for the task. She's a political outsider, but trust me, she knows what she's doing. Ladies and gentlemen, meet Nicole Farber."

And in that way a stunned Brian Sadler learned that his wife would be the next vice president of the United States.

She walked confidently to the lectern and spoke earnestly into the camera about her desire to make a difference and her willingness to be at President Perrin's side. And at the end, without mentioning her famous spouse by name, she said, "I want to thank my husband for his support. The input he gave me allowed me to be at peace about this life-changing decision I made." Brian wiped away a tear as he heard her positive, hopeful words and saw the woman he loved standing before the American people. He'd made her angry last night, but now he would support his wife and her decision, knowing full well that from this moment, their lives would never be the same.

The press secretary distributed an extensive biography when the conference was over, and within minutes the world began to learn everything about Nicole Farber. Brian wondered who would be first to text him, and he smiled when he saw a message from Cowboy, the Secret Service's nickname for Harry Harrison. He laughed when he read it.

"And you thought you were the only celebrity in your house! Tell Nicole congrats from both of us!"

The second message was from his mother, chiding him for not telling his own parents in advance. They had no idea that the announcement came as a shock to him too.

The confirmation hearings went on for days, mercifully absent the heated rhetoric some Supreme Court justice candidates had endured. The opposition focused on Nicole's lack of experience in politics and her ability to serve following a car crash in 2014 that nearly took her life. Some nitpicked, some made comments that were out of line, and others gave rambling speeches, but most from both sides of the aisle were cordial and seemed willing to accept her. Nicole was a brilliant attorney with a successful career, and her doctors testified that she was completely recovered mentally and physically from the wreck. She was apolitical and might just bring a breath of fresh air to the swamp.

Brian sat through every minute of the hearings, and he held the Bible on which her hand rested as the Chief Justice swore her into office. He kissed his wife, whispered, "I love you," and became first gentleman—the husband of the next person in line to the presidency.

# CHAPTER FOURTEEN

*Six weeks later*

Although it was April, Oklahoma nights could be cool and damp. A roaring fire crackled and popped in the huge fireplace, Sinatra crooned in the background, and four old friends shared after-dinner cocktails, reminiscing about the amazing things that had happened since Harry had left Washington five months ago.

Once Nicole became vice president, Brian had come to Washington most weekends, but often she wasn't available. The work never ended; the president worked on Saturdays and Sundays, and since he'd promised to involve Nicole in everything he did, so did she. Reminiscent of Dick Cheney, this vice president was an active part of the program and fully apprised of Perrin's agenda.

When the invitation to visit the ranch had come from Harry and Jennifer, Brian urged her to accept. She hadn't been out of town in six weeks, he reminded her, and it was time for a break. On a rainy Friday morning, she and Brian boarded *Air Force Two*, landed at Tinker Field in Oklahoma City, and went to the Nichols Hills area where Henry and Julia Harrison lived. It had been Harry's house before the onset of her illness, and they came to see how their old friends were doing. Henry greeted them at the door and brought them to the living room, where his wife was sitting in a chair. She held up her right hand to greet them, while her left remained in her lap, clenched like a claw.

# BILL THOMPSON

The Harrisons congratulated Nicole on becoming vice president and laughed about the difficulty getting anything accomplished in the crazy world of Beltway politics. At last the talk turned to the elephant in the room.

They didn't know many of the specifics of Julia's condition, but she wanted to talk about it. She told them that a neurologist in Houston who specialized in Parkinson's disease identified hers as corticobasal degeneration, or CBD. It was a rare disorder that robbed the victim of motor skills and coordination. Loss of speech and cognitive abilities followed, and no treatment or cure existed. One simply waited to die.

Brian and Nicole expressed their regrets and asked how things were going. "I can't make my left hand grip a cup or hold a fork," she answered. "Sometimes it will, but I can't rely on it. If I do, I could throw a glass of wine in someone's lap. Walking's an issue too. If I walk without Henry's help, I may fall, because my brain and my left leg don't always communicate these days. I have my faculties, which I'm told isn't necessarily a good thing. This damned disease can go two ways—it can strike you physically or mentally. I've clearly got the physical one, but the doctor says I might have been better off with dementia, not having to watch myself deteriorate. Sad thought, isn't it?" When she dabbed at her eyes with a Kleenex, so did everyone else.

"No more crying," she declared. "It is what it is. I have my family, a few good friends like you all, and a wonderful life I've enjoyed immensely. Never a dull moment, thanks to Henry and Harry! I'll be fine, don't you worry. If it comes down to sitting right here in this house, then that's what I'll do. Our agents can drive us out to the farm now and then to let me watch the sun set. I have months, maybe even a year. That means I have a little notice so I can set priorities and say and do what needs to be said and done."

*She's taking the short timeframe better than I would be.* Brian thought how horrific it must have been to hear that prognosis, but also how strong Julia Harrison had always been. Even now, this stoic wife, mother and grandmother was still hanging on, refusing to let the world pity her.

"The children are coming over this afternoon after school," she said brightly, changing the conversation to something positive. "I've asked Harry and Jennifer to let them visit as often as possible while I'm still doing well. Plus, you all need time to catch up. I know they're looking forward to having you at the ranch this weekend."

Julia's granddaughters, Lizzie and Kate, were eighteen and fifteen years old. They'd gone to private school in Washington, but now they attended the public schools in El Reno, Oklahoma, not far from the ranch. Secret Service agents ferried them around, and they seemed to be happy in the rural environs of Oklahoma compared to spending the past six years in Washington. Lizzie would be off to Oklahoma University, her dad's alma mater, next year.

After Brian and Nicole said their goodbyes, a helicopter took them from Wiley Post Airport to the family ranch sixty miles to the west. Harry and Jennifer greeted them at the heliport that had been installed a few years ago when Harry became vice president.

That afternoon Harry had prepped an enormous smoker and grill on which his father had often cooked what he dubbed the "Filet de Harrison," the world's perfect steak. Harry said his cooking would never equal the master's, but the slow smoking process would make them better than anything at a restaurant—even the steakhouses for which Oklahoma was known.

Every space on the grill held a steak. There were more than a dozen because the Harrison men always included the Secret Service detail, and tonight there were three extras who accompanied Nicole. Jennifer fixed a big salad and loaded baked potatoes. After Harry and his guests ate, he turned the dining room over to the agents, and the four of them retired to the library. They could hear outbursts of laughter as the men and women on the protective detail swapped stories about work, football and families.

The four old friends reminisced too, but more often they simply stared into the fire. Brian proclaimed himself stuffed to the gills—the steaks truly had been cooked to perfection, and he'd eaten more tonight than he usually did in a day. It was a time of reflection, a reunion of best friends tinged with the knowledge that the life of the Harrison family's matriarch was coming to a close in a tragic manner.

Nicole broke the silence. "Harry, I didn't properly thank you for that favor you did me when you twisted my arm and shamed me into helping Archie transition into the presidency. If I had just said no, he would never have picked me for vice president, and I might have been working back in Dallas right now. The horrific politician I've become is your fault, and I'm never going to let you forget it. You owe me big time."

Harry said she was the best choice Perrin could have made.

"Tell that to the Speaker. She should be thrilled to have a female vice president, but she treats me like I have the plague."

"That's because you're in the wrong party." Jennifer laughed. "If you'd been on her side of the aisle, you'd have been hailed as Nicole, Queen of the Nation!"

"You had a chance to be vice president too," Harry said to Brian. "Remember when I asked you?"

"Yeah, but I was smart enough to turn you down." He grinned at Nicole, and she snorted. That brought more laughter and more reflection, and then Brian unexpectedly changed the subject.

"Is there really a President's Book of Secrets?"

Harry looked up, a flicker of amusement in his eyes. "Have you been watching too many movies?"

"I'm serious. Obama said there was."

He laughed and wagged his finger. "No he didn't. Obama said, 'If I told you, I'd have to kill you.'"

"Come on, Harry. You're not the president anymore. Admit it. It *is* real, isn't it?"

To Brian's surprise, Harry's smile disappeared. "Don't push it, Brian. There are lots of things I know that I can't talk about, even with Jennifer. Matters of national security, things like that."

"My God. Are you saying the book contains things involving national security?"

"No, nor did I say there was a book in the first place. Drop it, okay?"

Confused by Harry's sharp retort, everyone sat in uncomfortable silence for a moment.

"I know you well, Brian. I've seen what happens when you think you're onto something exciting. You're tenacious and perseverant, but sometimes you push so hard that you go places you shouldn't."

Nicole snickered. "*Sometimes?* Come on, Harry. Brian's gotten himself in more messes than James Bond by going off without thinking things through."

Brian raised his hands in mock defeat. "Okay, everybody, go ahead. Pile on. Beat me up. Ignore all those great things I've found—the scroll, the artifacts, the relics, the lost treasures of the Hebrews—and call me an irresponsible Don Quixote. I've made a lot of mistakes, I'll admit. But I've had a blast so far, and I'm not done yet. You want to play coy about the Book of Secrets? Go for it. All you're doing is whetting my appetite."

"Believe me, I know that," Harry said, shaking his head. "I warned you not to read anything into my answer."

The silence lasted so long that one of the Secret Service agents peeked in from the dining room. "Sorry to interrupt," she said. "Awfully quiet in here. Just making sure everyone's okay." Harry assured them all was well.

As the others chatted, Harry's thoughts drifted to the book, and specifically to page 87. Some of the words—clues, it appeared—seemed to be about Oklahoma. He didn't know yet what the clues meant, but he got goosebumps just thinking about what secrets the poem held.

# CHAPTER FIFTEEN

Harry suggested they take a look at the Milky Way before everyone turned in. He doused the lights in the front yard so there would be nothing to impede the view and led them outside onto the grassy front lawn. "Guys, turn off your lights for a minute," he yelled to Secret Service agents sitting in two idling SUVs. When they did, the darkness enveloped them like a shroud. Out here, miles away from city lights, the heavens were a marvelous sight, a panoramic vista of glistening pinpoints surrounding a Cheshire-cat moon. Brian recalled camping out in the backyard as a kid, imagining himself as an astronaut up there among the stars. "Seeing the sky on a night like this reminds me that God's in charge," Jennifer whispered as she snuggled close to her husband.

When they returned to the house, Brian asked Harry to join him for a nightcap, a suggestion that surprised Nicole. It was almost eleven, and after her long day at the White House, they'd boarded a plane, then a chopper, and had eaten a hearty meal accompanied by plenty of libations. She was exhausted and knew he must be too. She shot him a glance, Brian raised his eyebrows slightly, and she understood. The men had unfinished business.

"Go for it, guys," she said, following Jennifer up the stairs. "Don't wake me when you come to bed!"

As a guard moved through the house securing doors and windows, Harry and Brian returned to the library. He tossed another log onto the fire and poured two cognacs. Once again they sat silently, watching the flames dance and flitter, until Brian said, "I guess I hit a nerve asking about that book. Sorry that I upset you."

Harry smiled. "I should be the one apologizing. You know me too well. I had a good poker face negotiating with Putin and Kim Jong-Un, but I can't fool my old roommate." He paused for an uncomfortably long time. Brian raised his head and looked into his friend's eyes, asking without asking. *Is it real?*

Instead of giving the answer Brian hoped for, Harry said, "I have a story to tell you. Have you ever heard of a legend called the cave of the iron door?"

"No. Tell me about it."

"Since the late eighteen hundreds, there have been rumors about a lost cave in southwestern Oklahoma. Back in the early seventies, an article about it appeared in a treasure-hunting magazine. I got a copy of that article when I was a teenager, and I must have read it a hundred times. I still have it to this day; it was fascinating, especially because according to legend, the iron door lay somewhere in the Wichita Mountains less than a hundred miles from my house in Oklahoma City. I fantasized about going down there and finding it."

"You never mentioned it when we were college roommates."

"There were way more important things in those days, like fraternity and girls and even studying, believe it or not. I did go to the mountains once while I was in high school. A fellow Eagle Scout and I drove to the Wichita Mountains Wildlife Refuge, trekked in and camped out on Elk Mountain, a site the treasure story says is close to the cave. We rappelled and hiked for most of two days, but we didn't find anything."

"What's so fascinating about a cave? Is something hidden inside?"

Harry walked to his desk, riffled through some hanging files and brought over a yellowed magazine. "You can read the article. I find myself going back to it every so often, and the words get my adrenalin flowing as much today as they did when I was a teenager. A lot of people claim it exists, and there were several sightings in a canyon called Shadow Gulch back in the early part of the twentieth century. But those who saw it went back for tools and could never locate it again. That makes sense; you won't believe how remote and rugged the area is."

Brian shook his head. "I won't believe it because I won't be there. There's no way I can take time off to go treasure hunting. My galleries are doing better than ever, we're holding auctions every couple of months in London and the US, and I'm finishing up the project for the British Museum. You may have settled into an early retirement, but I haven't." He laughed and clinked his snifter with Harry's. "The idea is interesting, but I don't have the time."

Harry looked at the fire and spoke quietly. "Neither did I, for a long time. I spent the last six years as president wondering how I might sneak away and hike those back trails again, but a vice president or president can't just do things like that. Now's a different story. Archie's the president, and I'm a has-been who's free to do his own thing once again. I have this friend—a guy who's been on one adventure after another his entire adult life—who simply has to come with me. What if I found a buried treasure? He'd never forgive himself if he wasn't by my side!"

Brian smiled. "You're right about the treasure, but there's been far too little adventure in my life since I signed up to help the museum. My work there's almost finished, but even if I was free, chasing folklore isn't my bag. The people who claim to have seen it never can locate it again. Nobody knows who built it or why. The entire story's fabricated on secondhand stories told by people long since gone. You have to admit there's not much substance there."

"I disagree. There's really quite a bit to it. I've collected a small library of books and articles related to the cave, including a story about who built it and why. A lot of people believe the cave is real, and if you ever see the Wichita Mountains, you'll understand how searchers can't find it a second time. Call me a hopeless treasure buff, but I was a believer from the day I first read that article. And after I became president, things got even better. I learned something fascinating. It's…it's a secret I'm not able to share just yet, but it just may prove the cave is real."

"You can't share something that might convince me the cave's real? What the hell are you talking about?"

"Something I'm trying to work through. Just give me a little time."

Brian leaned in close. "Come on, Harry. You can't pique my interest like this and then tell me you need more time. Let's have it."

"I know you don't understand, and maybe I shouldn't have brought it up yet. There's nothing I want more than to convince you to join me in the mountains. I…I came across something that may be a clue. But seriously, I can't discuss it now."

Brian picked up his snifter, settled back in the chair, and smiled. "It's real, isn't it? The book is real, and you've seen it. You're itching to tell me about it, but for some reason you can't."

Harry didn't have to say a word; his face gave everything away. "Let it go for now," he replied, fidgeting in his chair. "If I can figure a few things out, I'll tell you more."

*You've told me plenty, old friend. The President's Book of Secrets exists. And maybe that iron door does too.*

# CHAPTER SIXTEEN

Before they called it a night, Harry went across the room and took down a book from a shelf. He brought the well-worn volume to his chair and flipped through dog-eared pages until he found the one he wanted. "This is a compilation of Oklahoma treasure tales," he said as he handed the open book to Brian. "I bought this book after I read that magazine article. Here's the tale about the iron door. Back in the day, I could have recited most of it from memory. Like you say, it's based on hearsay and folklore, but I see no reason why it couldn't be the truth. Take it upstairs, and we'll discuss it tomorrow. It won't take long to read."

Brian eased into bed, listened to Nicole snoring softly, and flipped on the nightstand lamp. She rolled over, grunted, pulled the sheet over her head, and snored again. He was tired too, but after seeing Harry's enthusiasm, he wanted to talk more, so he opened the book.

*The Story of the Iron Door*

*After a successful train robbery in northern Texas in 1867, Cole Younger and Jesse James decided they needed a place to stash their booty. It was cumbersome and dangerous to carry around gold and silver bars, coins and currency. So they devised a solution.*

*The Missouri-Kansas-Texas railroad maintained regional offices and a telegraph facility in Lawton, Oklahoma, next to the train station. In a nearby switchyard* *sat old railcars that were no longer in service. One day a man walked in and offered to buy a boxcar for the scrap steel framework and door he needed to build a cattle pen on his ranch. The railroad was only too happy to get rid of a junked boxcar, and a deal was quickly made for $30 cash.*

*The next day several men arrived and dismantled the railcar where it sat, loading the steel frame and heavy door on a wagon and heading west out of town. They left behind the car's bed and wheels and never returned.*

*A few hours after their departure, that wagon snaked through a deep ravine in the Wichita Mountains. The men followed a crude map provided by their boss, Jesse James, winding through a dry creek bed until they came to a ravine called Shadow Gulch. Rounding a bend, they saw horses tethered up ahead. High up on a cliff, men were at work clearing the area around a cave entrance. They'd built a winch, and when the boxcar door arrived, the crew hoisted it up the side of the mountain. Once the steel frame was in place and the door set, the cave would be secure.*

*Over a year earlier, the outlaws Cole Younger and Jesse James, riding through this same narrow wash between two cliffs in the Wichita Mountains, had spotted the cave. The cliffs were dotted with others, but its lofty location made this one interesting.*

*After some exertion they reached it, discovering this was no natural cave; it was a mine that ran more than three hundred feet into the mountain. Spanish, they figured, for the conquistadors had dug other such mines in this area in their searches for silver and gold. They lit torches and ventured down the first passage they came to, seeing unmistakable evidence men had worked the mine for silver. Some veins remained in the walls, but long ago this mine had played out and been abandoned in the forbidding terrain.*

*In the months since they found the cave, the James-Younger gang had returned several times, relying on subtle markers to lead them back to Shadow Gulch. They weren't the first to mark the spot; hundreds of years earlier someone—perhaps Spaniards who worked the mine—had driven a spike into an ancient oak tree in the canyon floor. Anyone riding through the narrow ravine could see it, but unless one knew where to look, he would miss the partially obscured cave entrance far above.*

*Cole and Jesse had explored the cave, stooping to walk through offshoot tunnels, finding a cavern deep inside, then crawling on their bellies through yet another passageway that led to an air shaft. They chose the cavern as their depository and began stashing loot from their robberies there. Soon the small cave deep in the mountain held gold, silver and boxes of currency.*

*It concerned them that someone might accidentally find the mine as they had, riding through the canyon and looking up at the right moment. They didn't want their stolen loot filched by someone else, so one afternoon in the settlement of Wichita Falls, Texas, they sat in a saloon and decided they needed a way to conceal the cave entrance.*

*Days later as they rode away after robbing the Territorial Bank of Lawton, Cole pointed to a rail yard where rusting boxcars sat on side tracks. There they found their door, and one of the gang negotiated its purchase and removal. Once the door arrived on-site, they set it in place and padlocked it shut. At last the gang had their hiding place. It wasn't perfect—even though the old door was rusty, the rays of the setting sun sometimes reflected off the metal, but only when the sun's rays hit the door square on. All in all, it would serve them well.*

# CHAPTER SEVENTEEN

Nicole had been at her desk for half an hour when Perrin's assistant, Frances, said the boss wanted to see her. She thought nothing of being called to the Oval at eight, since Archie was at his desk by seven each morning, and early meetings were commonplace. Usually these impromptu summonses involved daily agenda items, and one or more others would join them. Today it was just him, and he pointed her to a chair without standing to greet her. That hadn't happened before, and she wondered if something was wrong.

"Sit down, Nicole. I have something to tell you."

He seemed exhausted—his eyelids drooped, he sat slumped in his chair, and he needed a shave. Archie didn't allow himself to be seen like this; his entire demeanor had changed. Was he ill? Perhaps, but when he spoke, she heard despair and defeat in his voice.

"I can't express how much I appreciate your agreeing to help me the day I was thrust into this job. You may not believe me, but I never considered then asking you to be my vice president. I needed guidance—help transitioning those first few weeks—and that's exactly what you delivered. Things couldn't have gone better."

*What's this about?* She sat patiently, waiting for him to get to the point, if in fact there was a point to this rambling dialogue.

"It's been one hell of a ride, I'll say that. Back when Barbara Whittington tapped me to be her running mate, I knew I'd be a powerless vice president, but look where I ended up instead. Power is a fickle friend, Nicole. Power can make incredible things happen, good and bad. Its hold over a man can cause him to do things he regrets…" he paused, fixing his gaze on the fireplace across the room.

"Mr. President, I think you've done a great job so far, especially since you had no time to prepare. Don't be hard on yourself…"

"*You've* done a great job. Let's be honest, Nicole. I'm the career politician who knows how to work the system and secure votes for the projects I want. I know people's secrets, their likes and dislikes, who'll sell their souls and who won't. I can tell the players from the moralists, and I work both sides. Most of us who've been inside the Beltway as long as I have know each other better than our own spouses do. Especially the things we keep hidden away.

"You arrived with none of that baggage. You came in as Harry's transition leader with a lawyer's businesslike approach to things, proved yourself to be a leader with the staff, and discovered you had a knack for working both sides of the aisle. When I nominated you, your confirmation hearing went through with almost no hitches."

Again he paused, and his mind seemed to wander. And again Nicole waited patiently. When he next spoke, his voice was a whisper.

"Always be careful, Nicole. I know people's secrets and who'll sell their souls. That's a two-way street. Likewise, certain people have known things about me for a long time. When you do something wrong…when you sell your soul to get power, it's a forever decision. You're at their mercy, and they'll destroy you. They say the higher you climb, the harder you fall."

"Mr. President…"

"For God's sake, quit calling me that!" he bellowed, slamming his fist on the *Resolute* desk. "I don't deserve that title…" He covered his face with his hands, sobbing.

"Sir, if something's wrong, let me help. Anything you need…"

"What I need, I lost a long, long time ago. The Tin

Man needed a heart, but that's not my issue. I've got a heart and a brain and courage—some, at least. I wish I'd had more. What I lost way back when is my conscience, and there's no wizard who can give it back to me."

His head jerked up, and he looked at Nicole blankly, as if noticing her for the first time. "I'm...I'm sorry about all of that," he said, his voice stronger now. "I don't know what got into me. Just forget all that I said, okay? Forget any of it happened."

"Of course, but you know you can call on me anytime, sir. If there's anything I can help you with, I'm right down the hall."

He dismissed her with a wave of his hand, leaving Nicole to walk back to her office wondering if her boss was having a mental breakdown. If not, what the hell was going on with him? It was as though he needed to confess, but suddenly thought better of it. What on earth had he done?

# CHAPTER EIGHTEEN

"Shelly, get in here!"

With a shudder, Frank Innocente's personal assistant jumped from her chair, sending it careening into the wall behind. She heard him yell through the heavy oak door that separated their offices, and she took a deep breath before opening it and stepping through. She'd stuck it out at Innocente Freight Lines for three years, making her one of the most senior employees. Office employees—those in close proximity to the boss—rarely lasted even a few months. The lucky ones—dispatchers, truck drivers, forklift operators and laborers—didn't have to see the boss every single day.

When she first hired on, Shelly had been thrilled. Executive assistant to the owner of a big company sounded like a great job. The pay and benefits were good—they had to be, she quickly learned, because her position had been a revolving door for years. People who worked in the office not only feared Frank—they detested him.

She cracked the door. "Do you need something, sir?"

"Could you for once *anticipate* something I need?" He was in one of his snitty moods, and confrontation was best avoided. Usually the tirades weren't aimed at her—she would sit at her desk as he ranted and raved into the phone or berated a hapless employee who'd committed a slight error that cost Frank a few dollars. This morning he'd been in his office with the door closed when she arrived, and she had crossed her fingers he was in a good mood. No such luck, as it turned out.

She drew another breath and told herself to stay calm. "I'm sorry, sir. What can I do to help?"

"What you can do to *help* is to brew me a cappuccino. And tell Sterling Lewis to get his ass in here. If he thinks I don't know what happens around this place, he's got a surprise coming."

She closed the door behind her, went to the coffee bar, and started his cappuccino. Then she called Sterling, an assistant supervisor on the loading dock.

"He wants to see you."

"Oh geez. Any idea what it's about?"

"He's on the warpath. He said something about giving you a surprise."

There must have been a hundred security cameras in the company's sprawling two-story office building, dock and vast truck yard. Veteran employees warned newbies that their boss spied on them using an ultrasophisticated audio-visual system. Although everyone knew the "spies in the sky" existed, they were easy to forget after a while. Offhand comments, snickers about their employer or their jobs, or camaraderie—which Frank Innocente described as "goofing off on company time"—earned people a trip to the second floor and a tongue-lashing by the boss. Depending on his mood and the offense, sometimes the unlucky employee got canned.

If you received a summons, the standing joke in the office was "better pack your box," an uneasy reference to the unfortunate few who went to the second-floor executive offices and never came back. Thirty minutes after the employee left, a security guard would appear with a file transfer box and empty out his desk while someone from IT removed his laptop. According to rumor, Frank would go through the files himself to see just what the worker had been up to.

As he rode the elevator, Sterling wondered about his offense and if this was his last elevator ride in the building. He also wondered how the CEO of one of the largest trucking companies in the southwest had the time to look at security tapes. When he arrived at Shelly's desk, she gave him a sympathetic smile, opened the door, and pointed to a chair in front of Frank's massive desk.

As she closed the door behind her, she heard the all-too-familiar mocking tone. "You think you're pretty damned smart, don't you?"

*Poor Sterling.* If those guys—and they were all guys, because Frank didn't believe women were cut out for the trucking business—if they didn't make so much money, they'd all quit. He paid them well because he had to. Turnover would have been far worse otherwise. So his men took the verbal abuse and the constant spying. Away from work they laughed and shrugged it off, although the humiliating dressing-downs kept morale at a low point and ensured the employees were always looking for a better job.

Sterling emerged ten minutes later, his shoulders drooping and his eyes glazed.

"You okay?" she whispered, and he nodded.

"I'm still employed, so I guess so."

"What did you do?"

"I shot the finger at the camera. Somehow I convinced him it was aimed at someone in another cubicle. If he knew the truth—"

She put a finger to her lips, pointed to the camera high above, and smiled conspiratorially. Everyone hung together at Innocente Freight Lines—it was a case of the staff against the tyrant. Sterling had been the whipping boy this time, and any of them might be next.

As he walked away, Shelly's intercom buzzed. "Call Denton," her boss snapped. "I want him here at ten in the morning."

As usual, Denton Kopaddy answered immediately. Shelly pitied the man every time he kowtowed to her boss. He'd have skipped a trip to the Super Bowl to be at Frank Innocente's beck and call, and when she told him what Frank wanted, he didn't hesitate a second.

"You bet, Shelly! I'll be there at ten sharp! You tell Mr. Innocente I'm looking forward to seeing him again!"

It would take Denton three hours to drive from the Native American Cultural Museum in Lawton, Oklahoma, to Dallas. Shelly knew he'd leave really early, because Frank didn't tolerate people who were late. It saddened her to think of the times her boss made the poor man jump through hoops for no reason. Whatever he wanted probably could have been handled by phone. But Frank relished ordering people around.

She entered the appointment in his calendar, and when Frank left for lunch, so did she. There weren't many restaurants in the industrial area of Garland where the company's office building and yard sat, so Shelly drove a few miles to Richardson's Chinatown and her favorite restaurant, Jeng Chi. The server she always requested, a friendly lady named Gigi, brought her a glass of Pinot Grigio without asking and took her order for the usual—steamed juicy pork dumplings and fried rice.

Before coming to work at Innocente Freight Lines, Shelly never drank in the daytime. Now it was a daily ritual to ease the occasional difficult afternoon when Frank returned after drinking his lunch. Today she watched the time carefully; sometimes he'd go to lunch and not return, but one never knew. She'd be back at her desk on time; not only was it her duty, it might avert a martini-fueled tirade.

She relaxed, ate slowly, and practiced the deep-breathing exercises her therapist recommended, reminding herself the employment package made it worthwhile. Tending to an egomaniac was a high-tension job, but she took home more than ten thousand a month, enough to keep Xanax in her medicine cabinet, expensive wine in her fridge, and plenty in the bank for nice dinners and exotic vacations. She had a health plan, a generous 401K, a company-owned Mercedes convertible, and a credit card that she occasionally used to make personal purchases. He signed off on her expense accounts without comment, and the company paid for whatever she charged. She'd gotten so used to the money that it would be a challenge to go back to the days before she came to Innocente Freight Lines. Her apartment alone cost nearly three grand a month, and nowadays she enjoyed having money instead of scraping by until the next payday.

There were other perks, like the hundred-dollar bills he'd hand her at the end of a particularly stressful day. Those rare gestures proved Frank knew he'd acted like an asshole. Incapable of apologizing, he used money instead. When managers and drivers and dock workers got Christmas bonuses, she did too—sometimes equivalent to six months' salary. Last summer he gave her a free first-class trip to Spain and an extra ticket so she could take a friend. It was bizarrely Jekyll-and-Hydeish how he ran his business.

Yeah, the stress and irritation were worth it. He'd never made a pass at her, which had surprised her at first considering his reputation as a Lothario. After a while, she decided somewhere in his narcissistic brain, he knew not to screw things up with her. Shelly wasn't bad looking—other bosses had tried and failed—but she was also an excellent assistant. In his own way, Frank recognized that.

*Sit back and enjoy the ride, sister,* she told herself today as she finished her lunch. *Quit whining and look at the bright side.* That little pep talk worked well. Checking the time, she decided there was time for one more glass of wine.

# CHAPTER NINETEEN

A proud member of the Comanche tribe, Denton Kopaddy had a degree in history and a minor in American Indian studies from Oklahoma State. A month before graduation, his advisor mentioned a job posting from the Native American Cultural Museum in Lawton, Oklahoma, Denton's hometown, which was seeking to hire a director. The pay wasn't great, which might have been why a twenty-four-year-old fresh out of college ended up getting the position. It had been a fun ride so far; the place was small, but the exhibits were unique, interesting and educational. The main building housed several rooms with rare artifacts from the Kiowa, Apache and Comanche tribes, mostly donated by private collectors. There was a reconstructed Apache village behind the main building that visitors of all ages enjoyed. During the school term, buses from across the state filled the parking lot, and the museum was alive with noise and laughter.

Denton was in his fifth year as director. The board of trustees loved him because they'd discovered a hidden talent even Denton himself hadn't been aware of. It turned out he was a whiz at fund-raising. Blessed with an engaging personality and an interesting Native American background, he wasn't embarrassed to talk about the museum's need for money, and he added several Oklahoma City millionaires to the museum's patron list. A year ago, fueled by modest success and convinced there were more potential donors out there, Denton convinced the trustees to spend a relative fortune—five percent of its $200,000 annual budget—on one lavish cocktail party in Dallas. The Oklahoma patrons sent personal invitations to friends and business associates in north Texas, while Denton combed the lists of Dallas's wealthiest to create a "who's who" invite list. More than a hundred people attended; Denton kept an anxious eye on the buffet and drink stations, fingers crossed that the food and booze didn't run out. He'd spent a fortune on this event, and there wasn't a dime left in the budget.

After a crazy, whirlwind evening of wining, dining, presentations, glad-handing, and putting best feet forward, the last guest had departed, leaving Denton, his trustees and a few patrons from Oklahoma to assess the evening. Everyone agreed it had been a wonderful party, but the proof lay in a crystal punch bowl by the door. Upon arrival, each guest received a pledge card, and now a lot of them rested inside that bowl.

As the caterers broke things down, they gathered at a table where Denton had dumped out the cards. "Would you like to do the honors?" he asked the chairman of trustees, muttering a little prayer they'd raised enough to cover the ten-thousand-dollar cost of the event.

Without looking at anything else on them, the man separated the cards into "indications of interest"—fourteen people who wanted more information—and "pledges," of which there were twenty-seven. One trustee commented that twenty-seven percent of attendees was an excellent response rate.

The chairman unfolded each card, studied it for a moment, and made notes on a napkin. *He's adding up amounts,* Denton knew, although from where he sat, he couldn't see the numbers. After recording them, the man passed the cards around the table, and the first one Denton saw made his heart skip a beat. The CEO of a Dallas-based airline had pledged fifty thousand dollars.

*Holy crap! Not only are tonight's expenses covered, this guy pledged a quarter of our annual budget!*

"Here's an interesting one," the chairman commented, holding up a card and turning to a lady next to him. "Kathryn, you suggested inviting Brian Sadler, even though we knew it was highly unlikely he'd attend. Now that his wife is vice president, I suppose that keeps Mr. Sadler busy these days."

The others laughed, and Kathryn Miller, the trustee who'd added Brian's name to the list, said she had been a longtime client of Brian's Dallas gallery. "I spoke to him last week," she added. "He sends his regrets and asked if his manager Meghan O'Brien could come in his stead. I hope you all had a chance to meet her; she's a fascinating person, and the fact she spent over an hour here demonstrates Brian Sadler's interest in the welfare of our little museum."

The chairman nodded and held up the card. "Here's another indication. She brought his pledge card. He wrote on it, 'Thanks for inviting me. I think I can help with potential acquisitions. If I turn up anything interesting, I'll contact your director.'"

"Does that mean financial help too, I wonder?" someone asked.

Beaming, the chairman looked at the card again. "Let's just say inviting Mr. Sadler turned out to be a smart move."

One of the patrons, a burly man named Tex Conover, who owned a fracking company and wore a Stetson hat and ostrich boots, bellowed, "Dammit, man, don't keep us in suspense! Give it up!"

"Mr. Sadler pledged twenty thousand dollars a month for the next twelve months."

The banging of dishes and muted conversation from the caterers across the room broke the stunned silence of the people around the table.

Denton stammered, "Are you...are you sure, sir? That's, uh, more than our annual budget."

"See for yourself." He tossed the card across the table. There was the number—$240,000, payable at twenty grand a month.

Denton let out a yell that in the days before political correctness would have been called a Comanche war

87

whoop. His chair tumbled backwards as he jumped up and danced around the table, high-fiving the others, the majority of whom were most assuredly not accustomed to high-fiving.

The remaining cards held a few more surprises, including another large pledge from a man named Frank Innocente. "I don't think I met him," the chairman said. "Did any of you speak with him?"

"I did. He owns a big trucking company in Dallas," Denton replied, and asked how much he pledged.

"Seventy-five thousand. He said he'll send a check next week." That was welcome news, although after the pledge by Brian Sadler, everything else paled in comparison.

At last the chairman tallied the amounts and said, "Four hundred twenty-seven thousand in pledges, and I expect we'll receive more from the fourteen people who requested information. Good job, Denton. Great job, in fact. My God, man. Half a million dollars! Who'd have imagined it could happen for us? You hit a home run with your cocktail party!"

That night a year ago had been the first time Denton met Frank Innocente. There had been a dozen meetings since, always in Frank's office in the suburbs of Dallas. From the beginning, it became clear Frank's pledge had strings attached. He'd send a check for five thousand and demand Denton arrange a lunch with one of the ultra-wealthy trustees, a demand that so far Denton had managed to avoid, blaming the members' busy schedules. A recent check for ten thousand bore a note, "Don't cash this until we talk." When they did, it was about Brian Sadler. Frank had learned Brian was the museum's largest patron, and he wanted to meet the man who was now the vice president's husband.

That one had been easy to sidestep. "I appreciate your support, Mr. Innocente, but I don't have that kind of pull. I've never even met him myself." Over the past twelve months when Frank had summoned Denton to his office other times, he didn't mention Brian Sadler's name again.

# THE IRON DOOR

*Such is the life of a museum director,* Denton told himself as he drove to Dallas this morning. *A big donor wants to see me, and I have to go to his office to talk about something we could probably handle over the phone.* He mulled the thought, knowing that Frank was no ordinary donor. Nobody else had ever treated Denton the way Frank Innocente did, but he took it in stride. For the good of the museum, he told himself. For the good of the museum.

After driving in dense fog for an hour, he stopped at the McDonald's in Wichita Falls for a coffee refill. The fog would burn off when the sun rose, and it was an easy drive. Highway 287 was four lanes all the way into Dallas, and this morning traffic was light. Denton set the cruise control on eighty and wondered what Frank wanted this time. It really didn't matter, because whenever he called, Denton responded.

# CHAPTER TWENTY

What Frank wanted this time was to show Denton a photo and ask his opinion about a poem in eight stanzas, prefaced by two intriguing sentences.

*My fellow presidents, can you decipher this puzzle? Believe you can and you're halfway there.*

Denton took his time reading the words, pausing to think about their meaning and then reading it all again. Then he asked, "What is this, and where did you get it?"

"The question is, what do you think about it?"

He'd never seen Frank like this. His overbearing demeanor had been replaced with a childlike excitement that was contagious. Denton felt light-headed at the thought of what secrets this rhyme might contain.

"Is this...was this poem written by a president?"

"I don't know," Frank lied. "It begins with 'my fellow presidents.' Sounds like it to me."

"My God, Mr. Innocente. Look at the references to southwestern Oklahoma—Quanah Parker, Pah-Che-Ka—that's a Comanche name, as I'm sure you're aware—and the word Cache is capitalized, like the author's referring to the town of Cache, Oklahoma. Where did you find this?"

"Let me toss out a hypothetical. Have you ever heard of something called the President's Book of Secrets?"

Denton said, "Heard of it? Oh my gosh! I was just thinking about that when I read this. Oh my gosh, are you saying..."

"I'm not saying anything. I'm asking. You've heard

of the book?"

Yes, like most everyone, Denton had heard rumors of such a book.

"Do you think it exists?"

"It's fun to think so. What a treasure trove of information that would be!"

"What if I told you I've seen it?"

"That would be exciting beyond belief. But how's that possible, sir?"

"Because I'm a very close friend of President Perrin's."

"The president showed the book to you? I thought it would be top secret. Presidents' eyes only and all that. Are you saying this poem came from that book? Oh my God!"

Frank sat back, laced his fingers behind his head and smiled. "So what do you make of the poem?"

"If I knew it came from that book, I'd be more confident to discuss what I think."

"You're beginning to irritate me, Denton. How about you answer the question? I called you here to tell me what it means."

*How should I know what it means?* "Uh, sir, with all respect, I have no idea. As I said, parts of it seem to be references to Oklahoma, but I'd need more time to consider each stanza and what it might mean."

"Shelly!" Frank yelled, and moments later the door flew open.

"Yes, sir?"

"Show Mr. Kopaddy to the conference room. He's going to be with us for a while. Denton, take the sheet and let me know when you have something to talk about. I'll be waiting."

Frank's assistant led him down the hall, got him situated, and told him where the bathrooms were. "If you need anything—coffee, water, a soda—you know where to find me," she said before leaving him alone.

He looked at the poem for an hour, then two, parsing each sentence, considering every word in and out of context, all while trying to discover a hidden message. He considered that the poem could be a whimsical bit of nothing, a rambling collection of disjointed facts designed to confuse and trick someone trying to decipher it.

But if it came from the president's book—and Frank gave Denton every reason to believe it had—then why would a president add a page of pure deceit as his contribution to an important repository?

He considered snapping a clandestine photo with his phone but thought better of it when he noticed cameras in either end of the room. Instead he continued working, jotting notes and pondering. At twelve thirty he went to Shelly's desk and asked to see her boss.

"He's out to lunch," she replied. "I'm about to leave too, and you're welcome to join me. You've been hard at it all morning."

"What if he comes back and I'm gone?"

"Everybody has to eat. It'll be fine. Have you ever tried dim sum?"

"I've heard of it, but in Lawton, most of the Asian restaurants are buffet style."

"Let's go to Kirin Court. They come around to your table with carts of dumplings and other stuff. It's one of my favorite places."

"Okay, but what do I do with this?" He had a handful of notes and the photo of the poem.

She locked them in her desk drawer and drove Denton to Chinatown in Richardson. When they returned, Frank was sitting in the conference room. He ordered them both to join him and asked where they'd been.

"What did you tell her?" he asked Denton.

"Sir?"

"What did you tell Shelly about the—uh, the project you're working on?"

"Nothing, Mr. Innocente. We didn't discuss it."

"You two went to lunch for an hour and never talked about why I brought you here?"

Shelly replied, "Frank, he's right. It's none of my business. I didn't ask, and he didn't volunteer. We talked about his work at the museum and what he does for fun."

Frank stood, pointed a finger at both of them, and said, "If I find out you're lying, you'll be sorry! Now get back to work." He stormed down the hall into his office and slammed the door.

"What the hell..." Denton began, but Shelly put a finger to her lips and gave a nod toward the camera. He retrieved the papers from her desk and worked until almost three, when he asked to see Frank.

"You'd better have something for me," the man snapped. Denton had spent the last fifteen minutes composing himself, practicing what he was going to say, and prepping for the usual abrasive meeting with Frank. Now he sat across the desk from him, cowed by his harsh words and stumbling to put his thoughts together.

"Uh, uh, you have to realize it's impossible to know for sure..."

"I don't *have* to *realize* anything, Denton," Frank sneered. "*You* have to realize I want information. Now get on with it."

"Yes, sir. What I, uh, what I meant was, it's filled with clues—at least that's my layman's opinion. Some stanzas are clues to very specific things, while others apply to the entire poem. Let's start with what I call the simple ones. First, we assume a president wrote the poem. He tells us he's Dutch Reformed, and if that's true, then he's either Martin Van Buren or Theodore Roosevelt. Three other clues allow us to nail it down exactly. First, you read the numbers in the poem like a Jew would read them—right to left, or the opposite of how we do it. The other clue says 'I, six two,' have hidden a secret in a frame. Reading the number backwards, we get 'I, two six,' or the twenty-sixth president, who is Theodore Roosevelt. The poem's second line is a quote. 'Believe you can and you're halfway there.' When you Google it, you learn who said it—Roosevelt. So we know the author."

"Good work," Frank said. "What else?"

"Those clues quickly came together, but I have nothing definitive about the rest. It appears there's something hidden in a framed picture with glass that he calls four four six one, which would be 1644 backwards. I have no idea what that refers to. Ditto the part about a cache—he deliberately capitalized the word, which maybe refers to the town of Cache, which existed as a settlement from the mid-eighteen hundreds. It could also refer to a cache of something such as treasure.

"He mentions the chief Quanah Parker, who saw it—whatever *it* is—from afar, and he also refers to the grave of a Pah-Che-Ka, which is a common Comanche name. I can't explain those clues."

Without further comment, Frank dismissed him, and as Denton drove back, he thought about the interesting poem and the other things he knew but hadn't revealed, like how Teddy Roosevelt knew Quanah Parker, hunted with him in the Wichita Mountains, and once dined at his house in Cache. What all that meant, Denton didn't know.

He hadn't dared copy it, nor did he commit the entirety to memory, but he had enough to whet his appetite. One thing was certain—that poem was no capricious bit of whimsy. It was a map of sorts—a guide to finding something special.

# CHAPTER TWENTY-ONE

Earlier, when Shelly and Denton were dining in Chinatown, Frank had been in downtown Dallas. He left his Porsche with a valet and took the elevator forty-nine floors up to Monarch, one of the city's new, posh restaurants. He was fifteen minutes late for his one p.m. appointment with Brian Sadler, but that was how Frank managed his appointments. People waited for him—never the other way around. Ignoring the amazing views of the downtown skyline through floor-to-ceiling windows, he announced himself to the maître d', who led him to a table by the window where he found an attractive young female.

Recognizing her, he snapped, "What are you doing here? My lunch is with your boss."

With a smile she stood, extended her hand, and quipped, "It's good to see you too, Mr. Innocente. Meghan O'Brien. I'm not sure if you remember me…"

He remembered, all right. The captivating Irish brogue and perfect figure that belonged to a girl almost young enough to be his daughter weren't easily forgotten. She was the manager of Bijan Rarities, Brian Sadler's Dallas showroom, and she had worked with Frank both times he went there, professing his ignorance about ancient artifacts before making substantial purchases. She later told Brian it seemed as though the man couldn't have cared less about which relics he acquired. He wanted to demonstrate that he had money, and plenty of it.

As he sat, he said, "Of course I know you. It hasn't been long since I met you at the gallery. Where's Brian?"

"I apologize for not calling you earlier. Mr. Sadler sends his regrets that he's unable to be here today and asked me to come. I hope I haven't inconvenienced you."

Unaccustomed to relegation, Frank suppressed his anger. When he required something, his money typically ensured deference. But not only was Brian Sadler vastly wealthier than Frank, he was a famous TV personality and the husband of the vice president of the United States.

*Dammit, I should have known he wouldn't show up,* he thought as she explained that her boss was rarely in Dallas these days. For several weeks he'd been shuffling between Washington, DC, and London, where he was managing a project for the British Museum.

*He would have come if he'd been in town,* Frank assured himself. Instead of cancelling the lunch, Brian had sent his second-in-command instead, who wasn't a bad substitute. In fact, that Irish lilt was sexy as hell. Lunch with a young, attractive stand-in might not get him what he was after, but this could turn out just fine. He leaned in closer and flashed the plastic smile he vainly believed women found irresistible.

A glass of white wine stood at Meghan's place. Most of Frank's lunches started and ended with martinis, but today he wanted to be on his toes to advance his plan. He ordered a merlot.

Earlier, when Brian received Frank's invitation to lunch, he had called Meghan. Wealthy clients often insisted on dealing with the owner when considering expensive acquisitions, but Brian wouldn't have flown overseas for a lunch even if he'd wanted to. Innocente had an agenda; that much was evident after he dropped over three hundred grand on two pieces Meghan said he chose almost at random.

Accustomed to celebrity status, Brian found himself in an unexpectedly odd quandary when Nicole became vice president. His business was acquiring and selling antiquities, but in recent years it had become secondary to the income from his television documentaries and speaking engagements. His was a household name, and he became careful about which invitations he accepted. With over a million followers of his TV shows, it would take only one kook to change his and Nicole's lives forever. And others who posed as potential clients of the gallery were time-wasters who wanted access to Nicole.

When Frank emailed Brian, touting his recent purchases and asking about lunch, he made casual mention of Brian's close relationship with former president Harrison. He asked if they got together often, and that raised Brian's suspicions about the man's motives.

"Something feels off about him," he told Meghan when she offered to stand in for Brian. "Way too pushy and prying, if you know what I mean. I'm sure he's harmless, but don't agree to meet him anywhere but the gallery or the restaurant. And Meghan," he added, "you don't have to do this if you don't want to."

"Part of the job, boss. I've handled lots of clients in the five years I've been your manager."

"Much of the time when I'm away," he agreed. "Of course you can handle lunch with him, and frankly I'm glad I don't have to deal with a barrage of questions about Nicole. At least you can keep the conversation on business. By the way, I did an internet search and a background check. Seems there are more scurrilous posts about our client than biographical details."

Frank was forty-eight, or two years older than Brian. Raised in Brooklyn, he attended Catholic schools and graduated City University of New York with a degree in business. After working in the borough of Queens with his father in construction, he moved to Dallas, started Innocente Freight Lines, and built its business with astonishing speed and success. In an early interview, Frank claimed to be a proud third-generation American, his grandparents having emigrated from Italy at the beginning of World War II.

The tidbits that turned up on the internet painted an unflattering picture of the man. He appeared to be wealthy, but he could be obnoxiously ostentatious about it. He wanted others to think he was worldly, but his self-

# BILL THOMPSON

aggrandizing bragging resulted in snickering behind his back. He was the epitome of new money in a city replete with the other kind. Brian had nothing against the *nouveau riche*—he'd risen from a rookie stockbroker to an internationally respected antiquities dealer and TV personality—but ostentation was another thing entirely. And Frank appeared to be filled with it.

Meghan had proclaimed herself ready for the luncheon, and today she sipped her wine, listening politely while he dropped names and charity events, casually interjected that he'd sprained his ankle last fall while boarding a private jet on his way to Napa for Thanksgiving, and at last he turned the conversation to a subject besides himself.

"I know Brian has other galleries. London, New Orleans, Jerusalem—between whatever project he's doing for the British Museum and running his businesses, you must not see much of him. When will he be back in Dallas?"

"He doesn't share his schedule with me. He pops in every two or three weeks, but I communicate with him all the time. Mr. Sadler appreciates your patronizing Bijan Rarities and asked me to assure you I'll help with anything you need."

"And how about you, Meghan? You're not wearing a ring; is there a significant other in your life?"

Flushed, she dropped her eyes. "With all respect, my personal life is private."

"I'm single myself. I know evenings alone can be boring. I'd welcome the company if you'd join me for dinner sometime soon. Maybe this evening if you're free."

He crossed the line, and she saw red. Her eyes flashed with anger.

"Mr. Innocente, I appreciate your interest in my welfare. As I said, my personal life is my business, and if somehow I found myself lonely, it'd be a cold day in Hell before..." She paused. She still didn't know what he wanted, and she was acting as unprofessionally as he. Now wasn't the time to piss him off.

"Before you'd have dinner with me? Is that what you're saying?" He smiled, and the words slithered out of his mouth like a snake shedding its skin. His slimy undertone made her shudder.

"That's not what I'm saying at all. Business is business, and I make it a point not to date clients. That said, I'm flattered." That was a bald-faced lie. "Anyone would be flattered." Another one. "So now let's talk about why you asked Mr. Sadler to lunch."

He knew what she was doing. She was playing hard to get, and he enjoyed that game. He'd seen it many times with many women, but he had ways of breaking down their barriers. When it finally happened with young Meghan, the feeling of conquest would be exhilarating.

*She'll come around because women can't resist me. For now, I'll let her have her way.*

"I wasn't suggesting anything inappropriate," he murmured with a leer that demonstrated his insincerity. "I apologize if I upset you."

She shook her head and he continued, "Your boss has some fascinating friends, doesn't he?"

She waited while he leered at her with that smarmy smile.

"I'm not sure what you're getting at."

"I have a few friends like that myself. President Perrin, for one. He and I are good friends. Very close, actually. Brian knows Harry Harrison, and he's a man I'd like to meet. We have something in common."

*Okay, now we're getting somewhere.* He wanted to use Brian to get to the former president.

"What would that be?"

"He has clues about a train robbery a long time ago. He even has an idea where the stolen goods are hidden. I have ideas about it too, and I want to discuss them with him. It could benefit us both—and Brian too. I could see it becoming his next big documentary."

"How interesting."

"Not nearly as interesting as you, my dear."

That was enough for Meghan. Now she understood

why he'd bought two relics without appearing interested in them. He was a wealthy opportunist seeking a way to meet former president Harrison. She knew Brian would support her in the action she was about to take.

She took out her phone, glanced at the screen, and said, "I'm so sorry, Mr. Innocente. Something's come up, and I have to get back to the showroom." She put her napkin on the table and stood.

He remained seated. "Are you sure? We haven't even ordered yet. I'm interested in talking about buying more pieces from the gallery, and I thought we could chat about them."

*Of course you are, now that I'm leaving.* "My apologies. Give me your number, and I'll ask Brian to call if he has a moment."

"People don't call me when they 'have a moment,' my dear," he sneered. "People don't send others to luncheon appointments with me without notice, even their beautiful young managers. Tell your boss what I said about President Harrison. I want to talk to Brian, face-to-face. Soon. Call my assistant and set it up."

He turned his head away and picked up his wineglass. She nodded to a couple of clients she recognized as she walked through the crowded restaurant. She called an Uber, and when she got in the car, she retrieved her phone to call Brian, but he called first.

"Is your lunch finished already?" he asked. "I was going to leave you a message."

"There was no lunch. The guy's a total asshole, and after he came on to me, I left."

"I'm sorry. Were you able to handle things?"

"With that creep? Yes, I think he got the message. I've dealt with pushy men, but this is the cockiest guy I've ever met. His attitude put me off from the beginning. But enough of that. Let me tell you what he's after." She explained the discussion about Harry.

# CHAPTER TWENTY-TWO

Horace Wilmington Fleming lived in a comfortable two-bedroom house in Greenbelt, Maryland, that his mother bought in 1983 when she retired from the federal government. Upon her death nine years ago, her only child inherited everything—the house, furnishings, personal effects and a 1991 Oldsmobile 88 that he maintained carefully and drove rarely. He'd lived with her his whole life, and she had been his only family. Mother meant everything to Horace because Mother had once saved his life. Not literally, although perhaps so. If she hadn't taken matters in her own hands, Horace might have lived an entirely different life, in juvenile detention and perhaps prison. When Mother died, Horace stayed in bed for days, sobbing and crying out for her. After a period of mourning, he assuaged his grief by burying himself in the one thing he loved—books.

Some might have considered Horace a penny-pincher, but that wasn't true. He spent little because he had few needs. A sensible man, he walked to the Metro station each weekday morning and rode the train to work, not because it saved on gas, but because it made better sense than fighting the traffic and ending up frazzled. He dined out rarely and always alone, never entertained or received an invitation, and had no friends either at work or on the street where he lived.

He contributed the maximum each month to his retirement plan, made regular deposits to a savings account, and spent weekends pursuing the only indulgence he allowed himself. On most Saturdays and Sundays, Horace would drive the back roads of Virginia and Maryland, visiting flea markets and garage sales. The owners of small-town antique shops knew the eccentric man well. He wore the same worn tweed jacket, corduroy trousers and golfing cap on every visit, regardless of the season. He looked like an awkward, eccentric uncle, his inquisitive eyes peering over old-fashioned horn-rimmed glasses as he examined every book in every store he visited.

Books were Horace's passion, and he called them his "babies." On rare occasions during his weekend jaunts when he found something special, he'd cry out in delight, his giddy excitement eliciting smiles—and the occasional derisive sneer—from other shoppers.

Money was no object when Horace found a new baby. He'd make a feeble attempt to haggle, but the shopkeepers knew him by now. He was like a novice poker player holding a winning hand; his entire demeanor changed the moment he saw what he wanted, and the sellers stood their ground until Horace paid full price. Now and then they let him win the bargaining because they pitied this lonely man who lived for books.

Until a couple of years ago, there had been books piled everywhere in the house. If anyone ever visited, which they didn't, they'd have seen what amounted to a hoarder's abode and would have had to snake their way through stacks of books in the living room, dining room and even the kitchen. Only two rooms were exempt—Mother's bedroom, which remained exactly as it had been on the day she died in her bed, and his own bedroom. He was a man of organization and neatness, and eventually these traits overcame his desire to accumulate vast quantities of books. He became disgusted at his own lack of self-control and decided to do something about it.

*I won't buy any more until there's a place to put them,* he told himself, but like a relapsed alcoholic, he went right back out the next Saturday, looking for new additions to his little family. At last he made a decision. He talked it over with Mother and felt better when he learned she didn't mind him creating a library in her bedroom. Mother was long-since dead, of course, but Horace often spoke to her in his mind, getting her opinion on decisions affecting his mundane life. She had always been his savior and the one on his side, after all.

*Just don't move my bed out,* she had admonished, so he didn't. He donated the rest of her bedroom furniture to the Salvation Army and hired a handyman. Two weeks later, the bedroom had floor-to-ceiling bookshelves that provided space for his current babies and plenty for new ones. He moved his favorite overstuffed chair, ottoman and end table into his new library. They had been in the living room by the TV, and he was thrilled to relocate them. Although Mother had watched television, Horace never did, instead getting the news on his office computer. Once the new library was complete, he could hardly wait every afternoon to ride the train to the Greenbelt station, walk to his house, pour himself a Coca-Cola and sit in his favorite chair, smoking his pipe and relaxing with his favorite friends.

Now that he had a special place for the things he loved, he implemented a plan he'd been thinking about for years. It was daring, outrageous and scary, but it was also the most exciting thing he had ever done. He created an area for the most special treasure babies of all.

He went into the bedroom-cum-library and walked past Mother's bed to her closet. He opened the wooden door; just behind it was another made of metal and reinforced steel. He entered numbers on a keypad and opened it. What had been a clothes closet was now a shrine.

Mother's clothes had been donated, the racks removed, and more shelves installed on every wall. In the middle of the small room was something Horace designed and his contractor built—an altar. It had a kneeler and a wooden shelf at chest level, allowing Horace to get on his knees in front of a book lying open on the shelf and read. He spent many an enjoyable evening kneeling and reading in what was tantamount to a religious experience.

The secret room contained only a few books, but

they were his pride and joy, ones he had carefully purloined from the National Archives. The books dated back to the founding of our country. Many were handwritten diaries of important figures in American politics, business and religion. He could study Abe Lincoln's thoughts about the Civil War, Bishop Fulton J. Sheen's commentaries on his struggles with the church, and Henry Ford's challenges as he built an automobile empire.

He carefully chose books no one ever asked about. He'd move them to the wrong place in the shelves, deliberately misplacing them for a month or two just in case, but one afternoon he'd put a book in his briefcase and go home. No one ever checked Horace's movements. He came and went at will, and his stolen books found a home in the secret vault.

There was one more book he wanted, but he had neither the nerve nor the opportunity to make it happen. Someday at exactly the right moment, he'd figure out how to make the Book of Secrets his own.

# CHAPTER TWENTY-THREE

On that fateful Tuesday morning, in the West Wing the political machine was operating in its typical frenzied fashion. Staffers scurried down the carpeted halls as reporters sat in the press corps office overlooking the west colonnade, reading advance briefings and preparing questions for the afternoon press conference. President Perrin's eight o'clock and eight-thirty appointments sat waiting outside the Oval Office, peppering Frances with snide comments. The Speaker and the senior senator from New York were pissed, and they demanded to know where the president was.

Frances would have gladly told them if she knew. Perrin was always in the Oval by the time she arrived at eight, and his unwillingness to let her manage his schedule meant appointments often got backed up. This was different, because it was first thing in the morning, when Frances booked the important people to keep them happy.

Since President Perrin didn't appreciate her nagging, she gave him until quarter of nine before ringing the upstairs residence. "Why isn't he downstairs yet?" she asked the valet, who advised he had come out of the bedroom around five, walked across the hall in his pajamas to the kitchen and returned with a cup of coffee, which he took to the private sitting room adjoining his and the first lady's bedroom.

"I checked on him about an hour ago," the valet added. "He was sitting in the dark and told me to leave him alone. He hasn't been out since."

He called Frances a few minutes later. "I knocked on the door, Miss Anderson. He didn't answer, so I opened it just a little. He's got all the shades drawn; he was staring into the empty fireplace like the last time I checked. I asked if he needed anything, and he said no, everything would be fine. He's not himself, ma'am. Something's not right. And now I'm wondering where Mrs. Perrin is. She's usually up by seven, and here it is almost nine. I don't have the clearance to enter their bedroom, especially since I know he's not in it."

Frances agreed something was wrong. After thirty years by Archie's side, she could read him better than anyone except Dee Perrin, and she knew secrets Dee would never know. As much as she wanted to barge upstairs, she waited. Perhaps he was having a medical issue. Or a little dementia—she'd begun seeing signs—or had something important on his mind. He'd been more agitated than usual lately, but she hadn't been able to learn why.

At nine thirty she made a command decision. She'd already rescheduled the Speaker and senator, and she took the elevator to the residence. "Where is he?" she asked the valet, who pointed to the private sitting room. "Nothing's changed since I spoke to you earlier. No sign of Mrs. Perrin, and he hasn't come out either."

There was an interior door between the sitting room and bedroom, and Frances wondered if Archie had gone back to bed. She knocked on the parlor door, waited a moment, and opened it. The darkness was pierced by meager rays of sunshine peeking through the almost-drawn curtains. She saw him sitting in his pajamas in a chair.

"Mr. President, are you all right?" He remained still, apparently unaware of her presence, and she stepped inside and closed the door. "Mr. President..."

"You can stop calling me that, Frances," he said in a hoarse whisper. "That's all behind me now."

"I'm...I'm going to turn on the light, sir." She flipped a switch, and the chandelier flooded the room with light. She would recall that she walked to his chair, looked at him, and gasped. A wave of nausea swept over her, and she grabbed the back of his chair to support herself.

President Archibald Perrin held an eight-inch butcher knife in his lap. His robe was covered in blood, and a set of red footprints led from the bedroom door to his chair.

"Oh Archie," she moaned. "Oh Archie, what on earth have you done? Have you cut yourself?"

"Frances, you're so good. Always taking care of me. No, dear, I'm fine. I just had to take care of a little business this morning. Regrettable, but something that had to be done." He pointed to the bedroom door.

"Is it Dee? Is she hurt, Archie?"

"No, she isn't hurting, thank God. That's a blessing. If she'd found out who I really am...I couldn't let that happen, now could I?"

His rambling words scared her, and she trembled as she walked hesitantly across the room and grasped the knob. Afraid of what she might find in the bedroom, she turned, saw Archie staring absently into the fireplace, and opened the door.

Her horrific screams brought the valet and two Secret Service agents crashing through the door. The valet went to check on the president, who remained silent in his chair, while the guards ran to Frances's side. She stood dumbly in the doorway, one hand stifling sobs while pointing with the other.

# CHAPTER TWENTY-FOUR

The White House is solidly constructed, and the commotion in the second-floor residence went unnoticed by more than a hundred people working one floor below. Staffers had begun to wonder why the president—and now his personal assistant—weren't at their desks, but it wasn't until Perrin's physician and two guards ran through the hallway and dashed into the elevator that everyone knew something was very wrong.

"The president's dead," someone whispered, and the rumor spread like a California wildfire. The press secretary called upstairs, and Frances answered, ordering her to remain at her desk and say nothing. A member of the protective detail ran to the elevator entrance and blocked it, telling anxious staffers no one was allowed upstairs without permission.

"Is it the president?" they asked him. "Is he dead?"

The stoic man said nothing because he had been told nothing. He wondered what was going on, just as they did.

Work stopped as everyone milled about the hallways, sharing theories and spreading rumors. Several congregated around the Secret Service command post, where the senior officer on duty directed the men who guarded the inside and outside of the White House. His attempts to shoo them away didn't work; they were hungry for information. One aide heard the officer make a call, telling the guards at the Seventeenth Street entrance gate to allow DC police vehicles to pass through.

"The metropolitan cops are coming," the aide reported to his co-workers. "What the hell happened up there?" At that moment, an announcement came over the public address system. All visitors were ordered to leave the building, and governmental employees were told to return to their offices and remain there until notified.

"You heard it, people," guards said to the staffers milling about. "Get back to work." They returned to the West Wing, passing groups of tourists and visitors being led to exits by the Secret Service. The more ingenious of the staffers—and those whose offices lay in proximity— kept an eye on the doors to the chief of staff and vice president's offices. Curiously, a guard stood in front of each closed door, barring entry. When the national security adviser, Perrin's chief of staff and Vice President Nicole Farber simultaneously stepped into the hall and marched toward the elevator, the rumors about President Perrin escalated throughout the West Wing like the headwinds of a hurricane.

"The DC coroner just arrived," an aide to the press secretary reported to her co-workers. "That's why they ordered us all back to our offices. It's so we can't see what's going on. He's dead. That must be what happened."

Two hours later, curious White House employees still hadn't been briefed, and they gathered in small groups around TV sets as CNN broke the news first. A letter invoking the Twenty-Fifth Amendment of the Constitution had been sent to the Speaker and the president pro tempore of the Senate. Specifics behind the request to remove President Archie Perrin remained a mystery, but the petition was signed by Vice President Farber and fifteen cabinet secretaries, sufficient to allow her to be immediately installed as acting president. The transfer of power had happened at 1:13 p.m. Eastern time.

To those witnessing things unfold inside the White House, the petition revealed two things. First, Perrin was alive. Second, something awful had happened to him that precipitated his immediate removal from office. On television, political pundits explained the Twenty-Fifth

Amendment, which had temporarily been invoked in the past when a president had a colonoscopy or routine surgery. It had never been used to force a president out of office. With no information flowing from the White House, the broadcasters pondered if Perrin's removal was consensual or forced. And what had happened overnight to cause this unprecedented, sensational turn of events?

Brian Sadler learned about his wife's new position in a dizzying way. He was in his office at the Dallas gallery when his cell phone rang, displaying the name Fiona Deloache, his wife's chief of staff. The moment he answered, rapid knocks came on his door. "FBI, Mr. Sadler. We're coming in!"

Stunned, he stood as four plainclothes agents burst into his office, leaving a bewildered Meghan O'Brien behind them. "Is that the White House on the phone?" one asked, seeing Brian holding it to his ear. He nodded, and the agent motioned for him to take the call.

He listened in silence for what seemed a long time, stopping to jot down notes. Finally he said, "Okay. There's no need to send a plane. I'll charter a jet here..."

Numb and in shock, he was told he must comply with instructions. There would be no charter; a government plane was already at Love Field waiting for him. "Tell me what happened," the agents in the room heard him say, and they watched his face turn ashen as he collapsed into his chair. He listened again before saying, "Is...is Nicole okay? Is she safe? Is she already president right now? And the president—Archie, I mean—my God, what happened?"

The only thing Brian learned was that his wife was acting president of the United States. The rest would have to wait until she called him. As soon as the call ended, the FBI agents took him in an armored SUV to the airport. He ordered a vodka martini as soon as the plane was airborne, and for most of the trip he alternated between staring out the window deep in thought and making a copious list of the questions that flooded his brain.

Realizing he'd dozed off, he awoke abruptly when a flight attendant touched his arm. "I'm sorry to wake you,

Mr. Sadler. President Farber's on the line." She pointed to a telephone receiver in the armrest. Suddenly dizzy, he stared at her. *President Farber.* The words hit him like a freight train. The flight attendant opened the armrest, removed the receiver, and handed it to him.

Nicole described the unimaginable circumstances that led her from learning of a tragedy to becoming leader of the free world in less than sixty minutes. Until now, Brian had known only what he saw on the news—First Lady Dee Perrin died in the White House residence, and the president experienced a psychotic episode, presumably because of his wife's tragic death. For the safety of the country, the Twenty-Fifth Amendment had been invoked, and Vice President Farber was acting president. "I'm glad you're on your way," she added. "You can't imagine how crazy everything is around here."

"So Dee just died in bed? I guess Archie found her; the news says he's taking it really hard. I can't imagine—"

She interrupted. "You really cannot imagine, and you don't know anything about what really happened. I can't talk on this line, and the chairman of the Joint Chiefs of Staff is waiting in the other room. We'll talk when you get here."

He had one last question that had crowded everything else from his mind. "This is temporary, right? You're acting president, but in hours or days you'll turn it back over to Archie. Right?"

She paused. "Brian, there's so much more to this than what's been made public. So much more. I'll see you soon." The call went dead.

Brian spent the rest of the flight unable to concentrate on anything except her words. How much more could there be? What would he learn when he reunited with his wife, the president of the United States?

The Gulfstream landed at Joint Base Andrews, and more agents whisked Brian into a waiting limousine. He noticed the small US flag on the right front near the hood and swallowed hard. Everything would be different now. Flanked by four motorcycle cops with lights flashing and sirens blaring, they made the trip to the White House in under a half hour. Fiona met him at the staff entrance and took him directly upstairs to a familiar place—the Treaty Room—where a guard opened the door and notified his counterpart inside that Brian was here.

When the guard led him in, he saw Nicole and a few others sitting around a table. Easels stood nearby, holding whiteboards covered with bullet points and diagrams, and he was ushered to a chair out of the way as aides scurried in and out, delivering papers to the men and women assembled.

The moment he entered the room, the conversation stopped abruptly. Nicole stood, walked over, hugged him, and said, "I'm glad you're here. Your extra set of eyes and ears will help navigate the craziness." She brought him over and introduced him. Some of the people he'd met before, but most—cabinet secretaries, the Speaker of the House, and the national security director—he hadn't.

"Come join us," she said, but the security head objected. The topics of conversation today were above top secret, and Brian had no clearance. "You may discuss things with your husband afterwards," he added. "Every president does, but I'm afraid he can't stay."

Unaccustomed to being excluded, Brian stood uncomfortably and mumbled that he'd see Nicole later. Out in the hall, he had no idea what to do next. This floor—the residence—was exclusive to the president's family. Archie and Dee Perrin lived here. As acting president, he doubted Nicole would be expected to move in, and today it saddened him that he felt a stranger here where he and his wife had been welcomed by Harry and Jennifer so many times.

"I need to wait somewhere while my wife finishes that meeting. Where should I go?" he asked the Secret Service guard outside the door. The man radioed Fiona, who instructed Brian to take the elevator to the first floor, where she would meet him. He rode down in silence, his mind spinning with possibilities of what might be ahead—none of them good.

# CHAPTER TWENTY-FIVE

Fiona suggested Brian wait in Nicole's office. The vice president's ceremonial office was in the Eisenhower Executive Office building, and Nicole rarely used it. Her functional office, the one she used every day, was a smallish room just down the hall from the Oval Office, allowing her to be at the president's beck and call. Brian unpacked his laptop and set it up, accepted a cup of coffee from an aide, and worked on his gallery's business. Trying to keep his mind on his projects and off the issues at hand, he lost track of time and two hours passed. He walked next door, got directions to the restroom, and returned, wondering how long it would be until he'd see Nicole.

Fiona came by around five to advise that Nicole had been working in the Oval Office for the past couple of hours. Things had wrapped up, and she wanted to see Brian. When he walked in, he saw her sitting behind the *Resolute* desk, holding her head in her hands, and he took a seat across the desk from her.

"I've come up with the title for my presidential biography," she said at last. "It's 'Holy Shit!'"

Brian laughed. "Hopefully you won't be around long enough for a presidential biography." She stared at him, and he added, "What I mean is, once Archie gets over the shock of Dee's death…"

She shook her head. "This is all so sad, Brian. There's so much that we can't make public. It's just tragic." She rose, took his hand, and led him to the couch across the room where he and Nicole sat so many times while Harry had been president.

"For now, all this is between you and me, period," she began, and he reminded her he was pretty good at keeping a secret. Much of what Harry had told them over his six years as president remained just between them to this day.

"You're right, and I trust you completely, but what happened in this building in the past twenty-four hours has no precedent. It's so bizarre and so unexpected that it could affect our relationship with allies and enemies alike. This is so delicate..."

"Why don't you tell me about it?"

She stood and walked across the room. "First I need a drink. I recall Harry used to press a button over here. Wonder if it's still there? Do you think anybody's waiting around to serve a brand-new president?" She pressed; in seconds an unobtrusive door opened, and Robert, the valet they knew from Harry's time, entered the room.

"Welcome, Madam President. I'm so sorry you've assumed this position under such awful circumstances. I know it must be difficult, but I'm here to help any way I can. May I bring you and Mr. Sadler a cocktail?"

"Robert, I'm so glad to see you! I didn't know if you would still be here after Harry left office. You're like a breath of fresh air on a crazy, crazy day. I can't think of anything better. I'll have—"

"I remember, ma'am. Dry chardonnay for you, XO vodka martini for Mr. Sadler. I've made sure to keep some on hand just in case President Perrin invited you in for cocktails."

She smiled. "Thanks for remembering the wine, but tonight I'll join Brian in a martini. It's been a hard day."

"Yes, ma'am. I can only imagine."

"Are the rumors flying around this place?"

He nodded. "Yes. I don't want to be presumptuous, ma'am, but I just wondered if I should keep President Perrin's favorite gin in the pantry, or if I should send it down to the locker in the basement. Just for now, I mean. I'm sure he'll be coming back. I don't mean to be out of line…"

"No worries. Nobody's sure about what's going on. For now, just leave it here."

"Yes, ma'am." The old valet shook his head, left, and returned with two ice-cold martinis. Alone once more, Brian asked if the office was under electronic surveillance.

"I'm told not. It's swept several times a day. What happens here supposedly stays here, at least until someone leaks a story."

They clinked glasses, took a refreshing sip, and she said, "We will always remember this as the day our lives changed forever." He waited, knowing she'd begin when she was ready.

"There's physical evidence for a lot of what I'm going to tell you, but parts are still conjecture, since Archie isn't cooperating. That's really not a fair statement. Apparently he *can't* cooperate. Around five this morning he came out of their bedroom, nodded to the guard in the hallway, and went to the kitchen across the hall. He returned with a cup of coffee and went into the sitting room next door. He'd also picked up something else in the kitchen—a butcher knife.

"The valet checked on him twice and saw him sitting in the dark. Archie said everything was fine. Shortly after nine, his assistant, Frances, entered the sitting room, turned on the lights, and found him in his bloodstained bathrobe, holding the knife in his lap. Bloody footprints on the carpet led from the bedroom, where she found Dee Perrin in their bed covered in blood. According to the medical examiner, the time of death was around five thirty a.m., or relatively soon after Archie returned from the kitchen. She was stabbed forty-seven times, any number of which could have been the fatal one. The guard was always in the hall but heard nothing, and no one entered or left the presidential suite except Archie. Apparently he got the knife, went into the bedroom where his wife was sleeping, and stabbed her to death for reasons unknown.

"He was incoherent when Frances spoke to him in the sitting room. He said he didn't need to be called president anymore, and that he was glad Dee wasn't hurting, because it would have hurt her to learn what kind of man he really was. As surreal as it sounds, the president of the United States brutally murdered his wife this morning in the White House. That's a fact, but nobody knows why."

"Will he be arrested?"

"Too soon to tell. They're taking him to a private mental facility, where he'll be under armed guard. He has some awareness of his action, since he told his assistant he didn't want Dee to hurt, but the horror and gravity of it doesn't seem to register with him. The ME said he could be in shock, but it's more likely some type of total breakdown. Why he killed her, nobody will know unless he recovers enough to explain."

"What have your meetings today been about?"

She sighed. "What have they *not* been about? Sudden transition of power to a person—that would be me—with no political background and no experience with Beltway shenanigans. The danger of attack from enemies who perceive us as vulnerable. Am I just a temp in this job, or is it mine to keep? Should I step aside and let people with experience run things? Just mundane little agenda items. And by the way, did you see the S&P closing this afternoon? Down thirteen percent. Nice way to start a presidency I didn't want in the first place."

Brian took her hand. "As I've told you in the past, I've never met a stronger person. That strength is going to benefit you and the country through challenges no other person has faced—or even could imagine facing."

"It's going to be insanely busy for a while," she agreed. "My assistant's working in tandem with Frances Anderson to ensure a smooth and quick transition. I'll have all his appointments plus a lot of my own. Little decisions just like Robert a minute ago asking if he should keep Archie's gin close by—there are going to be a thousand of those a day, I'm afraid. Do I clean out Archie's desk in the Oval or leave everything just as it is? As acting president, is it presumptuous to even work there? Should I stay in the

VP's office? See what I mean?"

"What can I do to help?"

"Not a lot, I'm afraid. These are uncharted waters, and ordinarily I'd ask you to sit in on every strategy meeting and planning session, but it's just not done that way. I have a hundred advisors, and it seems every one of them has a hundred. I must take counsel from people who know the ropes and hope I can separate the ones with my interest at heart from the greedy bastards.

"As the greenest novice ever to hit town, I have to stay on my toes. Harry has offered to help, and a couple of his staffers will be coming over to pitch in for the next few weeks. I'll make it, but you needn't waste your time in DC listening to everything I do. I think it would not only drive you crazy, but probably me too. And it may not even be allowed—most of the meetings are top secret and all that. So go home or to London or wherever, do what you need to do, and I'll call you back when I get a little free time."

Two days later he did just that.

# CHAPTER TWENTY-SIX

*Twenty-two days later*

"The usual, Mr. President?" the valet asked, and Harry smiled and nodded. When he served the Oban single-malt scotch over ice, Harry thanked him and asked, "Robert, does this feel as strange to you as it does to me?"

The waiter nodded. "It sure does, Mr. President. Not that long ago you were calling the shots." He turned to Nicole. "I apologize, Madam President. Sadly, it's the same thing with you. Three presidents in six months. My, my, what's this world coming to?"

"No apologies necessary," she assured him. It was an awkward moment for Nicole too, playing host instead of guest in the Treaty Room. This was the first time the tables were turned; it might become comfortable later, or Archie might somehow return and upend everything. The chance of that happening was nil, and everyone knew it. But tonight a tension hung in the air.

Although Jennifer and Harry were exes now, Robert, the valet, knew the Harrisons far better than Nicole and Brian. He'd served hundreds of evening cocktails during Harry's six-year term as president. But now Nicole was leader of the free world, and as he waited on the couples, the valet felt as if he were at a tennis match. "Mr. President, Madam President, Mr. President..." Back and forth between a former chief executive and the current one. *A unique and very sad occasion*, the old butler mused as he watched their interaction. He'd served other presidents, but never had one been close friends with another like these folks. It was a pleasant thing to observe two couples whose friendship was built upon other things than power and politics.

It had been Brian's idea to invite Harry and Jennifer to join him for his first trip to the White House since Nicole's transition. It had been twenty-two days since she told him to go home and wait until she had time to see him, and much had transpired during those three weeks.

President Perrin remained in a dark place, strapped in his bed, curled in a fetal ball day and night, and unable to comprehend the horrific crime he'd committed. Under the law, he'd had four days to challenge his removal under the Twenty-Fifth Amendment, but that challenge did not come. He'd experienced no periods of lucidity from that tragic Morning until the present. Despite the strenuous objections of a few on both sides of the congressional aisle who wanted no part of Nicole Farber's presidency, the Supreme Court Upheld the law, and here she was.

Tonight, Harry and Jennifer listened in rapt fascination as Nicole described her abrupt and unprecedented ascension to power. Harry had done it the usual way, by climbing the political ladder. He commiserated when she described the hundreds of decisions, the backbiting and lack of support from many who rightly called her an outsider, and the handful of sympathetic congressmen and senators who had taken her under their wing. With almost a month under her belt, she felt comfortable finally spending a weekend with friends at the White House.

For over an hour they talked about Harry's mother's medical issues, how well Harry and Jennifer were adjusting to life as private citizens, and how Brian was coping. "The first gentleman isn't exactly a happy camper," he grumbled, saying many of the sudden changes in their personal life were irksome. Almost every president had spent years in politics, and their spouses had an idea of the life changes that accompanied a move into the White House. Nothing— no aspect of a couple's personal life—would ever be the same. Nicole had been vice president for a short time, of course, but that invasion of their lives was minimal compared to this.

Decisions that affected national and world policy, strategizing, press conferences, public appearances, state dinners, and stumping for candidates were part of a president's life. And after being the spouse in the spotlight for years, Brian found playing second fiddle difficult.

Although he understood, Nicole's secrets irritated him because they prided themselves on sharing everything. From the moment it all started, Brian found himself eased out of the picture by a simple touch on his wife's arm. "A brief word, Madam President?" meant she and the Speaker, or the Majority Leader, or a cabinet official, or any of a hundred others would whisk her aside for a private conversation. Once he left Washington, they'd speak by phone every night, and she'd tell him most of the things she'd done that day. Every president shared sensitive information with spouses, but what he took as condescending snubs—the "for her ears only" moments— were hard for this type A to stomach.

Sometimes those whispered conversations remained a secret. "You really don't want to know," she'd told him more than once those first days when it involved matters of national security. She was right, of course; there were things he shouldn't know. It was none of his business, but he was married to the president, and certain parts of their new relationship stung.

In years past, Nicole had been a stellar performer in one of Dallas's most prestigious law firms while Brian had built his galleries, hosted History Channel documentaries, and traveled the world. It wasn't as though she had been a stay-at-home partner, listening eagerly when Brian came home at night to tell her about his day. They had been powerful people in their own rights, but now Brian had a feeling of emasculation he had shared with no one until tonight.

Harry deftly changed the subject, asking Nicole if she'd met Horace Wilmington Fleming.

"What a strange man," she commented, smiling.

Brian asked, "Who's he?"

There was an uncomfortable silence. She glanced at Harry and mumbled, "He's with the National Archives. He's a curator of things related to former presidents."

"So you've met him? What's special about him?"

Nicole fidgeted in her chair. "There...uh, there wasn't much to the meeting. It was just about..." She faltered.

"Good thing you're not on the red phone with the premier of Russia, since you can't seem to get your thoughts together," Brian snapped. "Cat got your tongue?"

Harry rescued her. "Ease up, buddy. It's not her fault. She's not allowed to say anything about what he does."

"A curator in the National Archives is the keeper of state secrets? Come on, Harry. Admit it. How much did you tell Jennifer when you were negotiating a tough agreement with Iran? Or North Korea? A lot, I'll bet. What's different about this?"

"I told her anything she wanted to know. I'm sure Nicole will do the same if a crisis arises..."

"And that's my point," Brian interrupted. "A president is given tacit consent to discuss matters of national security with his or her spouse. But some glorified docent from the National Archives imparts secrets she can't tell me?"

"That's right. Nicole signed an oath. We all did."

Brian's eyes opened wide in astonishment. "You *all* did? Every president? An oath about what?"

Nicole answered, "A promise never to reveal something exists, or anything related to it. The only persons I can discuss it with are other presidents who have sworn the same promise."

"How far back does this promise go?"

Casting a glance at Nicole, Harry replied, "Amazingly, it goes all the way back. Back to POTUS the first. I can't say anything more. Please don't play guessing games about this. We're sworn to secrecy."

"How about I grab my AirPods and listen to music so you guys can talk? Or maybe Jennifer and I can go downstairs and play gin rummy until you're finished."

Nicole stared at him in disbelief. "God, Brian, what's the matter with you? You're acting like a spoiled child. You know by now how things work around here."

After a period of silence, Jennifer said, "It's not easy, Nicole. Look at it from his perspective. I had a hard time, and I'm not a type A like Brian is. Second fiddle's not an easy thing to play, especially when you're used to being in the limelight." She turned to Brian. "You're fortunate that in addition to your role as first gentleman, you still have your place in the business world. In the rarified world of truly unique antiquities, you're the top dog. You have handled some of the world's rarest objects, you've been on dozens of treasure hunts, and every network turns to you for a sound bite when something new and interesting turns up. Be thankful for that."

Jennifer was right, of course. Brian had no reason to complain; instead of being at his wife's beck and call, he split his time between his four galleries, and for now he had extended his work with the British Museum, since he couldn't be with his wife anyway.

He said, "Okay, you're right. Go ahead, you POTUSes. Talk in riddles about mysterious things in the Archives. Jennifer, the weather was nice today, wasn't it?" He paused before breaking out in a grin. "Just kidding."

Harry asked Nicole how many times Horace Wilmington Fleming had met with her. "Just once so far," she answered. "It's hard to find a block of free time." Harry recalled having the same problem.

He added, "Check out page 87. Let's talk about it after you've seen it."

"Page 87," Brian quipped. "Isn't that the page where the guy kills his wife and his best friend because they communicate using secret codes?"

And on that note, Nicole changed the subject, and nothing more was said about the Book of Secrets.

# CHAPTER TWENTY-SEVEN

Harry tried to sleep, tossing and turning until he gave up and slipped out of bed at midnight. Careful not to wake Jennifer, he tiptoed around the Lincoln bedroom, found his robe, and walked into the brightly lit hallway. A guard sitting in a chair down the hall saw him, jumped to his feet, snapped to attention, and saluted.

"Hey, Charlie," Harry said, feeling foolish as he returned the salute in his pajamas. "I can't sleep. I recall there being a bottle of brandy stashed away in the Treaty Room. Wonder if it's still there?"

"I wouldn't be surprised, Mr. President. Let's take a look. If not, I'll summon the valet…"

"No, no, there's no need to disturb anybody else this time of night. I just thought a little brandy might let me rest." Sure enough, a mostly full bottle of Cognac sat where Harry had put it after the president of France brought it as a gift, and tonight he was glad to see it still around. He took a Waterford snifter from the shelf and poured.

The guard retired to the hallway, closing the door and leaving his former boss alone in an armchair with his brandy for company. Harry settled back, recalling good times here. The Harrisons had celebrated in this very room the evening after Brian and Nicole married in the East Room downstairs. They'd also entertained political and personal friends from around the world, and it was a time of wistful reflection for Harry. A year ago, he'd never have imagined visiting Nicole as the sitting president.

The dying embers in the hearth flared now and then

as Harry sat in a comfortable old chair, his feet propped on an ottoman and his brandy within reach. He alternated between staring into the flames and looking at the sheet of paper in his lap. In his six years as president, he had done only one thing illegal, and the crime he had committed— the technicality that even Horace let slide—rested in the words on that sheet.

The nagging question that kept Harry awake was how much to tell Brian. Despite signing a sacred oath, he wanted to show Brian the words he'd copied from memory. They were on a piece of paper and not "in the book." He struggled over that technicality in an attempt to rationalize it. If he were to ever understand the poem, he needed Brian's help, because he knew nobody better at unveiling the meaning behind mysteries.

The only penalty for breaking the rules was having to live with the knowledge he'd violated the sacred trust of George Washington, but that was reason enough. After thinking for a while, he conceived a plan he believed would work. He finished his nightcap, placed the snifter on a side table, and returned to bed, motioning for Charlie to remain seated as he walked past his post.

Harry slept soundly after settling his problem and awoke to find Jennifer gone. It was almost eight thirty, longer than he'd slept in ages. He donned a jogging suit and went down the hall to the family dining room, where he knew he'd find coffee. The others were seated at the table before a lavish spread of meat, eggs, fruit, bagels and jam. Jennifer was still in her pjs and a robe, Brian wore sweats, and Nicole, whose first meeting of the day was in thirty minutes, had on a pinstriped jacket and skirt with a starched button-down white shirt.

"Retirement must be fun." Brian laughed when Harry strolled in. "You're sleeping late these days."

"Yeah, I'm surprised myself. I had a hard time falling asleep, but I feel great now." He accepted coffee from a waiter and took a bagel from the plate. "There's something I want to discuss with you, but I want to run it by Nicole first. Can we step out of the room for a moment?

Don't get your feelings hurt; I'll have her back in no time!"

As they stood in the hallway, he explained that he had memorized the poem on page 87 during the curator's monthly visits, and he had the entire poem on paper. "I want Brian's help to decipher it, but you and I signed the pledge not to reveal the existence of the book or anything in it. I'm struggling to find a way around that oath, and I have an idea. I won't tell him where the poem came from or reveal anything that would indicate the book exists. I'll just show him some words I wrote down. I think that meets the spirit of the pledge."

Nicole said, "We're both lawyers, and we were taught the boundaries of legality. What you're suggesting is a stretch, but in my opinion, technically you're okay. The curator said we couldn't take pictures of a page, or photocopy anything from the book, or admit it exists. Your idea does none of those, but if you asked the curator, I'm sure he'd say no. So don't ask him. I'm with you—talk to Brian, but don't break the pledge."

"I'm really pleased you agree with my plan. I'll talk to him right away. Do you want to be in on that conversation?"

She smiled. "No thanks. As you know, I have a country to run. Besides, I get to look at the original poem, and now I can't wait until Horace Wilmington Fleming's next visit. I want to know what you find so intriguing about page 87."

They returned to the dining room, Nicole headed downstairs to the Oval Office to begin her workday, and the others moved to the Treaty Room, where they sat around an oval game table. Harry excused himself for a moment before returning with two sheets of paper, one of which he handed to Brian.

# CHAPTER TWENTY-EIGHT

Harry watched Brian's face as he read the eight three-line stanzas.

"What is this?"

"You tell me. I can't figure it out."

"Did it come from the book?"

Harry said nothing.

Brian smiled. "Did anybody ever tell you how frustrating you are?"

"And vice versa, my friend. How about spending your brainpower on deciphering the poem?"

Jennifer asked to see it, read it a couple of times, and handed it back to her husband. "It's all gibberish to me. What do you think?"

"It could be nothing—just a joke or a clever riddle, but I think it contains a message. Words like *hiding, clues and secrets* make me believe it needs deciphering. I'm certain I know the author's identity, and there are several clear references to Oklahoma.

"Quanah Parker, the Comanche chief who lived in Oklahoma Territory, apparently saw something from afar that's the subject of the poem. The author capitalizes the word *Cache* in *the Cache is real*. A cache can be a hidden treasure trove, but if that's the meaning, why is it capitalized? It could be because there's a town called Cache in what once was Comanche territory—another tie to Oklahoma. I just don't know how we figure out what the poet's hiding."

Brian took the paper back and read every word

slowly. "Since you won't tell me anything about it, I'll give you my theory. It's in your handwriting and you copied it from the original, which is in the Book That Shall Not Be Named. You swore an oath, and that's why you're so secretive about it."

Harry stared at him, his face an impassive blank.

"I'll take that as a yes—"

"Dammit, Brian, you won't take that as anything! How many times do I have to tell you—"

Brian had gone too far. "Sorry. You know how I get when something seems interesting. You and Nicole stepped out into the hall to speak privately, and I assumed..."

Harry resisted lashing out. Brian had been his best friend for decades, and until now, his enthusiasm for adventure had been one of his most endearing traits. *This is my problem, not his,* Harry thought as Brian rambled an apology. *I can't blame him for being curious.*

"Listen instead of talking for a minute," Harry said. "I need your help to decipher the meaning of this poem and who wrote it. You can presume anything you want about the origin of the words, but I will not—do you hear me, Brian?—I will not condone any discussion about the book you think exists. None."

"Because you pledged an oath of secrecy..."

Harry jerked the paper out of Brian's hand and wadded it into a ball. "This goes in the fireplace unless you agree to my conditions."

"I don't have much of a choice. Can I have a copy of the poem?" Brian asked, and Harry tossed the ball of paper back, saying that copy was his to keep.

In Harry's opinion, the only surprising thing about Brian's curiosity was that he hadn't asked about the Book of Secrets during the six years Harry was president. Of course Brian was interested; rumors about the existence of such a book had circulated for two hundred years. And most likely he had respected Harry's position as president, waiting until after he was out of office to inquire. He couldn't have known the oath Harry swore was for his lifetime.

Would Nicole tell Brian about the book? Would he even ask now that he knew it was shrouded in secrecy? Harry had no idea, and that was her decision, not his. He'd cast his own lot; he would share the poem with Brian, but he would never confirm where it came from.

Brian flattened the crumpled paper, straightened it carefully, and said, "Okay, boss. I promise not to bug you about its origin. Now can we talk about what it might mean?"

Harry laughed. "We could have been talking for half an hour already if you hadn't been such an ass about everything."

"I'll let that go since you're a doddering old ex-president who deserves everyone's pity. I'll talk loud so you can hear me."

Ready to move on, Harry suggested they take the poem stanza by stanza. Sharing his copy with his wife, he read the introduction.

*My fellow presidents, can you decipher this puzzle? Believe you can and you're halfway there.*

"The first line reveals that a president wrote the poem," Brian commented, looking intently at his copy. "The second line contains our first enigma. What strange words. Any thoughts on what they might mean?"

"Not offhand. It may be a simple phrase to motivate the reader."

Jennifer thought the sentence sounded old-fashioned, perhaps a clue that the author lived long ago.

Leaving it for the moment, they turned to the first of eight stanzas. Harry read aloud, *"Four four six one has frame and glass, and something hid—a needed clue to find the pass.* It's pretty clear that it refers to a picture or something else mounted in a frame with glass. It contains a clue to help find a pass."

"I agree, but what does 'four four six one' mean?" Brian asked. "Why would he call a picture by a number?"

Jennifer stood, walked across the room to where a small, framed portrait of Abraham Lincoln hung, and removed it from the wall. "I have an idea," she said, turning the painting over to reveal a sticker from the White House Collection. "This one is number one hundred ten. When we moved in and had to decide what art to hang, the White House curator gave us a list to choose from. I picked a few, ordered them by their numbers, and the men brought them over for us to consider. Some we hung, and others we sent back. The author of the poem was a president, and I think he's referring to artwork that hung in this building while he was in office. I think he hid a clue in it."

"Good thinking," Harry said. "Can you get that list that has the numbers?"

Jennifer opened the door, asked a Secret Service agent to come in, and told him what they needed. Ten minutes later he delivered a large three-ring binder with hundreds of laminated sheets, each with a picture, description and identification number for items owned by the White House Collection.

"We may not find it here," she cautioned as she scanned the index. "Presidents are allowed to borrow from the Smithsonian, the National Archives and other places. If the item isn't part of the White House Collection, it'll have a different number, it won't be listed here, and our job will be a lot harder."

She found the item numbered 4461 and said, "Dead end, I'm afraid." She removed the page and held it up to reveal a gold chalice adorned with rubies. "It was a gift from Czar Nicholas II to President William McKinley to honor his inauguration in 1897. It certainly doesn't have a frame and glass like the clue says."

Brian thought a moment. "So maybe the clue doesn't refer to a number on a painting. It could be something else. We'll put that down as enigma number two. Everyone ready to move on for now?"

*Inside the frame, wings in the air protect a secret I, six two, have hidden there.*

"Are we still talking about the frame from the previous stanza?" Brian asked, and Harry said it appeared so.

"The first stanza says there's frame and glass. This

one says, 'inside the frame,' apparently a reference to that same frame. What wings in the air are, I don't know. And we get our first clue as to the author's identity—he refers to himself as 'six two.' Clearly that's not his presidential number, because we haven't yet had sixty-two presidents. What's he trying to tell us?"

"Wings in the air and six two. Enigmas three and four."

Harry smiled. "I never said this was going to be easy. Here goes stanza number three."

*The Cache is real, tho many doubt or laugh in scorn, and yet tis true what it's about.*

"We talked about the word 'cache' already," Brian said. "Let's jot down the two possible meanings—a hidden stash, or a town in the Comanche territory. Maybe other parts of the poem will make it clearer. Keep going, Harry."

*When Quanah Parker fought a war he said he saw it, and could view it from afar.*

"I know quite a bit about Quanah Parker's life," Harry said. "He was a fierce Comanche warrior but later integrated into society, built a house—in Cache, by the way—and died there."

Jennifer said, "So the Comanche chief is connected to Cache. And he saw something far away during one of his battles."

Reluctantly, Brian had to call a stop at that point. He and Cory Spencer, the manager of his London gallery, had a standing conference call at the same time every week when Brian was away. He excused himself and went to the private sitting room down the hall.

While he was gone, Harry and Jennifer continued to study the half of the poem he had read aloud. And he told her his theory about what it all meant.

# CHAPTER TWENTY-NINE

By the time Brian's call ended, Harry and Jennifer had departed for Georgetown to have lunch with the senior senator from Oklahoma and his wife. Harry himself had been Oklahoma's senior senator once, as had his father for three decades before him.

Brian had several favorite restaurants in Washington, but since his wife was president, he lacked the freedom these days to spontaneously select a place and pop in for lunch. He was "first gentleman," an awkward term that he considered demeaning and refused to use. He was President Farber's husband, and that was how he chose to be known, even though her use of her maiden name sometimes resulted in his being called Mr. Farber.

Annoyed that he couldn't go out to lunch without causing a ruckus, he ordered a sandwich and a beer and ate alone in the upstairs dining room while working on the British Museum project from his laptop. It was midafternoon when the Harrisons returned, and around 4:30 Nicole came upstairs too, her workday finished.

They gathered again in the Treaty Room at five. Two muted televisions on a buffet across the room broadcast CNN and Fox News, and as the valet brought cocktails, Harry and Nicole talked about the subject that was currently airing on both channels—increasing concern over the danger of China invading Taiwan. She'd spoken with the president of the Republic of China and promised increased naval presence in the area. Harry appeared interested, but he commented he liked it better on his side of the fence than being in the hot seat.

Jennifer said, "Harry, you're torturing Brian. He's about to jump out of his skin to get back into the poem, and you're making small talk about geopolitics."

Brian protested, "What are you talking about? I'm sitting here calmly enjoying a cocktail. The poem never entered my mind, to be honest."

"I don't believe you," Harry said. "Speaking of being honest, how much time did you spend looking at the poem after we left this morning?"

"I had a lot of work to do. I worked most of the afternoon..."

"How much time, Brian?"

"A couple of hours, maybe more," he admitted with a rueful smile. "I carefully read the rest of it, I took some notes, and I want to discuss some theories."

"You're going to have to hold your thoughts," Nicole said. "You and Harry can play after dinner. Right now we're going to have a conversation that includes all four of us, not just the men."

"I kind of got interested in the poem too," Jennifer admitted. "I'd also like to know more about it after dinner."

Brian retorted, "Three of us want to talk about it now. Majority rules. You lose."

Nicole smiled and gave an expansive wave around the historic old room. "I win. You're in my house, and I make the rules." That brought chuckles from the others, who changed the discussion to old times, Harry's parents, Oklahoma football, and how the couple was adapting to rural living on a ranch outside Oklahoma City after decades in the frenzy and mayhem of DC.

Brian participated in the conversation during cocktail hour and dinner, but once the plates were cleared, he insisted they get back to the poem. In the Treaty Room around the table once again, Harry ceded the floor to Brian since he had ideas to present. Jennifer sat with Nicole by the fire after making the men promise they'd let her know if they came up with anything interesting.

"First things first," Brian said as he picked up the paper and explained the three clues that revealed Teddy Roosevelt as the author. Then he read the next stanza.

*Pah-Che-Ka's face from Post Oak grave conceals a clue, and with it you might find a cave.*

Harry said he didn't know what it meant.

"Gotta love the internet," Brian said as he looked at a yellow pad filled with notes. "I Googled 'Post Oak grave Oklahoma,' and the first result was Post Oak Cemetery in Indiahoma, just nine miles west of Cache."

Harry's eyes widened. "Amazing! Another connection. Who is Pah-Che-Ka—someone buried there?"

"Yes, but not just someone. Pah-Che-Ka was a common Comanche name, and nineteen of them are buried in Post Oak Cemetery. There could be a lot more whose grave markers have been lost over the years; plus there are a variety of spellings. To make things harder, the earliest graves have the name Pah-Che-Ka only, while many of the later ones also have a first name, such as Samuel Pahcheka. Some are men and some women, so the grave mentioned in the poem might be one of many, many possibilities."

Harry added, "But I'll bet not all the grave markers have a 'face' like the poem says. In old cemeteries, a lot of the stones have pictures of the deceased affixed to them. I'll bet the right Pah-Che-Ka's does too, if it still exists."

"So presuming we found the correct grave in Post Oak Cemetery, the face 'from the grave' would conceal a drawing. You're right; the reference could be a picture in the gravestone, but it could be something else. We'd have to go there to find out. And that brings us to the most interesting sentence so far—the revelation that with the drawing someone might find a cave." He leaned back, crossed his arms and grinned. "A cave, Harry. In southwestern Oklahoma, near Cache. Like that cave with the iron door you told me about earlier. Could it be the poet is talking about the same cave?"

"Maybe," Harry agreed, "but it's possible both this poem and the article I read about a cave are pure fiction. It's going to take more work to find a connection. Let's keep going."

*My numbers aren't as they appear. To understand, read like a Jew to make them clear.*

"You already figured out who wrote the poem by switching the numbers," Harry said. "That means the thing with frame and glass that's called 4461 is actually number 1644. Maybe that one's an item in the White House collection."

"Way ahead of you. I used my First Gentlemanly privilege to have the requisition book brought back to us. It's sitting over there on the coffee table, turned to that entry."

As they walked over, Harry asked if this one looked more promising than the last.

"Oh, I'd say it looks promising, all right. This is starting to make sense. If a few more things fall into place, I'll know for sure." The relevant page showed Item 1644, an oil painting by renowned American artist Frederic Remington currently in the hands of the Smithsonian American Art Museum. The painting depicted Native Americans on horseback pursuing a pack of timber wolves on a grassy plain.

"Could be something straight from Oklahoma history," Harry commented. With a smile, Brian turned the page to a checkout log on the back side of the sheet. The last time this painting had hung in the White House was in 1906. Brian said, "Want to hazard a guess who was president in 1906? See what I mean about things making sense?"

Brian asked how the requisition process worked, and Harry explained Nicole could requisition the painting as long as it wasn't on display as part of a permanent exhibit. Nicole made the call and advised the painting would be delivered in the morning.

"To more revelations soon," Brian said, raising his glass in a toast.

"The suspense is killing me," Harry admitted. "I hope that painting is hiding a clue, because if it isn't, we're all working on erroneous theories."

"Trust me," Brian said with a smile. "I think I'm onto something."

# CHAPTER THIRTY

As it turned out, object number 1644 was gathering dust in a storage room at the Smithsonian. A courier brought it to the White House at eight the next morning, and soon it stood on an easel in the Treaty Room. Frederic Remington painted the sixteen-by-twenty-inch work in 1893, and today it hung in an ornate gilded frame. They had seen the image on the sheet—Comanches on horseback chasing a pack of timber wolves—but the photo didn't do it justice. The painting was a stunning piece, and they marveled at the artist's attention to detail.

Nicole was already at work, leaving Jennifer, Harry and Brian to appreciate it, but the men were more interested in what secrets it might hold. Brian read the first line of the relevant stanza aloud.

*Four four six one has frame and glass, and something hid—a needed clue to find the pass.*

"There's a frame but no glass," Brian remarked the moment the delivery person dropped it off. He turned it over and found a backing of cardboard with an identification sticker from the Smithsonian. It was held together by small brads tacked into the frame on all four sides.

Harry said, "The next line refers to wings in the air inside the frame that protect a secret. We need to remove the backing. Maybe there's glass underneath."

"Think we're breaking any laws?" Brian commented as they carefully removed the tiny nails from around the frame.

"Breaking and entering, I guess." Harry grinned. "But for God's sake, let's don't damage that painting. Destruction of public property—especially a Remington—might be a little hard to explain away."

Brian slipped a knife blade under one side of the cardboard and slowly raised it. Beneath lay a surprise, another painting maybe a quarter the size of the Remington that was simply a sketch in ink—an eagle taking flight above a rugged cliff—drawn on a yellowed piece of paper and affixed to a thin piece of glass to protect it.

"Wings in the air inside the frame," Harry whispered. "I can't believe it. Wonder what secret the wings protect?" He turned the sketch over, but the back was blank.

"I think that's the secret," Brian said, pointing to something in the sketch. "Look closely under the eagle's wings. See how it's rising in the air above a cliff? What's that?" He pointed the tip of the knife blade at a small black dot on the face of the cliff near where two mountains converged.

Harry squinted at it. "Do you think that might be a cave?"

"I don't think. I'm absolutely certain of it."

They took pictures of the hidden artifact before replacing it and the cardboard backing. Then Harry demanded answers, leading Brian to the sitting area by the fireplace.

"I haven't been entirely forthcoming about what I've learned," Brian began. "I was waiting to see what secret was hidden in the painting, and it only corroborated my theory. I know what the poem means because I deciphered it. I want Nicole to hear this too. When we gather for cocktails this evening, I'll tell you everything."

"Dammit, Brian, don't do this to me. Tell me now, and then you can tell her later. Who put that pen-and-ink drawing in the back of the painting?"

Brian knew it wasn't fair to keep Harry in the dark, frustrated at not knowing everything. "Okay, here goes. The person who drew the sketch and put it in the back of that painting was Theodore Roosevelt. In my opinion, he drew something he saw. It's a sketch of the cliff face where your fabled lost cave of the iron door lies."

"But that's supposition, right?"

"It's way more than supposition," Brian explained. "Roosevelt wrote the poem. He also requisitioned the painting to hang in the White House in 1906. It wasn't a random piece of artwork; he chose it for a reason. It's another confirmation that TR is behind all this."

"Whoa, whoa! Slow it down a little. I'm not following your logic."

"Because you don't know everything yet. Yesterday afternoon I did some research into TR's life. While president, he became friends with Quanah Parker, and the chief participated in his second inauguration parade in 1905. That same year, the president and Parker were together on a wolf hunt in Oklahoma, after which Roosevelt ate dinner at Star House, Quanah Parker's home in Cache."

Harry was intrigued. "So Roosevelt wrote the poem filled with clues, and with the hunting reference, I get your theory that he sketched the drawing and hid it inside a painting of Native Americans on a wolf hunt. I admire his cleverness, but why go to all this trouble? Having been president myself, I can tell you there's not a lot of free time to sit around and dream up a mystery filled with clues. What was his motive?"

"You've hiked the mountains there. Did you see caves?"

Harry nodded. "There were lots of dark spaces in the cliffs that might have been cave entrances or fox dens. I was looking for one with an iron door, so I didn't really give much thought to it, but yes, I think there were a lot of caves."

"Teddy Roosevelt wrote a cryptic poem about one of them. It says Quanah Parker once saw it from afar when he was fighting a war. Parker fought other tribes and the US Army too. He'd use the wild ravines and gullies of the Wichita Mountains to hide and ambush his enemies. I think

TR capitalized the word 'Cache' to lead us to the town where Quanah Parker lived. It's also a few miles from the cemetery. See how all the clues seem to point in one direction?"

Harry nodded. "One big clue remains, though. We have to find the right Pah-Che-Ka's grave, look at his face, and figure out how it conceals a clue. Roosevelt said if we found it, we might also find a cave. Maybe *the* cave. Damn, Brian, this is getting really exciting. Now the big question is, do I tackle this adventure solo, or will the famous treasure hunter Brian Sadler join me?"

"I'm working in London, in case you've forgotten. It's already taking longer than I expected. I took it on, and I have to finish it so I can get back to my real life."

"That's great. How soon can you be ready to leave?"

"Didn't you hear what I just said?"

"It shouldn't take more than a couple of days for our initial visit. Want to leave from here or meet me at the ranch and go to the mountains from there?"

Brian gave him a quizzical look, then gave up with an outburst of laughter. "How'd you and Jennifer get to DC this trip?" he asked, and Harry said they flew in a friend's Gulfstream jet that was waiting at Andrews to take them back.

"Got enough room for me and a couple of the Secret Service guys?"

"Plenty. Once we get to the ranch, I'll charter a helicopter to take us to Fort Sill. From there it's just a few miles to the Wichita Mountains, the town of Cache and the cemetery."

"Are you thinking we'll actually go look in the mountains?"

Harry nodded. "While we're there, we might as well rent some horses and look around."

"You think our bodyguards will like us going off on horseback in the wilderness? You said the Wichita Mountains are rugged as hell."

"The agents go where we go. There's no discussion

148

on that topic. Now as I asked earlier, how soon can you leave? Your wife is the president; don't worry about how quickly the Secret Service can arrange the manpower."

Their adventure began the next afternoon. Harry, Jennifer and Brian left Joint Base Andrews in the Gulfstream and flew to the Harrison ranch west of Oklahoma City, where they would spend the night. After dinner Brian and Harry worked until almost midnight planning what to see and how to make it happen. The next morning a Bell 205A helicopter landed at the ranch to pick up them and four Secret Service agents.

No-fly regulations over the Wichita Mountains Wildlife Refuge and Fort Sill, an active Army base, were temporarily lifted for the government chopper carrying a former president and the husband of the current one. Ultimately they would land at Fort Sill and transfer to Army vehicles, but before touching down, Harry wanted to check out the rugged canyons and passes from the air. From high above the deep ravines, they could see things on the cliff faces invisible from below. Harry didn't expect to find anything, but it was worth a try while they had the chopper.

The hundred-mile flight took less than twenty minutes, and when they reached the mountains, Harry switched seats with the copilot so he could point out places he wanted to see up close. The ruggedness of the terrain and how deep some of the canyons were surprised Brian. The mountain range extended across more than a hundred square miles, and many of its ravines and gorges were accessible only on horseback or on foot.

The sheer cliffs would have challenged a seasoned rock climber, Brian realized as they descended into deep gorges, studying features in the cliffs. They passed by dozens of dark indentations in the rocks that might be caves or maybe only shady places under projecting rocks where mountain lions might nap.

After traversing miles of canyons for almost an hour, the pilot turned back to the Army base and landed. The base commandant—a colonel named O'Reilly—

snapped to attention and saluted as Harry and Brian left the chopper, and two SUVs pulled up.

"Welcome to Fort Sill, gentlemen," Colonel O'Reilly said. "If there's anything you need, please let us know." They exchanged pleasantries and thanked the man for his hospitality, then left for the mountains.

"When do we pick up the horses?" Brian asked.

"There's a visitor parking lot near Elk Mountain. People hike in from there, and that's where we'll meet the guy bringing them."

Brian recalled the name Elk Mountain from Harry's treasure magazine article. Almost everyone who claimed to have seen the iron door put it near Elk Mountain and north of Treasure Lake. The fact that those place names existed today should have made it easier, although today's helicopter excursion into the gorges showed how tough exploring from the ground would be. The Rocky Mountains might have been better known, but in some ways the Wichitas could be just as challenging.

# CHAPTER THIRTY-ONE

The SUVs pulled into a small gravel lot, empty except for two pickups pulling long horse trailers. At any other time, the lot would have had several cars belonging to day hikers and people with overnight camping permits for Elk Mountain. Rarely did the refuge close to the public, but today Brian and Harry were free to roam the place alone. Almost alone, actually. Three Secret Service agents would ride with them, and a military helicopter would follow from above as they made their way into the canyon.

Two men wearing Stetsons and chaps waited next to five horses tethered to the trailers. They met Brian and Harry, introduced them to their horses Double-Oh-Seven and Minnie Pearl, and confirmed everyone knew how to ride. Ten minutes later, the party left with two armed agents on horseback leading the way, Harry and Brian in the middle, and the other agent in the rear. Two of the horses carried packs with food and emergency survival gear. The former they'd need for lunch; the latter was protocol.

Harry consulted a crude map he'd created using information from the old article. Although frustratingly vague, each person quoted had revealed where his journey began and ended, and some described features in the canyon at the place they reputedly spotted a cave. Four lines intersected in a ravine called Shadow Gulch that lay about three miles ahead of them. Harry knew Shadow Gulch well, because every story about the cave called it the most likely spot from which others had seen the door.

The horses picked their way along a dry stream bed

that led them from one gorge to another, forcing choices when narrow passageways through the rocks led in different directions. For the first couple of hours the air was cool and crisp, but as midday approached, the sun appeared over the canyon's rim far above them, and the temperature rose quickly. They spotted the chopper now and then as the horses meandered in and out of shadows.

Lunch consisted of sandwiches, chips and water they ate on the shady side of an arroyo. A little after one, they mounted up and continued, keeping an eye on the cliff faces above. The people in the article had seen the door at different times in the afternoon, and they knew only the sun's reflection would allow it to be seen.

As the hours passed, the shadows deepened, and the air turned cooler. Around three the lead Secret Service agent told Harry it was time to head back. It would take more than two hours to return—faster than the trip in because they wouldn't be stopping as often to check out possibilities—but the sun would set less than an hour after they reached the parking lot. They had to leave now, the agent cautioned, to be out of the canyon well before dark.

They headed back, maneuvering one turn after another in the deepening shadows, unaware they had been observed throughout their journey. A man on horseback stood at the rim of a sheer cliff and watched until they were out of sight. Familiar with the art of evasion, he ducked under trees each time the chopper approached. He rode a paint pony bareback, as was the custom of his people, and once they were out of sight, he waited, glancing at the sun, and at the right time he looked across the narrow gorge. He considered himself fortunate; when the sun set on certain cloudless days, its last rays illuminated a spot on the cliff face several hundred yards across the canyon. For a few seconds he watched something glimmer brightly amid the rocks and scrub. As quickly as it had appeared, it was gone.

The man turned his horse away from the canyon and urged him into a gallop. Soon, like the sun and the iron door in the canyon, he disappeared as well.

# CHAPTER THIRTY-TWO

Enthused after exploring the canyon, Harry and Brian flew back to the ranch for the night. There was more work to be done, and by daybreak they were back in the air, returning to Fort Sill. The SUVs met them and took them directly to Post Oak Cemetery outside the town of Indiahoma. The little graveyard was neat and well groomed, demonstrating the love and respect caring people had for their deceased kin.

Nineteen markers bore the name Pah-Che-Ka, a few of which had last names too. Many other markers they saw contained an engraving or photo of the deceased, but none of these did. "Roosevelt wrote the poem before 1909, when his term ended," Brian said. "A hundred and ten years have passed. Maybe the marker he referred to is lost, or it's lying broken somewhere in the weeds, or vandals hauled it off."

They searched for another half hour, turned up a few toppled and broken stones that weren't what they were looking for, and went back to the SUVs. Their next stop was a small museum in Lawton that Brian had discovered while researching the history of southwestern Oklahoma. According to its website, it housed more documents and artifacts relating to three tribes—Apache, Kiowa and Comanche—than any other. Pah-Che-Ka was a Comanche name. So was Quanah Parker, and both were in the poem.

———

When he came to work this morning, Denton Kopaddy had placed a sign on the front door of the Native

American Cultural Museum advising it was closed until noon. Except for school field trips, he rarely saw more than a dozen visitors in a day, so he doubted anyone would be inconvenienced. Not many people came to Lawton just to visit the small museum; most came to see friends and family at the Army base, and others to hike in the Wichita Mountains. Lawton wasn't a tourist destination, and the museum existed more to preserve culture than to display artifacts. In fact, only one showroom held cases and wall mountings, a far cry from the extensive collections on display at big western heritage museums in Oklahoma City, Texas and New Mexico.

After a phone call that came around suppertime, Denton hadn't been able to sleep a wink. An agent of the United States Secret Service asked if it would be convenient for two Washington dignitaries to visit the museum first thing tomorrow. An agent would come at eight sharp to reconnoiter the premises. Denton agreed immediately.

An advance party! That sounded exciting; from reading spy novels, Denton knew that an advance party meant his visitors would be big shots of the first magnitude. Whom did the Secret Service protect, anyway? Presidents and vice presidents, that's who. Tomorrow would be an opportunity to show off the place and maybe even get a photo op that could assist with the museum's publicity and fund-raising efforts.

Precisely on time at eight, an agent arrived and walked through the premises, radioed an okay, and joined Denton in his office. When asked who was coming, the agent replied, "Be patient, Mr. Kopaddy. They'll be here soon."

Half an hour later, two SUVs pulled up, and Denton watched eagerly as agents emerged from the front seats of one, looked in all directions, opened the back doors, and efficiently ushered the two guests inside. He recognized both men immediately, of course, since one was a past president and the other was husband to the current one.

*What the hell are they doing here?* Nothing

remotely like this had ever happened in his life. Barely able to contain his excitement, he couldn't wait to learn the purpose of their trip. There had been nothing on the news this morning, and he wondered if they were traveling secretly. *How exciting!*

First Gentleman Brian Sadler's face was familiar to millions of armchair adventurers—Denton included—who followed his exploits on History and Travel Channel documentaries and watched his interviews on cable news. His insights and opinions on archaeological discoveries, buried treasure and legends about early civilizations in the Americas brought interesting and exciting ideas into the lives of his viewers.

Denton introduced himself, showed them around the exhibits room, responded to questions and comments, and learned they were interested in the Comanches.

"We just came from Post Oak Cemetery," Sadler said. "How old is it?"

"The original cemetery dates to 1896, but the one you visited began in 1957. That's the year the Army moved the old graveyard, lock, stock and barrel, to make room for a missile firing range."

"So the government exhumed the bodies and moved each stone? Did they keep a record, and did anybody oversee the job to be sure they got it right?"

"The museum has some pictures taken by tribal Elders who were there as observers. It would have been a big deal, Mr. Sadler. The Corps of Engineers team physically moving the graves took a lot of flak, as you might imagine. Comanche leaders raised a huge stink over it, and rightly so. But despite their anger and criticism, it happened anyway. The Army was the biggest employer in the area, the Native Americans had far less power in those days, and nobody in Washington stopped it."

"Was it because the Elders considered the land sacred?"

"Absolutely; it was a hallowed burial ground. After the relocation, they made other accusations. Several tribal leaders claimed old burial records didn't jive with the ones

155

in the new cemetery. Those Elders have long since passed away, but you can find Comanches today who still don't believe all the graves got moved. Many still think the Army went too fast, did a half-assed job and left some of their people behind."

Harry shot Brian a glance and said, "Is there a list of people they think were left behind?"

Denton raised his eyebrows. "Why? Are you looking for someone in particular?"

"Is there a list?"

"Not really. Our museum has memorabilia but not a list per se. Some individuals wrote letters, others submitted formal complaints against the Army, and some contacted their congressional representatives. Those documents contain names and other information, but they're not in one place, and although many of them were real grievances, undoubtedly some people filed false claims in hopes of getting restitution. In my opinion, even if you had a list of possible missing persons or lost grave markers, it wouldn't be accurate. For instance, a body might have been relocated, but the stone got lost. The reburial happened, but nobody knows exactly where the body lies."

"So you believe there were stones that never made it to the new cemetery?"

"I'm saying that's possible, although I wouldn't know where to look. If the Army found themselves with extra tombstones and surreptitiously disposed of them, they might have ended up as part of a sidewalk or the foundation of a barn. I'm happy to help if you're looking for something specific. I'm a Comanche myself. My relatives are buried in Post Oak, and I probably know as much about it as anyone."

Brian took Harry aside. "How much should we reveal? We know nothing about this guy."

"He knows the cemetery, and he's willing to help. I say we tell him a little more. What can it hurt?"

Harry turned back to Denton. "We're looking for the marker of a man named Pah-Che-Ka. We discovered that's a common Comanche name, since we found nineteen

THE IRON DOOR

in Post Oak Cemetery. But we didn't find the one we want—a stone with that name and a photograph or engraving on it."

Denton nodded. "I know exactly what you're describing. You probably saw other stones in the cemetery with photos; some people still do it. I don't know about the specific stone you're looking for, but the museum's full of resource material. If you can tell me more, I'll dig in and see what I can find." He leaned forward with an expectant look on his face that made Brian wary.

"There's supposedly something interesting about the picture—"

Brian interrupted Harry mid-sentence. "I think we've said enough for now."

The man pushed on. "Does this have anything to do with your interest in trains, Mr. President?"

Harry chuckled. "I didn't realize the American public knew I was a train fanatic."

"I read something about it a while back. So does your visit concern trains?"

Brian opened his mouth, but Harry shot him a look and replied, "Trains may be involved in what we're looking for, but it's too early to know for sure. It's more about an article I read as a kid—something about a lost cave in the Wichita Mountains."

*Aha. Now I get it.* Denton smiled. "The cave of the iron door. I wish I had a dollar for every amateur treasure hunter who's come to this museum asking about it. Now I understand the train connection, since some people think it's an old boxcar door. You two are on a treasure hunt, and you think Pah-Che-Ka's picture holds a clue."

Brian was having no more of this. "With all respect, Mr. Kopaddy, we've told you enough. We need to be going…"

Denton observed Brian's body language. They knew a lot more than they had revealed. "I think I can help you, gentlemen. I have access to a wealth of information about this area and the tribes, and there may be things in the Archives that you should see. I also know the Elders, some of whom are almost a hundred years old. Wise men, we call them. It's surprising how much even the oldest ones can remember."

"We really appreciate your help," Harry said. "We've taken enough of your time, but if anything else develops, we'll be in touch."

"Sure. Happy to oblige." Denton watched the Secret Service agents usher President Harrison and Brian Sadler into the idling SUVs and drive away. He locked the door and left the sign turned to "Closed."

He had told his VIP visitors the Archives might contain things that could help them, and that statement had triggered a memory. He recalled seeing an artifact in the storeroom a long time ago, something that might provide answers to the questions these men asked. He searched the database but couldn't find what he was looking for, but that was no surprise. The storage area held thousands of things, and so far no one had taken the time to catalog them all.

Denton had read that 1970s treasure article too, and like the people interviewed for it, he had seen the iron door himself. It was back when he was a kid, riding through a remote canyon called Shadow Gulch late one afternoon. As he looked up, something shone like a beacon when the sun's rays hit it. It disappeared so quickly he thought he might have imagined it, but then he wondered if it could be the iron door. He'd gone home eager to return, but like the others, he never found it again.

As he walked into the storage area to look for that artifact, he thought, *wouldn't it be exciting to help someone prove the legend true?*

# CHAPTER THIRTY-THREE

After leaving the museum, Harry asked one of the agents to contact Colonel O'Reilly and arrange a visit to the site of the original cemetery. The area was strictly off-limits to civilians, but given who was doing the asking, the commandant agreed at once.

They made a brief stop in Cache to tour Star House, Quanah Parker's home. Teddy Roosevelt had dined with the chief there, but like the cemetery, the house had been moved from its original location. Other than being historically interesting, it yielded nothing that could help them.

When they returned to Fort Sill, Colonel O'Reilly met them and introduced them to a captain who was director of the base museum and an authority on the old cemetery.

Their SUV followed the captain's Jeep several miles before coming to a twelve-foot fence with signs every few feet warning that this was an active firing range. A sentry opened a gate and saluted as they passed through, crossing acres of prairie grass before reaching their destination.

"In case anyone's wondering, there's no artillery practice today." The captain grinned as they disembarked. "We wouldn't want Fort Sill to be remembered for blasting you gentlemen to smithereens!"

An engraved marble stone marked the location of Post Oak Cemetery and briefly described its 1957 relocation. They saw neither boundary markers nor gravesites. As they stood in the tall grass surveying the property, they asked the captain to tell them about the move.

"The Native Americans fought to stop the relocation, especially the Comanche, whose people had the most burials, but the government prevailed. They removed the remains; the record shows the more recent ones were in modern caskets, but many of the older burials were crude wooden coffins that were in various stages of deterioration. Back at the base museum, I can show you pictures taken at the time. Some of it was pretty grisly—decomposed bodies, even skeletons, all carefully removed and tagged. When everything was finished, they smoothed out the dirt and left." He swept his hand around the area. "As you can see, there's no sign of where the cemetery lay."

Brian asked, "Is it possible they left tombstones behind? Or even bodies?"

"To this day, the Comanche people claim they did. But from reports, it appears the Army workers were meticulous and careful. They invited Native American spiritual leaders to act as observers, so it seems unlikely they missed any marked grave. But here's a problem—the first burials took place over a hundred years ago. Some had wooden grave markers, and others simple wood crosses. Some markers might have disappeared long before the move in 1957, so they wouldn't have known to exhume a body. As far as tombstones, every marker that still existed, however crude, would have been transported to the new site."

"Are you absolutely certain of that?" Harry asked. "Every single marker they found intact would now be at the cemetery near Indiahoma?"

Puzzled by so many questions about tombstones, the captain asked, "Is there a particular grave you expected to find? I've told you what I know, but if you believe something's missing…"

"No, not at all. I didn't mean to infer that. Brian—Mr. Sadler—and I are doing research on a train robbery in the eighteen hundreds. I found a legend that mentions a gravestone in Post Oak Cemetery with a drawing or picture on it. We looked for that marker today but couldn't find it. I just want to confirm that all the markers were relocated.

"Yes, sir, they all got moved. Now it's possible one might have been stolen afterwards, but you all saw the new cemetery. The graves are almost all Native American, the stones aren't valuable, and I can't imagine someone would steal one."

They returned to the helipad, thanked the officer for his assistance, and boarded the helicopter to return to the ranch. On the trip back, Harry apologized for wasting Brian's time on a fruitless mission.

Brian disagreed. "I got to see how rugged the Wichita Mountains are. The people in that article you read saw the iron door once but couldn't find it again. Now that I've been there, I get it. There could have been screwups when the cemetery was moved, and stones might have gone missing."

"And maybe not by accident," Harry replied. "How coincidental would it be to lose the exact stone that Teddy Roosevelt mentioned in his poem? In my opinion, that stone disappeared on purpose."

"Maybe it's something else," Brian said, pulling a copy of the poem from his pocket. "Roosevelt's words were, 'Pah-Che-Ka's face from Post Oak grave conceals a clue.' I thought of the gravestone, but could it be something else?"

Harry wondered if Pah-Che-Ka had been buried with a photograph or clue inside his coffin. "If that's what TR meant, then we're finished. I don't see us getting permission to dig up nineteen graves in a Native American cemetery."

Brian said, "That's not it. Roosevelt wouldn't have looked inside a casket."

"He actually might have. What if the man we're looking for died and was buried at the time TR was hunting in this area? What if Quanah Parker showed him something inside the man's coffin before he was buried?"

# BILL THOMPSON

"I guess it could be possible, but I think the poem refers to something a person could find without disinterring a body. We need to keep an open mind, but I'm sure we're looking for another marker."

# CHAPTER THIRTY-FOUR

At the same time Harry and Brian were at the former cemetery grounds, Denton Kopaddy poked around in a cavernous old sheet-metal building adjacent to the museum. Once part of a lumber yard that closed when Home Depot came to town, now it served as the storeroom for thousands of things the museum had accumulated over the years.

Since the former president and first gentleman left, he'd been busy moving boxes, looking behind ancient artifacts, and sifting through hundreds of things lying randomly throughout the massive building. In the five years he'd been curator, Denton had laid eyes on most of the things in the storeroom, and often his fine-tuned sense of recall led him back. He felt certain he'd seen an old grave marker…but where?

It took over two hours of searching amid thirty thousand things of varying sizes, weights and ages, but at last he found the artifact he'd recalled seeing once before— the rough end of a piece of stone standing tilted between two rusty file cabinets. How to remove it proved a challenge because of the awkward place where it rested. Once he determined it was too heavy to slide out, he took the easier but more time-consuming course—he emptied out one of the cram-packed file cabinets and pulled it a few feet away from the stone. Now he could see the back of the rectangular marker, but the front rested against the other cabinet. He maneuvered a dolly under the hefty stone, lifted it, and moved it a few inches.

It was the tombstone he'd seen sometime in the past, and he looked fruitlessly for anything that might show where it came from. Near the top was a round indention containing a sepia photo in a gold frame. A piece of isinglass protected the picture, its opaqueness blurring the face slightly. The man, clearly Native American, had a stern face. His identity was no mystery, thanks to engraved letters and numerals on the stone.

*Pah-Che-Ka*
*1906*

Denton took his penknife and pried around the rim of the frame until it was loose enough to remove. When he pulled it from the stone and saw a hollow space, a bead of sweat ran down his brow, and he felt the hair rise on his arms. Wedged behind the photograph was a folded scrap of paper. *This is what President Harrison and Brian Sadler were looking for!*

He unwrapped the yellowed paper carefully to find a series of random numbers and symbols written in faded ink. He studied them for a few minutes but had no idea what they might mean.

**34/43\28/98\43/23 ☼ ✓□ ☉ ➤**
**5-20-05-TR**

*This is some kind of code! But what a strange place to hide it.* He carefully pocketed the scrap and replaced the frame in its socket, then laid the stone back against the first cabinet, pushing the other back into place and refilling each drawer. Once things were as they'd been before he found the stone, he returned to his office in the museum.

Denton faced two choices, the first one expedient and self-serving, and the other that his conscience told him was the right thing to do. He weighed the options and potential results of each and made his choice—the obvious one, and the same one he always made. He'd do the expedient thing, not the right one.

*Good old Denton. Always ready to share a secret with somebody powerful. Always ready to accept a smidgen of recognition from a person who couldn't care less about him.*

*Why do you keep doing this, you gutless, spineless, servile piece of shit?* His conscience ate at him as he speed-dialed the number and waited. When Frank Innocente answered, he said, "This is Denton, sir. Bet you can't guess who showed up at the museum this morning." He regretted the choice of words the moment they came from his lips, because this man hated small talk. Denton sometimes thought the man hated him too. Although it might have been true, his lack of self-esteem exacerbated the feeling.

"*Guess who?* I've told you before how irritating that is, Denton. If you have something to say, just say it."

"Harry Harrison and Brian Sadler came here this morning with some Secret Service guys, looking for a missing tombstone with a picture on it. It has something to do with a legendary cave. I wasn't surprised to hear Brian Sadler might be looking for a lost cave, since that's what he does. But to have the former president tagging along? Now that surprised me. After they left, I thought about something. Guess what...oh, sorry. They're looking for a certain grave marker, and I vaguely remembered seeing a tombstone in our warehouse. And guess what? I found it! It took a while, but I found the stone. I pried out the photograph, and there was an old scrap of paper hidden behind it that had a series of numbers and symbols."

"I want to see it," Frank snapped.

"The tombstone?"

"For God's sake, Denton. What do I care about the tombstone? I want to see the paper. Send me a picture of it ASAP."

*Why does he always treat me like a dog? I don't deserve this.*

"Okay, sure, Mr. Innocente. I'll get right on it..."

Denton realized he was talking to no one. He'd been hung up on. Again.

# CHAPTER THIRTY-FIVE

Although his actions were servile, it infuriated Denton when others took advantage of him. Since his teenage years, he'd been intimidated by certain people. Powerful figures like Frank or Brian Sadler, millionaires like the directors and wealthy patrons of the museum—around such people he had a deep feeling of unworthiness. When it happened, his lack of self-esteem manifested as subservient weakness, and some of those powerful people used it against him.

*I'm entitled to respect too,* he thought as he unfolded the scrap of paper with the symbols on it. *Just because they have a gazillion dollars to donate to the museum doesn't give them the right...* He paused, realizing he was in the same old pattern, berating himself for something he refused to change.

*You're weak. You're a lily-livered, spineless...*

*Stop it!* With a scream, he banged his fists on the table.

*Today it ends. Right now, right here. I won't allow this anymore.* He took a picture of the symbols, put the paper in an envelope, and locked it inside a desk drawer. Then, instead of forwarding the picture as Frank Innocente demanded, he went on to other things.

It didn't take long. When his cell phone rang once, then twice more in rapid succession, Denton didn't answer, nor did he listen to the voicemail Frank left. It wasn't easy—it took courage and restraint, but he was determined not to capitulate this time, even though there would be consequences. He would no longer be someone else's doormat.

Emboldened by a surge of adrenalin, he made another gutsy move. He looked up a number on the internet, dialed it, and heard, "White House switchboard. How may I direct your call?"

"Uh, I'd like to speak...I mean, can I leave a message for Mr. Sadler?"

"One moment, please." After a short hold, someone answered. "First Gentleman Sadler's office. May I help you?"

Denton explained who he was and that Brian and President Harrison had visited his museum yesterday. "I have something important to tell them—something I found. Please tell Mr. Sadler it's about the tombstone they're looking for." The person took his number and said the message would be delivered to Brian's executive assistant.

A little giddy after having spoken to people in the White House, Denton wondered if the message would reach Brian, and if so, would he get a return call from the president's husband?

A nagging doubt replaced his euphoria. *Why do I think he would call me? He doesn't care what I have to say...*

Denton forced the negativity away. *Dammit, he is going to call back. He will want to know what I found out, and he'll think my information is important. Of course he'll call.*

That felt better, and he fidgeted at his desk, trying unsuccessfully to do something productive, until his phone rang at last almost two hours later. The area code was 214—Dallas—and that made Denton nervous. It wasn't Frank's cell phone, but he could be calling from a landline. To avoid a confrontation, Denton let it go to voicemail.

As it turned out, the caller had been Meghan O'Brien, who introduced herself as the manager of Bijan Rarities, Brian Sadler's Dallas gallery. She referenced the message he left for Brian in Washington and asked him to return the call.

# THE IRON DOOR

He'd gotten a response from Brian Sadler after all! Denton quickly called, and Meghan advised if he had information for Brian, she'd take it and relay it on.

"With all respect," he replied, "what I have will be very interesting to Mr. Sadler and former President Harrison. I can only discuss it with one of them. Just tell Brian...uh, Mr. Sadler, I found something hidden behind a photograph in a tombstone from Post Oak Cemetery. He'll understand exactly why I want to talk to him."

Meghan took the message, said that Brian was flying to Europe with President Farber, and that a response might be delayed.

An hour later his phone rang, showing an unknown caller. He answered, breaking into a wide grin as he heard, "This is the White House switchboard, Mr. Kopaddy. Please hold while I connect you to *Air Force One*."

*Air Force One!* Denton shivered in anticipation.

"Denton, this is Brian Sadler." The connection was as clear as if he were next door. "I hear you found something interesting. Tell me about it."

He explained about the stone in the warehouse and what he'd found behind the framed photograph on a stone from 1906. Brian gave him a secure email address and asked him to send the picture of the scrap of paper while they were connected. Denton sent it off, and moments later Brian opened the attachment and asked Denton what it could be.

"I have no idea. Looks like gibberish, but it must be important. This is what you were looking for. This is what President Harrison called 'something interesting about the picture,' right?"

"It seems so." Brian paused a moment before deciding to lay his cards on the table. "I'm going to tell you something absolutely confidential. No mention of this to another soul. Do I have your word?"

"Yes, sir. You have my word."

"We found a clue—a poem, actually—that mentions Pah-Che-Ka's grave and his picture. When Harry and I visited the graveyard and found no relevant marker with a picture, we asked you about it."

"I don't mean to pry, but if the clue has something to do with the lost cave of the iron door, I think I can help you."

Hoping his intuition wasn't misplaced, Brian recited the stanza.

*Pah-Che-Ka's face from Post Oak grave conceals a clue, and with it you might find a cave.*

Denton replied, "That's amazing. A little background—I was born in Indiahoma thirty years ago. I grew up in Comanche County, and I heard the Elders of my tribe tell stories of spirits that protected an old mine hidden in the mountains not far away. I knew the man who wrote that magazine article President Harrison mentioned. I also knew someone who claimed to have seen the cave. He lived just around the corner from our house, and I'd sit on his front porch for hours listening to him talk about who built the cave and why. As he spun his tales, I was absolutely enthralled, and I began spending a lot of Saturdays out tramping around the canyons and gullies."

"So is the cave with the iron door real?"

Denton chuckled. "Every so often someone comes in the museum and tries to get my thoughts about it. I tell them the truth; I say it's a legend that's been told and retold for generations. But I'm not going to lie to you and President Harrison. It's all true, Mr. Sadler. I know the cave exists, because I saw the iron door once myself, a long time ago. And just like the people in that article, I could never find it again. Back to what the symbols and numbers on this paper mean, I can't say."

Brian ended the call, promising he and Harry would be back to Lawton as soon as their schedules permitted. In the meantime, each would work on deciphering the clue hidden behind the photograph.

Denton couldn't have been happier about that call. First, he had chatted with a very important person as an equal, not as a deferential lackey. Second, he had provided substantial information that Brian Sadler needed. Now the famous treasure hunter and the former president were coming back to see him. How satisfying! He put the enigmatic document in a desk drawer and leaned back in his chair, closing his eyes to savor the moment.

"Hello, Denton. You're a hard man to get hold of. Something wrong with your phone?"

He sprang to his feet and saw two men standing in the doorway, one stocky and muscular, with a thick neck and a boxer's flattened nose. The other was Frank Innocente.

"Are you surprised to see me? You wouldn't answer the phone, so you forced me to take time away from my busy schedule to come see that piece of paper you found."

"I...uh, I don't have it. I sent it off..."

"You just sent a picture of it to Brian Sadler, you lying bastard. I heard every word." He pointed to the man with him. "Forgive me for failing to introduce my friend Oskar. Oskar works for me. He collects money from people who owe me."

Denton stammered, "Okay, but I don't understand. I don't owe you money..."

"But you do owe me *something*. Give me the paper you found. This can be easy or difficult. You've been a coward since I met you, and trust me, you'll want things the easy way. Oskar's very persuasive, so be a good boy and hand it over."

*I am not a coward. I am not a coward.* He struggled to steady his nerves. "Okay, it's right in here," he said, opening the desk drawer and closing his fingers around the grip of a .38 pistol he kept inside. He pulled it out, trying to steady his shaking hands as he aimed and fired.

The shot went high and wide, and Denton's last conscious thought was about how fast that big man Oskar could move. He literally flew across the desk before slamming into Denton's chest like a locomotive.

# CHAPTER THIRTY-SIX

Brian forwarded the picture of the scrap of paper to Harry; then he called. "Denton found this behind a picture on a Pah-Che-Ka tombstone in his storeroom. What do you make of it? Does anything pop out?"

"I don't understand the numbers and slashes on the first line, but the second looks like a date and Teddy Roosevelt's initials. He told us in the poem where to find this paper, so there's no question he's left us another clue."

Brian agreed; the gravestone was dated 1906, one year after President Roosevelt hunted wolves and dined with Quanah Parker. What if on that trip, Roosevelt found something in the Wichita Mountains and left a coded clue? How would it have ended up a year later in a grave marker? Did Pah-Che-Ka have a connection to the president?

Harry thought they not only needed to figure out the first line, but also to see what they could turn up about the Comanche man. Harry's having been president gave him wider latitude to ask people in government to do a little research for him. If President Farber's husband—a man famous for exploring archaeological mysteries—asked the same favor, an inquisitive clerk might just leak it to the press.

"You take the line of code, and I'll work on finding out what our friend Pah-Che-Ka has to do with all this," Brian said. They would communicate again when one had something to report.

In the end, Harry learned a lot, while Brian found no connection between the Comanche man and Teddy

Roosevelt. Harry called back twenty-four hours later to advise he'd contacted a friend at the National Security Agency, the bureau responsible for collecting and processing counterintelligence information worldwide. The computer power at its disposal was second to none on Earth, and it had taken mere seconds to create probabilities for the numbers and symbols.

Harry said, "First I'll tell you what the NSA came up with. Then I'll tell you what the numbers mean." The computer's first guess, with a ninety-one percent probability factor, was that the numbers were coordinates—longitude and latitude—and the slash marks in between were separators with no other meaning.

"The symbols after the numbers are a sun, an arrow, a face and a marker pointing to the right. The computer gave these a thirty-eight percent probability of meaning 'look to the right when the sun sets, while standing at the spot marked by the coordinates.'"

"Good job!" Brian said. "Did you enter the coordinates to see what spot they mark?"

"Oh yeah, but let me finish first. The second guess, with a nine-point-three probability factor, is that the numbers are a twelve-digit international telephone number. The first two numbers—three and four—are the international dialing code for Spain, and the rest of the numbers might be a ten-digit phone number. Again the computer believed the slash marks were immaterial. And this time, with a four percent probability, the symbols meant 'look in the eastern part of Spain during the daytime.'"

"That makes no sense," Brian said. "I like the sound of those coordinates better."

"You're really going to like it once you hear this. I plotted the grid coordinates using the numbers on the sheet. The spot they mark is in Shadow Gulch!"

After years of adventure, Brian didn't excite easily, but he broke into a broad grin as he processed what this discovery could mean. The numbers on the paper were coordinates; that much was certain now that they pointed to the canyon mentioned in the article. Roosevelt's poem had led them to Pah-Che-Ka's tombstone, and that meant Teddy himself had left those coordinates. Now they had to decipher the meaning of the four symbols.

A sun, a slanted arrow, a face and a right-facing marker arrow. It was Brian's opinion they wouldn't learn what it all meant until they searched some more.

"I'm back from Europe tomorrow," Brian said. "We could go on the nineteenth. That might be good timing, because I'm thinking the numbers next to TR's initials are the date May 20, 1905. We can be there the same day he was. If he saw the iron door, maybe so can we."

Brian said he'd call Denton and make sure he'd be at the museum that day. Having found the paper, he deserved to hear what they'd learned about it. He reached voicemail, left a brief message, and after four hours he tried again. As enthusiastic as the man had been about helping, Brian had expected a return call in minutes, not hours. This time, after a series of clicks, an unfamiliar voice answered.

"Who's calling?"

"I want to speak to Denton Kopaddy. Who are you?"

"This is the FBI. Who's on the line?"

*The FBI?* Brian smiled; this agent was about to get a big surprise.

"This is Brian Sadler. I'm calling from Washington, DC. Put Mr. Kopaddy on the line, please."

Sure enough, there was dead silence for a moment, and then a different voice, authoritative and irritated. "This is Special Agent in Charge Quentin Phillips, FBI. Who is this?"

"I just explained who I am, Agent Phillips. I'm Brian Sadler. Where's Denton Kopaddy?"

"Sir, if you're really Brian Sadler, my apologies. I'm going to disconnect and call you back through the White House switchboard. Is that satisfactory?"

"Sure. Do you need the number?"

"No, sir, I'll get it independently." Moments later the two men were reconnected, and the agent's tone was far more conciliatory.

"I apologize, Mr. Sadler. I hope you understand what a surprise it was that you called..."

"No need to apologize; I understand. Why is the FBI answering Denton Kopaddy's phone?"

"Because Mr. Kopaddy appears to have been kidnapped. We have an APB issued for this area and north Texas. May I ask, why were you calling him, Mr. Sadler?"

"The reason for my call isn't relevant..."

Suddenly the agent was all business. "With all respect, sir, this is a federal investigation, and we'll judge what's relevant. Is your attempt to contact Mr. Kopaddy connected to the visit you and former president Harrison made to his museum earlier this week?"

"That's correct. In fact, President Harrison and I plan to be in Lawton again the day after tomorrow. We'd both like to hear what's up with Denton, so give me your number, and I'll let you know a time we can meet up. You talk to us, and we'll talk to you."

"No, sir. Please answer my question. Why did you call?"

Brian ignored him. "Give me your number, and when it's convenient, we'll get together."

Brian sensed the agent's indignation as he snapped off numbers. Phillips was used to giving orders, not taking them, but when dealing with two of the nation's most powerful people, he knew when to back off. He promised to make himself available whenever they could meet.

After Brian told Harry about Denton's disappearance, they wondered if it involved the scrap of paper. They agreed when they met the agent, they wouldn't mention their search for a lost cave. Instead, they would press for information about Denton.

————

Back from her European trip, Nicole sat alone in the Oval Office that evening and listened for perhaps the tenth time to the recording of a phone call that came through the White House switchboard to her assistant. The digitally enhanced voice had spoken briefly before disconnecting. Her aide forwarded the recording to Nicole without comment. This was one she'd stay out of unless the president directed otherwise.

"Tell President Farber I want to make a trade—my video for her document. The video was taken a few years back and shows the president in—well, there's no need to describe it. She'll know immediately what I'm referring to, and I'm certain she'd like the video and all copies destroyed.

"I want page 87 from the president's book. Not a copy—the original. After she's torn it out, tie a yellow ribbon on the lamppost in front of the barbecue restaurant at Seventh and D. When I see it, I'll call and arrange a swap so everybody's happy. The call will be from her uncle Charles, so put it through when it comes. The president has forty-eight hours."

Nicole knew exactly what the caller was referring to. Several years ago as a corporate attorney, she had been asked by her boss to represent a notorious mobster named John Spedino. He and Brian Sadler were sworn enemies, and he drugged and raped Nicole one night, capturing it all on camera. She mistakenly believed she had the only copy, but as often happens, that apparently wasn't true. Without context, the video was damning; thanks to the effects of the drug, she appeared to be a naked, willing participant in a steamy sex scene.

Brian wasn't the problem, she'd told him everything at the time, and he'd been instrumental in taking down Spedino, who was now serving a life sentence in a New York prison. The problem was perception—as a political novice and the first woman in the office, Nicole was subject to constant criticism from most in the other party and some in her own. A small cadre of older male congressmen fed irksome, false rumors to the mainstream media that kept the pot stirred. A real story—a lurid porn video starring the president—would mean the end of her short career in politics.

In other situations, resigning might be an option,

since Nicole hadn't signed up to be president in the first place. But this was different. She was determined not to let John Spedino's video take her down. She began making notes on a legal pad, listing the pros and cons of the possible responses to the call, from ignoring it to complying. Her brilliant legal mind had served her clients well, but as her famous predecessor Abraham Lincoln noted, a man who represents himself has a fool for a client. How could she objectively assess the courses of action when her own future was at stake?

# CHAPTER THIRTY-SEVEN

Upstairs in the residence, she played the message for Brian, who asked if she'd checked on Spedino's whereabouts. She had; he was still behind bars in the state penitentiary at Ossining, New York.

"What should I do, Brian? I can't talk to anyone else about this…"

"I get it, but I think you must. Harry and Jennifer know us better than anyone else. They would understand why you never told them about the video, and having been president himself, Harry can give you insight nobody else can."

She agreed to a Zoom call, and he said he'd set it up. "May I change the subject a moment?" he asked.

She nodded, and he said, "The guy who placed that call knows about the President's Book of Secrets. There's no reason not to tell me about it since I know it exists."

She shot him a vicious glare. "Dammit, Brian. Let it go. I can't talk about that, and neither can Harry. I think my problem's a little more important than a book. We destroyed the original of that video, but damn! I can't believe how stupid I was to think there wasn't a copy. I should have known better."

"You still don't know. It's certain four people know it exists—you, me, the person on that call and John Spedino. He may have told someone, who's attempting to blackmail you. There may not be a copy. All we know is that someone is aware of a video that could damage you. We can explain to Harry and Jennifer how it came about.

They'll understand."

She nodded, sat thinking for a moment, and said, "I can't give the man what he's demanding. It's impossible. You don't understand...you *can't* understand, but there's no way I could give him an original page or even a copy."

He took her hands in his. "I can't understand, but Harry can. That's why you must talk to him." She agreed and went back to her office. Brian called Harry, filled him in and arranged a Zoom call at six.

For the rest of the afternoon Nicole couldn't concentrate, barely listened to her visitors and finally told her appointments secretary to cancel the ones remaining. Alone in her office at four p.m., she made a decision and picked up the phone. Brian might have felt differently, but this battle was hers alone to fight.

Fifteen minutes later Horace Wilmington Fleming entered the Oval Office, trademark briefcase in hand. "Good afternoon, Madam President," he said, placing the case on his lap as he sat. He unsnapped the locks, removed the book, and put it on the desk.

She nonchalantly thumbed through the pages, attempting to appear mildly interested as she cast furtive glances in his direction. Each time she saw him watching her intently while his stopwatch ticked quietly on her desk. Finally she could wait no longer. She turned to page 87, and there it was—the poem that had created so much attention and become the subject of an extortion.

She fingered the page, pretending to read while testing its thickness. How hard would it be to remove? Not easy, she decided as she gave it a little tug.

At that moment, Fleming said, "Perhaps I can be of help, ma'am."

She jerked her head up and saw him sitting there with a piece of paper in his hand.

"What...what are you talking about?"

He placed it carefully in front of her. "Might this be useful?"

Lying next to page 87 in the book was an exact copy—the same yellowed paper, handwritten words almost identical to those on the original, and a jagged tear line on the left side. Even to someone who had seen the Book of Secrets, the page looked real. To a blackmailer who had never seen it, it would pass without question.

She cast off a shiver and stammered, "What is this? How...how did..."

"You aren't allowed to remove a page from the book," he said quietly. "But this replica will suffice for your needs."

Concerned that her dark secret might already be circulating in Washington, she snapped, "Tell me what you know."

"I know very little. 'Need-to-know' is the phrase civil servants all over town operate under. I am aware you are under a great deal of pressure to produce the original of page 87. I cannot allow you to do that, but fortunately for you I made a perfect copy. My little cubbyhole of an office is filled with old things, and luckily I came upon some paper from the early twentieth century that worked perfectly. How does my forgery look? Not bad, in my humble opinion."

In no mood for chitchat, she marched around her desk and jabbed her finger into his chest. "Who is he? Who's the man who wants this page? Tell me right now, or I'm calling the Secret Service."

Horace neither flinched nor did his voice tremble even a bit. He looked at her and said, "Please be calm, Madam President. There's no need to involve anyone else, nor do I think you wish to do so. Here's why I brought this paper to you. Every man and woman on earth has secrets— some may be minor and inconsequential, while others are monumental and carry tremendous consequence should they be discovered. Some people fear being shamed or blamed, while others may face prison or something even worse. The gravity of one's secrets determines the lengths to which one will go to keep them hidden.

"It appears both you and I have our secrets. I assure you I am not privy to what yours are, nor do I intend to reveal my own. But one individual—the person who wants this sheet—has brought us together. President Perrin allowed him to photograph the page, and I'm ashamed to admit I did nothing to stop him. He and I both broke our oaths, and afterwards the man threatened to expose me if I didn't give him the page. I saw him, but I don't know who he is. What I do know is that he knows my past, Madam President. But I would rather die than remove that page.

"I made this copy, but before I could offer it to him, he said he would get what he needed another way. That would be you, Madam President, since you and I are the only ones allowed to see the book. I deduced you had something to hide too, and that he'd use it against you, so I waited for your call."

"He has a photo of the page. Why does he want the original?"

"So that no other person will be able to decipher the words on it. It contains clues to a hidden treasure, ma'am. At least that's my opinion after having studied it for years. This man wants that treasure for himself."

As he spoke, wild thoughts spun in her brain. She felt nauseated and above all else, pissed off at the blackmailer and his seemingly unwilling accomplice sitting before her.

"Get out. Take the book and get out of my office," she snapped. He carefully returned the book to the briefcase and walked to the door, leaving the copy behind.

Having trouble focusing her eyes and with a migraine forming in the back crevasses of her brain, she ignored the phone when it rang quietly. She stared blankly at the paper in front of her, thinking about the keeper of the book, who had his own secrets, ones so serious he violated a sacred oath that had existed since the founding of the nation.

The next time the phone buzzed, she answered it. "Your husband would like to come in," her assistant said, and moments later Brian joined her. She hugged him tightly, told him everything that had happened, and handed him the copy.

"Why shouldn't I show this page to you?" she

rambled, mostly to herself. "I'm not violating any oath. I didn't tell you there's a book, and I didn't show you page 87. This is a reproduction, and frankly, it's the least of my worries right now."

He looked at it, recalling the words Harry had memorized and copied, and said it looked like a passable forgery, although he hadn't seen the original. He said, "I want to talk to the book keeper. Call and tell him you want to see him again. We have the Zoom call at six. Get him back here at five."

"He was just here, and he won't come back. I'm only allowed to see the book once a month."

"Tell him you have new information for him. He can leave the book; I don't care about it. I want to find out what he knows. We must find out who the extortionist is and how he's connected to John Spedino."

# CHAPTER THIRTY-EIGHT

Horace seemed surprised to get another summons from the president half an hour after he'd rather abruptly been dismissed. When she asked him to come back, he replied as she'd expected, reminding her that she was allowed just one visit a month. She explained she wanted to talk not about the book, but about the things he had said. About his secret...and hers. About an extortionist and his motives.

He declined at first, but she Insisted, saying she'd have him brought by force if necessary. Her threat didn't faze Horace, but his curiosity was aroused, and he agreed to come right back. When he arrived, his jaw dropped when he found not only the president but also her husband.

"This is highly inappropriate," he said, turning to leave. "I'm surprised, Madam President. I told you about President Perrin allowing an intruder, and now you're doing it as well. You know it isn't allowed, and I mustn't stay. You brought me here under false pretenses..."

"Sit down," Brian snapped. "She didn't bring you anywhere; you came voluntarily. We want to know about the extortionist. What's your secret?"

Horace struggled to think his way out of this dilemma, then collapsed into a chair. "Why can't you just give him the sheet? I made it easy for you. There's no need to complicate everything."

"Who is he?"

"As I told the president, I don't know his name."

"What do you know about him?"

"He wanted information. He learned I was the keeper of the book. President Perrin showed it to him, and later he ordered me to give him page 87."

"Then why didn't you? Why involve my wife?"

"I couldn't do it, Mr. Sadler. It's a sacred trust. I have my secrets, as I told your wife earlier, but I also have my integrity. He threatened to...well, to ruin my life, truth be told, but I held fast. He asked if President Farber had seen the book, and I nodded. Another transgression, I'm sorry to say."

Brian pushed harder. "You were there when Perrin showed him the book. That's when you violated that sacred-trust bullshit you seem so hung up on. In for a penny, in for a pound, the way I see it. You don't want to break any more rules, but you're happy to let Nicole do it. You've already committed the ultimate sin, so start talking. What do you know about these people?"

He hung his head. "My contact—a man named Oskar—called me at home. He said his employer was a very influential person who knew things about my past. He told me things no one else knows. He pressured me, but I refused to give him anything more. A few days ago Oskar called again and said I was to forget the conversation ever happened. His boss was going to get what he wanted from you, President Farber. Oskar's boss wanted to settle a longstanding grudge with you and Mr. Sadler."

Nicole glanced at Brian. "What did he say it was about?"

"He didn't say, nor did I ask."

Brian said, "Have you ever heard the name John Spedino?"

Horace stroked his chin for a moment. "The name sounds vaguely familiar. Should I know him?"

"He was a New York mob boss. Back in the day, his name was as familiar as John Gotti's, but he's in prison now. We had a run-in with him a few years ago, and I wonder if he's behind all this."

"Why all the interest in page 87?" Nicole asked. "The book..." She cast a glance Brian's way. "It's...well, filled with all sorts of tantalizing secrets."

"It is that, and with all respect, Madam President, I believe you know the answer. I've watched other presidents spend a few minutes looking at page 87, but your friend Harry Harrison was mesmerized by it. He was interested enough to memorize it one stanza at a time. To be honest, I found it fascinating myself, and over time I cracked the code. I presume you, Mr. Sadler, and President Harrison did as well. Which would of course be in violation of the promise he signed."

"My, aren't we hypocritical?" Brian snorted. "Technically, Harry didn't reveal anything. He showed me a piece of paper with a poem he'd copied."

"What did you learn from that paper?"

Brian replied evasively. "So far, not much. You say you cracked the code, so what does it mean?"

"Teddy Roosevelt wrote it, the numbers are backward, there are several oblique references to southwestern Oklahoma, and there's a direct one to Quanah Parker, whom Roosevelt once visited. The thing of frame and glass hidden inside object number 1644 I believe you've already found. Am I correct?"

"How did you know that?" Nicole asked, and he said it was simple. He checked the records just as they had done, and learned the president had requisitioned the painting a few days ago. He added, "It appears Oskar's boss is also trying to solve President Roosevelt's tantalizing puzzle."

Nicole snapped, "Excuse me, but you seem to be enjoying all this, like it's some kind of game we're playing. I don't know what your deep, dark secret is, but you certainly don't have the same level of concern that we do. What'd you do...steal a bar of candy?"

"It's far graver than that, I'm afraid. And it shall remain confidential. I don't mean to make light of the situation, Madam President. Transferring the burden of the problem to you makes me no less vulnerable to exposure, trust me."

Brian said, "Let's go back to Oskar. How does he

contact you?"

"The first meeting was the only one face-to-face, on a bench near the Lincoln Memorial. I felt like a spy for the CIA. That day he gave me a cell phone, I've never owned one, and he's the only person who calls it. I never saw him after that."

Brian asked more questions, learned almost nothing, and they dismissed Horace, who promised to call if Oskar contacted him again. The moment he left, Nicole rang for the valet and ordered drinks. It was half past five—cocktail hour on a distressing, tense day—and she needed a drink before the Zoom call at six.

Harry and Jennifer sat in silence as Nicole told them about John Spedino's video and offered their full support. Brian held up the duplicate of Teddy Roosevelt's poem and asked if Harry had any suggestion on how they might avoid handing it over.

"What if we get Horace Fleming to change a few words and alter the meaning?"

"Good idea, but we don't have the time. We should get another call about making the drop any time now."

Harry said even with his having the exact copy, they held the advantage. They had found the secret drawing that only someone with White House access could have done. And thanks to Denton Kopaddy's discovery in the grave marker, they had what appeared to be grid coordinates.

"Yeah, but Denton's missing," Brian pointed out. "I'll guarantee our extortionist is the same man who kidnapped him, and I'll bet he has the coordinates too."

Harry asked, "Do you think Spedino really might be masterminding this?"

"It must be him. Nobody else fits."

"I agree, but why now, after so many years? And how's he doing it from prison?"

"The *how* is easy. He was one of the most powerful Mafia bosses in the country, and I'm sure he still has a network of loyal people. As to why, I can't imagine what he wants with Roosevelt's poem. Even if he knows it's about treasure, why would it matter to an old man destined to die behind bars?"

Jennifer asked if they'd considered there might not be a copy of the video at all.

Nicole said, "Am I willing to risk my presidency, which I couldn't care less about, and my reputation, which matters a great deal to me? I was a victim, but it won't come across that way. So we must go on the assumption there's a copy."

Brian asked what she thought about bringing in the FBI and the Secret Service. Although it would be reassuring to have law enforcement working to find the extortionist, the risk of exposure would grow as more people became involved. Nicole thought about it and said, "Let's do it. This is a big deal, I have nothing to be ashamed of, and I'll be damned if I'll let that bastard John Spedino get the best of me."

Harry agreed it was a good idea. Their vast resources might quickly put a stop to the extortion attempt. With that, they ended the Zoom call with a promise to stay in touch.

The next morning a female FBI agent drove to Seventh and D Streets. In front of the Southern Pit, a popular barbecue joint, she tied a yellow ribbon around a streetlight post, while in the White House, another agent sat in the Oval Office. When the blackmailer called two hours later, he reached for a phone handset, counted down from three to one, and he and Nicole picked up simultaneously.

"Write down these instructions," the caller said. "This is where you're going to deliver the page. I know it won't be you, of course, because you're the *president*—the sarcasm was unmistakable—so your flunky needs to do exactly what I say."

"Not so fast, Oskar," Nicole said. "I don't know anything about a video. And it is Oskar, correct?"

He paused. "So you had your guys put a yellow ribbon on the lamppost just for kicks? You want that video, Madam President, so I suggest you stop trying to figure things out. You'd better shut the hell up and listen to me."

"Tell me something that proves you have it."

She heard him chuckle. "Okay, but remember, you asked. You have a very cute mole about two inches south of your belly button."

Nicole shot a glance at the FBI man listening ten feet away, who averted his eyes. After taking a deep breath, she said, "Give me the instructions, you bastard." Two minutes later the call ended. A trace would soon show it came from a burner phone that went out of service thirty seconds after it disconnected.

# CHAPTER THIRTY-NINE

That afternoon, an FBI agent in an unmarked sedan drove to Union Station in downtown Washington. In the passenger seat lay a cardboard mailing tube containing the replicated page Horace Wilmington Fleming had created. Inside the busy terminal, he retrieved a key taped behind a toilet in the men's room, opened a locker, and removed a burner cell phone that rang before he could get back to his vehicle.

Per President Farber's instructions, no backup vehicles tailed the agent. Knowing the phone tracked his whereabouts, he listened as the caller directed him south into rural Fairfax County, Virginia, and eventually onto Ox Road. He drove for miles in silence until he heard the caller say, "Now! Stop the car!"

He pulled to the shoulder and drove as instructed to a rusty mailbox a hundred feet ahead. "Put the paper and the phone inside the mailbox and keep driving south. Take another route back to Washington. If we see anything suspicious on this road, the deal's off."

"When do we get the video?" the agent asked, but the call went dead. He relayed the drop location to his office and returned to DC. Twenty-five minutes later, another agent checked the mailbox and found it empty. Now all Nicole and Brian could do was wait.

After twenty-four hours with no call, Brian was going stir-crazy. He had to get his mind off the situation; it was slightly easier for Nicole, who had a full schedule every day with little time for reflection or worry. He and

Harry were scheduled to return to Oklahoma tomorrow, May 19, but he didn't want to leave Nicole alone to handle this awful issue.

"Go on," she told him. "There's nothing you can do here. I've done what he asked, and he's failed to do his part. I can't stop the country from running while I dwell on it, and if something comes up, you're just a few hours away. Take Harry and go back to the mountains."

Harry made the final arrangements. Brian had committed to meet the FBI agent in Lawton, and Harry's personal secretary lined up a conference room. Then she called Special Agent Phillips, who agreed to be there. The other logistics of the trip fell into place, and the next morning Harry and Brian returned to Fort Sill.

Colonel O'Reilly's driver took them to headquarters, where Special Agent-in-Charge Phillips waited. Brian and Harry introduced themselves and sat across a conference table while their two Secret Service bodyguards stood near the doorway.

Before Phillips could speak, Brian asked who reported Denton's kidnapping.

"A banker friend of his had a lunch date with him. When he stopped by the museum to pick Denton up, he found the front door smashed in and called the police. After a preliminary investigation, they called the FBI, since it appeared he'd been kidnapped.

"The museum is equipped with cameras, but the video was on the blink. From the audio, it appears two men entered the office. Only one spoke; he mentioned your name, Mr. Sadler, and he demanded the paper that Mr. Kopaddy had sent to you. When he refused, the man introduced the other man as Oskar, a debt collector. From there it sounds like Mr. Kopaddy opened a drawer, perhaps to get the paper. A single shot rang out, and a scuffle followed. Nobody spoke, but the audio seems to indicate Mr. Kopaddy was attacked and rendered unconscious before all three left the premises. My question to you is, what was on that piece of paper?"

Brian looked at Harry, who said, "I have no

problem with telling him so long as it stays within the bureau." He removed it from his shirt pocket and put it on the table. "President Harrison and I are looking for something, and Denton found a paper that seems to have clues. I have a copy, and we think we know what it means. If I let you see it, this goes no further. No disclosures to media, other agencies or anybody else, period. Agreed?"

When Phillips agreed, Brian pushed the copy across the table. He studied it for a moment and asked what the numbers and symbols meant.

Harry replied, "We don't know yet, but that's why we came back to Lawton. We're going back into the mountains to test a theory. Once we finish, if there's anything to report that relates to Kopaddy's disappearance, we'll let you know."

Phillips wasn't having it. "Sorry, Mr. President. If Mr. Kopaddy has been abducted, you two are in danger as well. They want something, and they'll come after you to learn whatever this is about. I'm asking you to tell me everything you know, and if you insist on going into the mountains, I'll send a team along to protect you."

Harry shook his head. "Thanks, but that's not gonna happen. You know as much as we do, and we have the best protection in the world." He pointed over his shoulder toward the Secret Service agents who stood behind them, suppressing smiles. The rivalry between the agencies was legendary, and they appreciated the kudos from a former president.

Phillips wouldn't let it go. "You may need more firepower than that…"

Brian and Harry stood; he picked up the paper and said, "Thanks for meeting us. We'll be in touch." Everyone walked out, leaving the frustrated FBI agent fuming by himself.

As before, they rode in Army SUVs to the parking lot near the canyon opening and met the men with their horses. Brian, Harry and the same three agents mounted their steeds and entered the narrow passage that led them back into the maze of canyons and ravines. They rode for nearly an hour, stopping at every junction while Harry followed the GPS on his iPhone, frustrated by the increasingly sporadic internet connectivity as they went deeper and deeper into the mountains.

They came to a place in a dry riverbed where everyone dismounted for a break in the shade while Harry rechecked the GPS. He took Brian aside and said, "The place marked by the coordinates is about a mile ahead. Are we sticking with the plan?"

Brian nodded. "Let's tell them what's going on."

Harry gathered the three agents and said, "I'm sure you've been wondering what the hell we're doing out here in the wilderness, and it's time to let you in on what we know. Anybody want to hazard a guess what we're after?"

The lead agent said, "Since Mr. Sadler's here, I'd say you're looking for Spanish treasure." Another, a man named Spurgeon who grew up in this area, suggested outlaw gold, because of the myths and legends surrounding the Wichita Mountains and its inhospitable terrain. The third, a New Yorker born and bred, said he didn't have a clue, but if he had to ride a horse much longer, he was going to need an ass massage.

"We're following a set of clues left a long time ago," Brian explained. "We think we've deciphered most of it, and the museum director in Lawton who was kidnapped gave us more. The guys who took him are after the same thing we are, hence the possible need for firepower."

Harry added, "We have a set of numbers that appear to be grid coordinates. They mark a spot not far from here, and hopefully they will bring us closer to what we're looking for."

"Which is?"

Brian glanced at Harry. "I want a promise from each of you that you won't reveal anything that happens here, no matter what. Agreed?"

Each nodded.

"We're following a legend called the Lost Cave of the Iron Door."

Agent Spurgeon said, "I know it well. Growing up

on a farm outside Lawton, I heard lots of stories about lost treasure buried in these mountains. The iron door legend is one of the most compelling. Damn, I'm excited to be along on this one!"

"It'll be a hell of a lot more fun than guarding a president at a political rally." Harry laughed. "I can only imagine how much you guys loved doing that kind of stuff."

The lead agent shrugged, said it came with the territory and that he also enjoyed being part of the adventure, especially in the company of Brian Sadler. His televised archaeological adventures enthralled millions, and today these three agents might see him in action.

They headed deeper into the canyon, with Harry keeping an eye on the GPS as they meandered through the gulches in the increasingly oppressive afternoon heat. About a mile along, he stopped and pointed to a high cliff face on his right and said, "We must be in Shadow Gulch. Our site is up there somewhere." He consulted the paper again and double-checked his coordinates.

### 34/43\28/98\43/23

"If we've interpreted these numbers correctly, then we've found the spot," Harry said. "It could be on the east wall or the west."

"I can tell you which wall it's on," Brian said, pulling out the copy of the drawing they'd found behind painting number 1644 and pointing up. "See where those two mountains converge at the top of the east wall? They're the ones in Roosevelt's sketch. The cave's up there somewhere. Grab your packs, gents. Let's go up there and solve a mystery."

# CHAPTER FORTY

Brian had identified the east wall, so it was the western face they climbed so they could find a place to study the cliffs as the sun's rays moved lower in the western sky. It was slow going as they maneuvered up the cliff face, slipping and sliding on loose rocks until they found a ledge jutting out twenty feet from the wall. It provided the perfect shady spot to check out the east wall opposite that now lay bathed in sunlight.

Brian handed the paper to the agents and asked for their ideas, saying, "We think the first set of numbers are coordinates and the second line is a date and the writer's initials, but we're not sure about the four symbols."

**34/43\28/98\43/23 ☼ ✓☐ ☉ ➤**
**5-20-05-TR**

Agent Spurgeon asked where the paper came from, and Brian said it had been hidden in an old graveyard. As they ate lunch—sandwiches and water from their backpacks—everyone tossed out ideas about the four symbols. Harry and Brian interpreted them as saying when the **sun** shone **down** on the canyon wall, **look** to the **east**. That was why they chose the west side. As the sun illuminated the opposite wall, maybe they'd see the door.

They discussed the notation "5-20-05-TR." Brian said he believed President Roosevelt wrote the note May 20, 1905, when he visited and hunted in these mountains. That was why they chose to return on that same day.

After two boring hours, Brian said he was going to the east side to look around. Harry went too, accompanied by two of the agents, leaving one on the west ledge to shout if he saw a reflection. They clambered down to the canyon floor, walked a hundred feet across the dry gulch, and started up the much steeper eastern face, one agent in front and one bringing up the rear. Erosion and loose rock made climbing this side a bigger challenge. Every step on the unsteady surface required careful testing before putting down full weight, and Brian, just behind the lead agent, dodged rock missiles as the man's feet dislodged a hailstorm of stones with each footfall. His climb created the same issue for Harry, who in turn rained pebbles and rocks on the agent in back.

They planned to climb to the same altitude on the east side of the ravine as that where the agent sat opposite. They'd be directly on the grid coordinates and wait to find out if he saw anything as the sun dropped. It was after three now, and they knew from their earlier visit that the canyon would be draped in shadows as the last rays disappeared around five. They should be leaving already, but nobody mentioned it this time. If darkness came, it would only mean a slower ride back.

Everyone plodded upwards, concentrating on the trek and dodging rocks, until the man in front yelled, "Snake! Shit, it's a snake, guys! Son of a bitch bit me!"

They'd been warned about them by the men who brought their horses. Several types—including the western diamondback rattlesnake—lived in the rough terrain, sunning themselves on rocks until the heat of the day, when they crawled into shady places. It was one of those crevices, a small indentation that seemed a good handhold, where the agent had stuck his hand. As the others reached him, they could see two nasty holes where the serpent's fangs had dug deep into the fleshy part of his palm.

"I've got a snakebite kit," yelled the agent in back. Brian and Harry moved aside, giving the agent room to reach his companion on the precipitous incline, retrieve the kit from his backpack, and work on the wound.

"We're going on up," Harry advised. "We're just in the way here."

"Take this with you," the lead agent said, passing up a red backpack that was the emergency kit. As Brian and Harry climbed on, it was apparent the wounded man needed medical care fast, and they'd both have to ride out of the canyon, leaving only the agent on the western ledge to protect them. He radioed, saying he was coming down.

The lead agent insisted Brian and Harry descend too. Everyone had to go back with the injured man; it was too dangerous to leave them with only one member of the security detail left. But neither would agree.

Brian radioed the agent on the other side, telling him to stay put. "Watch for the iron door when the sun drops lower. If you see something, we'll set a homing beacon and meet you at the bottom before it's too dark." Although it would leave them with almost no protection, the two agents rode away because they had no choice.

When they reached the correct height, Brian radioed that they had found an outcropping wide enough to sit. By four thirty their ledge was deep in shadows, and they waited, hoping for a frantic radio transmission from across the gorge alerting them to check something out.

And it happened in exactly that way. At twelve minutes before five, the radio crackled to life. They looked across to see the agent sitting in the gloom with his walkie-talkie in one hand and his phone in the other. "The sun's reflecting off something maybe forty feet to your left and five or so up. I'll shoot video…damn! It's already gone, but it sparkled like a diamond for a moment."

Excited, they prepared to move. The reflection had lasted mere seconds, but the agent's estimate of the distance would help pinpoint the location. On level ground, forty feet would be an easy distance to cover, but moving along a canyon wall, clambering to find handholds and footholds, it took more than twenty minutes, and now the canyon was getting dark quickly.

"That looks about right," the agent radioed. "Set the beacon and let's get out of here before we can't find our ways down. I'll meet you at the horses."

As Brian continued moving slowly along the cliff face, Harry pulled a Garmin inReach satellite communicator from his pack and switched it on. The unit would transmit a continuous locator signal to a cloud-based website, allowing them to easily find it again.

Harry watched Brian move past an outcropping and out of sight around a slight bend. Across the narrow gorge, he watched the agent descend the opposite side, but before he reached the bottom, Harry lost sight of him in the shadows. As the canyon was plunged into an inky blackness, they realized they'd misjudged how quickly things would change.

"Brian, come on back. We have to get out while we can!"

A muffled shout. "Harry! Harry, you gotta come see this!"

"I set the beacon. Come on back!" Harry yelled, but Brian didn't answer. Grousing to himself that they might end up spending the night on the side of a mountain, he carefully inched his way left, missed a step that sent debris flying downward, and grasped for a handhold until his feet were back on solid ground. He rounded the corner where Brian had gone, stepped onto a slightly wider ledge, and sidled across, keeping his body pressed hard against the rock face. In the inky blackness he could see only a foot ahead. He called Brian's name and heard a faint, "In here! To the left of the iron door."

*The iron door?* His arms tingled with excitement as he saw it—a cave entrance beside an old boxcar door, battered and rusted to a shade that blended perfectly with the environment, set into the side of the cliff and mostly obscured behind brush and rocks. A door impossible to see from even a few feet away—except for a few seconds on the twentieth of May as the sun's last rays played across its rusted surface.

# CHAPTER FORTY-ONE

Once Brian kept moving along the cliff face, he realized he could no longer see Harry. Now he found a slightly wider ledge, kept his face pressed against the rock, and his fingers wrapped tightly around an outcropping. His breath came in feverish gasps; never a fan of heights, it took every ounce of courage to slide one foot to the left, then the other, while choosing rocks he hoped wouldn't move when he gripped them. The deepening gloom helped only because he could no longer see how high he was above the canyon floor. He knew, as Harry did, that every step became more treacherous as he depended on feel rather than sight for solid footing.

*I should go back while I can. But I'm here, and if I quit, we may never find it again.* Truthfully, going back was the last thing Brian wanted; in his current situation, the only thing scarier than staying put was thinking about slip-sliding his way back across the cliff face in the dark.

At the same time Harry was yelling for him to come back, he maneuvered around scrub brush, searched for the next handhold, and felt something else. Behind the scraggly bushes against which he pressed his body, the wall of rocks became something different—a surface solid and smooth and warm from earlier, when the sun's rays had touched it.

He ran his fingers along the surface, noting its height and width. *It's metal,* he thought as his heart raced. *Oh my God, Harry's never going to believe this. We found it! We really found it!*

He shouted, "Harry! Harry, you gotta come see

this!"

He wanted to shoot a picture, but the narrow ledge left no room for missteps, and he dared not risk throwing himself off-balance by reaching into his back pocket for the phone. It was precarious enough balancing his weight to account for the backpack and emergency kit he wore as he inched his way a little farther and breathed a sigh of relief when he felt the outcropping widen by several feet. At last he could take a few steps away from the wall without fear of falling.

His fingers found the edge of the metal wall. Where it ended, there was a narrow, deep-black void—a hole, partially hidden by the iron door, that opened into the rock face. He realized the momentary reflection at sunset happened because only a fraction of the door was exposed. He swept the area for snakes, took out his phone, and entered what he realized was not a natural cave, but a tunnel cut into the rock that was around six feet wide and six tall. It sloped gently downward off into the darkness.

From somewhere outside, he heard Harry call his name.

"In here! To the left of the iron door."

A moment later, Harry stepped inside, his face beaming. "Do you realize what we've found here? This is it! I'll be damned if the iron door's not real! And it covers a tunnel entrance. When I read the article, I pictured men on horseback riding through these very canyons, watching the sun's reflection on a mysterious door set high in the cliffs, I dreamed of being the one who found it. All these years later, here we are!"

Forgetting all about the Secret Service agent who was waiting for them down below—and the encroaching darkness outside the cave—they began to inch their way into the cavern, playing their flashlights across the low ceilings and the pebble-strewn pathway ahead.

About twenty feet down, the passageway dog-legged to the left and widened, and as they ventured farther, a light, cool breeze swept over them. They descended on a gradual slope until the tunnel opened into a vast cavern.

Here the ceiling reached up into inky blackness, and they could no longer touch the walls on either side. Gusts of chilly air swirled about them.

Brian's voice echoed. "I wish we'd brought more powerful flashlights. It's impossible to see how big this cavern is." He took a few steps along the wall but jerked his hand away as he felt the stones begin to tremble. A low growl turned into a rumble as first pebbles, then larger stones began raining down from above.

"Earthquake!" Harry yelled. "Run back into the passageway! It's not safe in here!"

They scrambled through the opening and waited as the walls of the corridor shook. Brian turned his light up into the passage they'd come down and saw a smoky cloud cascading toward them, filling the narrow tunnel with choking dust and debris. Within seconds it was so thick that just inches apart, they couldn't see each other. The trembling stopped, and they went back into the cavern to escape the suffocating dust.

Brian said, "As soon as everything settles, we have to go back up the tunnel to see if we can reach the entrance. If the corridor has collapsed, we're trapped!"

Conserving battery power, they sat in darkness and checked the tunnel occasionally. After an hour the dust began to clear, and they started back up the corridor to find their means of escape blocked by rubble and rocks. They had no idea the extent of the damage out in the canyon, but if a rockslide had covered the iron door and the tunnel entrance, it could take days—weeks, perhaps—before they'd be rescued. They had an emergency pack and their own backpacks, but by then it would be too late. They hoped all three Secret Service agents were safe—the two who would have been halfway back to the parking lot, and the one who had remained with them.

They wondered if this was the destiny intended for them—to die of starvation or thirst in utter blackness. At last Brian broke the silence. "I sure hope there's another way out. We have two flashlights and the lights on our phones, plus a couple of power charging banks, but that's all. We must make everything last as long as possible."

Given the sobering likelihood that rescue might take days rather than hours, it was high time to assess what supplies they had. First they opened the emergency kit. It weighed almost twenty pounds, and Brian had almost declined because he didn't want to carry the extra weight. Now they considered themselves fortunate because what it held might save their lives.

Designed for four persons and seventy-two hours, it contained water pouches, a hundred protein bars, water purification tablets, coffee pouches, a small cooking pot and kits for basic hygiene and first aid. Practical items included two powerful LED flashlights, a compass, work gloves, nylon rope, a pocket card multitool, a hammer and a screwdriver.

There were lightweight blankets, body warmers, a tent, hooded ponchos, firestarter sticks and a ten-pack of twelve-hour light sticks. Almost everything would be useful, including a survival whistle that Harry suggested they could blow if searchers got close. The emergency kit would sustain them for a week, maybe two, hopefully giving rescuers time to find them.

Their personal day packs contained other useful items—puffer jackets, which they were already wearing in the dank cave; more energy bars and water; portable chargers, which would keep phones and iPads going for a few days; and something that Brian pulled out that made Harry smile—a half-pint of cognac.

"Holy moly, that's a welcome sight! Why on earth did you pack that?" Harry asked.

"Because it's always five o'clock somewhere, even in a cave," Brian replied. "Would you like a nip?" Since it was midnight out in the real world, they decided to wait until the afternoon to do a cocktail hour, and to ration it so it would last until their rescue...or the end.

# CHAPTER FORTY-TWO

*FORMER PRESIDENT HARRISON,*
*FIRST GENTLEMAN SADLER MISSING*

At eight thirty p.m. Washington time, newscasters around the world interrupted broadcasts for breaking news. Brian Sadler, husband of President Nicole Farber, and former president William Henry Harrison IV were missing after riding horses into a remote area of the Wichita Mountains National Wildlife Refuge near Lawton, Oklahoma. A third man, a member of Harrison's Secret Service detail, was missing as well. The president issued a statement asking the nation to pray for the safe return of the three men.

ABC News reported, "The men and their bodyguards arrived at the Fort Sill army base this morning by helicopter from President Harrison's ranch in central Oklahoma. Just after noon local time, First Gentleman Sadler, former President Harrison and three agents rode on horseback into the Wichita Mountains." Video accompanying the newscast showed the rugged terrain and steep, winding gorges.

The newscast continued, "Two of the detail assigned to guard the men left the area after one was bitten by a poisonous snake and needed urgent medical attention. One Secret Service agent, who remained with Harrison and Sadler, is now unaccounted for. Quentin Phillips, Special Agent in Charge of the FBI's office in Oklahoma City, is heading a joint team of Secret Service, FBI agents and military police from Fort Sill searching for the three missing men."

The broadcast cut to a live shot from the visitor center at the wildlife refuge, where Phillips introduced Colonel O'Reilly. "It's too dark in the canyons to search tonight," he said. "With hundreds of canyons and pathways leading in every direction, it's easy to get disoriented in the mountains, even in the daytime. If necessary, we'll begin a ground search at dawn, but already we have Army helicopters and drones equipped with searchlights and thermal imaging cameras canvassing the area from above."

Phillips said nothing about his meeting with Brian and Harry before they left for the mountains, although he wondered if the mysterious scrap of paper filled with numbers and symbols played a part in their disappearances. He also considered foul play a remote possibility; authorities had closed the refuge to tourists when Brian and Harry arrived, but given the vast area, hikers or campers could still be inside without permission.

Agent Phillips kept to himself his thoughts about who might be in the refuge. Most visitors were families or outdoors fanatics, but some Okies were rabidly independent and distrusted the government. What would they do if they found these two Washington VIPs?

Radar picked up dozens of heat signals from nocturnal creatures large and small roaming the gulches and arroyos, and around two a.m., a helicopter captured a significant heat concentration in a remote area at the bottom of a two-hundred-foot canyon. A drone was dispatched, and soon the searchers saw video footage of three saddled horses grazing idly along the dry riverbed.

By dawn an astute investigative reporter at the ABC affiliate in Lawton connected the sensational story to another. Denton Kopaddy, director of a local museum, vanished one day before they did, and only days after Harrison and Sadler toured his museum. In an opinion piece aired nationally, the journalist posed questions the country was asking as well.

"Four disappearances in twenty-four hours in a city

of less than a hundred thousand people is no coincidence. Mr. Kopaddy, former President Harrison and Mr. Sadler were together earlier in the week. Should searchers be looking for him too? What were two luminaries doing in the Wichita Mountains anyway? Could our past president and the husband of our current one be off on some kind of adventure? Brian Sadler is a renowned treasure hunter, a frequent guest on television talk shows, and the star of thrilling archaeological documentaries. What if—and all our thoughts must be what-ifs until they are found—these men became entangled with current-day outlaws protecting something in the remote canyons? And where is the missing Secret Service agent assigned to guard the VIPs? We must keep these men in our prayers as law enforcement mounts one of the biggest manhunts in history. May they return safe and sound."

After one received treatment, the two agents who left early—the snakebite victim and the man who accompanied him back to the staging area—faced separate interviews, and their stories matched. After traveling far into the canyon through a maze of twists and turns, Harry and Brian pinpointed a location using GPS. They and the two agents began an ascent that had stopped when a snake bit one of them. The agents went back down while they continued, refusing to return to base or let the other agent join them.

Why did they leave the men they were sworn to protect? The interrogators asked.

One man required medical attention, another had to take him back, and the third did as Sadler ordered.

What exactly were Harrison and Sadler looking for? Why all the GPS and climbing and pinpointing locations?

"They didn't say," each agent dutifully lied.

At dawn, armed FBI and Secret Service agents rode in and found the three horses. When they dismounted and began searching the area, they heard groans from somewhere nearby and found the Secret Service agent who had been stationed on the west wall. Barely conscious, his badly bruised torso showed severe trauma, and back at the

Fort Sill hospital, he would tell interrogators he came down from the ledge in the dark, missed his footing and fell. He tumbled to the bottom, apparently hit his head and passed out.

"Why didn't you go help them earlier, once you knew they were alone on the other side?" the interrogator asked, and the agent verified the stories told earlier. Once it got dark, he started down because he thought Harry and Brian were doing the same, and they'd meet up at the horses. In the blackness, he lost his footing.

"What were they doing?" his interrogator asked, but the agent refused to break his pledge of secrecy.

"That's something you'd have to ask them. Our job was protection, not to get involved in whatever they were up to."

The frustrated interrogator sarcastically reminded the man that they all worked for the same agency, and thanks to their protection—or lack thereof—President Harrison and Sadler were unavailable to answer questions. "They've disappeared, and you're withholding information that could help us find them. You could face criminal prosecution."

This was the first the agent had heard about their having gone missing, and he told the investigator everything.

By midday, agents were scouring every square foot of land, vertically and horizontally, within a quarter-mile radius of where the agent had been found. Rappellers dangled from ropes attached to descenders on the canyon's western rim, search and rescue dogs roamed the dry creek bed, and agents combed the dry gulches for clues, however small.

# CHAPTER FORTY-THREE

Brian awoke with a start as something brushed his cheek. He cried out and waved his hand as he heard the rushing of wings. *Bats,* he realized as he came fully alert. They'd dodged guano when entering the cavern, and when Harry had played his light around the room earlier, they had seen the creatures lodged in cracks and crevices high above.

"I guess we fell asleep," Harry mumbled, clicking on his flashlight. Using his jacket as a pillow, he'd lain on the chamber floor, and now he clutched his aching back as he sat upright. It was 7:22 a.m., fourteen hours since Brian had found the iron door and they'd entered the cave. Surely people would be searching for them now, but how much damage had the quake done to the cliff face? Was the door more visible now, or buried forever? Would the Garmin beacon Harry left on the ledge transmit their location, or did the rockslide crush it to bits?

After sharing a protein bar and a few sips of water, Brian suggested they check out the cavern. They set out in opposite directions, measuring paces as they walked alongside the cave walls. They called out frequently to ensure all was well, and after some time they met up again, each having traversed half of the room, which they now knew was a rough circle of about one hundred and fifty feet in circumference. Harry calculated the diameter and said it was about fifty feet directly across the room from where they started. Neither had encountered obstacles other than rocks and detritus, but both had come across side tunnels leading off the main room.

"Now we know how big our prison is," Harry said, "and we know there are three side tunnels. Since we can't go back the way we came, I say we explore the other ones. Preferably together. I don't relish the thought of getting lost in here. Or being alone, for that matter."

They took a light stick to save their batteries and entered the first tunnel. It was so narrow and cramped they had to bend at the waist and sidle through. It extended only twenty feet before ending at a rock wall. After looking at it, they decided this was not another cave-in; it was merely the end of a very short shaft.

Within moments after entering the second tunnel, they found something exciting. Every ten feet, wooden beams—probably old-fashioned railroad ties—supported the five-foot-high rock ceiling. Long ago, men had worked this part of the mine.

The tunnel sloped downwards, and forty feet along they emerged into another chamber. They stepped inside, shone the light stick around, and found a much smaller room with two tunnels branching off it. Brian let out a shout when he saw a stack of wooden crates across the chamber…and a man sitting atop them.

"Denton!" Brian cried as they ran across the sandy floor. "Denton, are you all right?"

Denton Kopaddy was decidedly not all right. In fact, he was stone dead, his body propped up in a sitting position on the boxes. They lifted the corpse down and put it on the ground as Harry dropped to one knee to examine it. He noticed ligature marks on the neck that revealed Denton's likely cause of death was from strangulation.

"Those two men must have brought him here and then killed him. But why? Why did they go to all this trouble? They could have dumped his body in some remote ravine."

"It's about the gold," Brian suggested. "That paper in Pah-Che-Ka's marker had the coordinates, and I think they brought him here to show them where the iron door was."

# THE IRON DOOR

"So they killed him and propped his body up. Why would they do that? And where are they now?"

Brian shrugged, walked over to the stack of boxes, and brushed dust off the top of one, revealing faded, stenciled letters. "Property of US Government."

"Look at this! As soon as I saw that iron door outside, I knew we'd found the place in your treasure story. But check out this writing. Wanna bet what's inside? Silver or gold, I'm thinking. I'm going back to get tools so we can break one of the boxes open."

Harry ran his hand across the dusty wood and read the words. "My God, I can't wait! But you're not going back for the hammer without me; we only have one light stick. Either I go and you stay here in the dark with a corpse, or we both go." And so they set off back up the passageway, returning with a hammer and screwdriver.

In moments they had loosened the top from one crate, but instead of lifting it, Brian stepped away. "You do the honors, Harry. This is your adventure; you've believed this legend since you were a teenager, and it's only right you get to see what's inside the box."

Brian snapped photos as Harry carefully removed the wooden top and held the light stick up. Gleaming rays of reflected light shimmered off the cave walls as Harry moved the light stick over the contents of the box.

"It's full of gold, Brian! It's packed solid with twenty-dollar gold coins. They call these double-eagles, and these boxes are chock full! We found the treasure! This really is the lost cave of the iron door, and *we* found it!" He began to chuckle, then broke out in a boisterous guffaw that went on and on. Holding a handful of coins in the air, he danced a little jig in the semi-darkness. It was impossible not to smile at Harry's giddy enthusiasm, even though the reality of their situation weighed heavily on Brian.

*I hope we live to tell people what we've discovered, instead of their finding our bodies along with Denton's weeks or months or years from now. We must face facts. If that quake blocked the entrance, they may never locate us. Let Harry have his moment of fun. Then we have to talk about our options, however limited they might be.*

———

A few hundred yards away on the opposite side of the canyon, the bare-chested rider stood silhouetted in the rays of the rising sun. Yesterday he'd observed five men traversing the canyons. Two appeared to be in charge, while the others, who had sidearms and long guns, guarded them.

Last night as Mother Earth groaned, he'd moved away from the rim, guiding his steed to a safe place where he could keep watch. Although a small quake—he had experienced far worse—the rocks and detritus it dislodged destroyed the narrow ledges across which the two men had inched their way over to the iron door. One had shouted he was placing a homing beacon on the ledge, and surely now the instrument lay somewhere in the debris. The men were trapped inside the mountain...in a place the rider knew well.

This morning through binoculars he watched the frenzied activity as searchers found the horses unscathed and grazing idly in the arroyo, along with one of the guards, who had been knocked unconscious as he fell during the tremor but was now awake. He must have given directions because some searchers rappelled down the cliff face. Moving under a tree, the rider raised his glasses toward the eastern cliff face and smiled. The men on ropes couldn't know how close they were, because the dull metal door visible yesterday at dusk now lay at the bottom of the canyon, covered by debris. The searchers didn't know exactly where to look for the missing men, and that was good. The fewer who knew the secret, the better.

He turned his horse, spurred him into a trot, and rode away. There was work to be done.

# CHAPTER FORTY-FOUR

Brian and Harry brought two of the twenty-dollar gold coins back to the main cavern. Both dated in the early 1860s, they remained bright and shiny. Harry said, "You saw the treasure article and the book about the James-Younger gang. After reading both, I became enthralled with tales of trains and train robbers in Oklahoma. It took time and effort in the days before the internet, but I found another book in the Oklahoma City library that put it all together. I read a story about the outlaws that connected them to the cave of the iron door. That did it for me; I was officially a fanatic. While we have nothing else to do, I want to tell you what it said."

Brian insisted on preparing a camp first. It was time to face the likelihood that they'd be trapped for days at the least. It was noon, and the blistering sun would be beating down on searchers in the canyon, but in here it was damp and cool. Exhausted after their amazing discovery, they spread blankets, gathered wood chips that lay in the tunnel beneath the timbers that supported it, and used a firestarter to build a small fire. Soon water was boiling, and they ate a meal of a protein bar and shared a coffee. Afterwards, Brian reclined on his pallet, resting his head on a rolled-up blanket, and said he wanted to hear the story.

Harry sat cross-legged on the floor and began. "A lot has been written about Jesse James and his gang. After so many years, it's impossible to separate fact from folklore, and parts of what I tell you probably aren't true, but a lot of what I read makes sense now that we found the iron door. We already figured out this cave is really an old silver mine, probably built in the 1500s by the Spaniards, and I know that those boxes of gold were stolen during a brazen train robbery in 1868. I found only one reference to it, because the government and Pinkerton's Detective Agency kept it quiet to avoid copycats. The title of the story is 'The Train Robbery and the Payroll of Gold.'"

Incredulous, Brian said, "You memorized it?"

Harry laughed. "No, but it's almost that bad. I didn't have access to a Xerox, so I copied the words on my brand-new 1984 Macintosh computer. And like the nerd I am, I put it in my backpack in case I needed to refer to it. He retrieved some yellowed pages printed on old-fashioned dot-matrix feeder paper, the kind with holes on both sides.

"God, Harry, and you laughed at me for bringing cognac! Talk about something useful. Let me see." Harry handed them over, and Brian laughed again when he saw the old ink-jet printing.

"I'm interested, but I'm too tired to read this now," Brian said, passing the sheaf back.

"If you're awake enough to listen, I'll read it aloud. I love this story; it gives me goosebumps every time I think about it. I can't wait for you to hear it too."

"No promises, but I'll give it my best shot." He handed Harry the light stick, reclined on his pallet, and adjusted the extra blanket that was his pillow. Harry looked at the faded sheets and began.

*The Train Robbery and the Payroll of Gold*

*The steam engine chugged its way down the tracks toward Denton, Texas. Since 1867, nearly two years ago, the Missouri, Kansas and Texas Railway, which the locals called the Katy, had been running three trains a week through Oklahoma Territory from northwestern Kansas to Denton. Today's train had an engine and five freight cars; four were filled with cattle destined for the Fort Worth stockyards. The fifth was a boxcar, carefully positioned in the middle of the train halfway between the engine and*

214

*caboose. It was sheathed in steel plates and had windows covered by heavy iron bars. Two men rode in this car, their chairs positioned near the windows so they could observe their surroundings. One worked for the Katy Railroad, and the other was an agent for Pinkerton's, the detective service hired by the United States government to guard the precious cargo.*

*This was familiar territory to the railroad man. He'd made this run a hundred times, and when he spotted the craggy hills and a cloud of dust in the distance, it was time to act. He reached into his jacket pocket, unholstered his revolver, and turned to the detective, a man named Jim, who snapped to attention.*

*"See something out there, Bill?"*

*"Take your gun out and drop it real careful on the floor," Bill said, pointing his pistol at the detective. Jim complied, not comprehending what his friend was up to.*

*"Now unlock the cage."*

*"What? What are you talking about, man? I can't unlock it until we get to Denton."*

*Bill had to be careful; he knew how well Pinkerton's had trained Jim. They were friends, they'd teamed up on other jobs like this, and Jim knew how to handle himself. A shotgun lay on a table three feet from them, and Bill picked it up.*

*"Go on now. Unlock the cage. I don't want to have to hurt you."*

*"Dammit, Bill. What the hell have you gone and done?" Jim turned to a wall made of iron bars that ran from floor to ceiling, bisecting the railroad car. It was like a jail cell with a padlocked gate in its center. Behind it, stacked floor to ceiling, were a hundred wooden boxes.*

*"Handcuff your left hand to the top of them bars. Then your right."*

*With only a moment to act, the detective's hand slid under his coat.*

*Bill fired a single shot, narrowly missing his friend's head. "We've had many a good ride, Jim," he said, "and I ain't out to harm you. But if you try that stunt again,*

# BILL THOMPSON

*I'll have to say I enjoyed knowing you. Drop that derringer on the floor nice and easy, and get them cuffs out like I said."*

*Once Jim's hands were cuffed to the bars above his head, Bill kicked the man's guns to the opposite end of the car. The Pinkerton's man charged with guarding a treasure was trapped.*

*Bill glanced outside; the cloud of dust was much closer now. He moved to the end of the railcar toward the engine, opened a door, and breathed the stench of manure from the cattle car just ahead. The cars rattled and swayed as the train moved along at twenty-five miles an hour. Hanging on to the door frame so he wouldn't fall between the moving cars, Bill knelt and removed two pins that secured a joining coupler and unhooked a heavy safety chain. Now the only thing connecting the rear three cars to the front three was the "handshake" coupler, and without the pins, any pressure on it would cause it to open automatically.*

*Bill knew exactly what to do, he'd ridden this route many times, and he knew when the terrain would start a gradual rise. As soon as the train reached it, the coupler would release, the train would continue south, and the back three cars would roll off in the opposite direction.*

*As he watched his friend uncouple the cars, Jim understood what was happening. "Bill, my God, man. What are you thinking? You know you'll hang for this."*

*Bill's friend spoke the truth. If someone stole what was in this car, they'd hang for sure, but only if they were caught. Out here in the wild Oklahoma Territory, with the forbidding Wichita Mountains looming to the north and west and Comanche raiding parties a constant concern, anything could happen. It was a huge risk, but successfully robbing a government payroll train and evading the law would reap a huge reward.*

*As the tracks began a slow rise through the foothills of the mountains, the engineer throttled down for the climb. He felt a jolt, stuck his head out the window and looked back. His heart sank as he watched two cars carrying cattle and another filled with gold roll slowly away in the opposite direction. There was no doubt what happened; despite having the Pinkerton's detective and his fellow employee guarding, someone managed to uncouple the cars. This was a well-planned heist, he thought as he watched six mounted riders approach the cars as they slowly came to a stop.*

*The only weapons on the train were in the payroll car. Pinkerton's had seen no need to arm the engineer since their own man, plus one of the Katy Railroad's senior people, could withstand almost any attack in a steel-plated boxcar. Everything would be fine...so long as people stayed on the right side of the law.*

*The engineer never considered going back; there was nothing he could do anyway. Those people on horseback were train robbers, and he hoped his friend didn't get killed. He'd known Bill Anderson for ten years, and they worked together almost every day. He had no idea who uncoupled the railcars, but he'd have bet a week's pay that it wasn't Bill.*

*He estimated he was around a hundred and fifty miles north of Denton, Texas, where other Pinkerton's men would be waiting for the gold to arrive. That meant it would be hours before authorities would learn about the theft of half a million dollars in gold.*

*Jesse James and Cole Younger had planned today's heist well. This particular train was hauling cattle to the Texas stockyards, but its primary mission was to deliver payroll in gold coin to military installations along the route from the Kansas border all the way to north Texas. The specially outfitted payroll car was like an armored fortress, and it had contained over two million dollars in gold coins when the journey began. That was an unusually large amount for one shipment, but Indian skirmishes had prevented payroll from reaching the outposts earlier.*

*Before the Cole-Younger gang arrived, the train had offloaded gold at Fort Reno and Fort Sill in Oklahoma Territory. The latter was under construction near Lawton, and the gold coins would be used to pay the soldiers building the military post.*

*The robbers knew that two armed guards were in the boxcar—a Pinkerton's detective and a longtime railroad employee who had turned to the dark side for $10,000 in gold. They also knew that half a million dollars remained, because Bill Anderson, the turncoat railroad man, told them so. It was to be handed over to soldiers in Denton, Texas, and hauled under heavy guard to Fort Belknap, a recently reopened military outpost a hundred miles to the west. But it would never make it across the Texas state line.*

Harry paused for a sip of water, looked over at Brian lying stretched out on his pallet, and wondered how long he'd been asleep. He chastised himself; even though these tales held lifelong fascination for Harry, he had no business forcing Brian to listen. Here they were, facing the possibility of an agonizing death deep in a cave, and he'd gone off into a tale of legendary treasure.

# CHAPTER FORTY-FIVE

As she sat behind her desk, worry over the fates of her husband and his best friend made it difficult for Nicole to perform even the most mundane duties. After learning of their disappearance, she called Jennifer, who was monitoring the situation from the ranch outside Oklahoma City. Nicole wanted to come there where she'd be closer to Lawton, where the men disappeared, but Jennifer wouldn't hear of it.

"Don't forget that my husband's missing too. I know how you feel, but you're the leader of the free world. Believe me, you don't want to be sitting here like I am, staring at the four walls and waiting for the phone to ring. As frightening as this situation is, you have responsibilities that can keep your mind occupied. You have no vice president, and if you temporarily invoked the Twenty-Fifth Amendment, you'd make the Speaker president, and you don't want that. Stay there, stay strong, and handle the country's business until we learn something. The minute they give us news, then by all means, come on out."

She was right, of course, so Nicole bucked up, sitting behind the *Resolute* desk, slogging through her agenda hour after hour, forcing herself not to cry, and thinking of nothing but Brian and Harry. The first day passed, then a sleepless night, and the second morning broke with no news from Lawton. The Secretary of Homeland Security stopped by to advise her that the directors of the Secret Service and the FBI were on the scene along with more than a hundred members of various law enforcement agencies. Workers had searched tons of rubble from the minor earthquake that sheared off part of the cliff face, but no bodies had turned up, which he called a good thing. The director voiced hope that Brian and Harry had made it into the cave they were looking for, and that they'd survived the tremor.

"If they're inside the mountain, we'll find them. We're utilizing the greatest resources on earth in the search effort," he assured Nicole, who asked questions he couldn't answer. "When? How quickly will you find them? What if they run out of air, or food and water?" He couldn't promise the one thing she wanted—an assurance they'd rescue Brian and Harry in time.

An unprecedented manhunt was underway in the remote canyon and at the rim above. Cranes lowered workers who examined the cliffs inch by inch, looking for the location. There wasn't time to erect platforms and bring in borers to penetrate the canyon's rock walls, nor did those looking know the exact place to search. After the earthquake, the Secret Service agent who had watched them ascend could no longer identify the ledge they'd found. All they could do was search and rappel and listen and hope and pray.

———

Nicole had to think of something to do. Sympathetic visitors paraded through the Oval Office, offering prayers and comforting words, but these people weren't her friends. They were political allies and nothing more. They didn't know Brian, nor did they really know Harry, even though he'd been their leader for six years. Along with Jennifer, those two were the closest people in her life.

Perhaps Horace Wilmington Fleming could offer some clue from the poem about exactly where Brian and Harry had gone. It was worth a try, since there was nothing else she could think of. She picked up the phone, dialed the number, and was surprised to hear a stranger's voice. "Who is this?"

"Henry Barclay, Madam President. Are you calling

about the book? If so—"

She interrupted. "Where's Horace Fleming?"

"Mr. Fleming is no longer with the Archives, ma'am. I'm his replacement. How may I help you?"

Something in the man's smooth answers grated on her. "I asked you where he is."

"Yes, ma'am. Well, it seems no one knows. He failed to appear for work yesterday and isn't answering his home phone. Is there something I can do?"

"I have some questions for him about the book."

"Ah yes, the book. That brings us to another problem, Madam President. I'm afraid not only is Horace unaccounted for, but so is the book."

"Have you notified the authorities?"

"No, and I can't. As you know, the existence of the book is a secret known by a select few. I can't call the police."

"You can tell them to look for Horace Fleming."

"It's not my place, Madam President. That order would have to come from someone else."

*Like me,* she thought as she disconnected.

Half an hour later, agents from the Secret Service arrived at the modest house in Greenbelt, Maryland, where Horace Wilmington Fleming lived. An old, well-preserved Oldsmobile sat in the driveway. They knocked, and when no one answered, they broke one small glass pane in the back door and entered the home. It was meticulously neat and clean—no dishes in the sink, no mussed-up bedcovers; in fact, it appeared the house was furnished but unoccupied.

They went room to room, finally coming upon a steel door hidden behind a wooden one. Outfitted with a numerical keypad, the door appeared impregnable. But when an agent looked more closely, he discovered that only the door itself was solid and secure. The walls around it were made of sheetrock and wooden studs. The lead agent, whose orders came directly from the top, ordered the men to break through the wall and see what lay behind.

Inside what had been a closet was a room filled with books neatly arranged on shelves, and in the middle of it, agents discovered something very unusual.

An altar, a padded kneeler and a bookstand stood in the middle of the room with a man's body sprawled upon them. An empty pill bottle—hydrocodone, it turned out— rested on the bookstand next to a thick volume, which was open to page 87, and a sealed envelope.

A note in neatly printed letters read, HE WHO FINDS ME MUST NOT LOOK AT THE BOOK OR SHOW IT TO ANY OTHER PERSON. DELIVER IT AND THE SEALED ENVELOPE TO THE PRESIDENT IMMEDIATELY.

Even in death, Horace Wilmington Fleming had carefully ensured George Washington's instructions would be followed.

# CHAPTER FORTY-SIX

*President Farber,*

*As you are the sitting chief executive, I direct this letter and my sincere apologies to you for betraying the trust of the Father of our Country not once, but time and again. I allowed Archibald Perrin to view the book, even though I knew he had broken his sacred vow by telling others about it. In my presence, he broke his vow by allowing an outsider to look at the book, and in my weakness I brought it back to him again.*

*I continued the same indiscretions with you, Madam President. I discussed the book with you, your husband and President Harrison, despite knowing Mr. Sadler wasn't allowed to know it existed.*

*As I have said, I have a secret of my own. I kept it hidden since my adolescent years, but through a twist of fate, Frank Innocente learned about it. After he threatened to reveal it and ruin my life, I told him about the book. I gave you a copy of page 87, knowing that it would in turn go to Mr. Innocente, an outsider. That was yet another breach of my sworn oath.*

*The Book of Secrets is my pride and joy—my precious, special baby, as I consider it—and I have been a shameful father. For years I contemplated stealing it, hiding it away in a secret place, putting it on an altar to be revered, perused and loved. No one could appreciate it as I, yet I could never completely have it.*

*Facing the gravity and repetition of my*

*transgressions, I realized death was my only release. In one last act of selfish deception, I removed the book from the Archives and brought it to the sacred place in my home. I knelt before it, took the medicine, and now I will fall into eternal slumber while caressing its pages.*

*It is my sincere hope that Brian Sadler and Harry Harrison find the fabled lost cave of the iron door. It exists, for Theodore Roosevelt said it did, and I believe him. I regret that I will not be alive when the poem on page 87 springs to life, provides clues, and reveals a legendary treasure trove.*

*Good luck to you. God bless you and the noble men who served our nation before you.*

*Horace Wilmington Fleming*
*Keeper of the Book*

# CHAPTER FORTY-SEVEN

Brian awoke, thought he'd gone blind as he blinked his eyes in absolute darkness, and then remembered where he was. He sat up with a groan, his muscles and joints aching from lying on the thin pallet. He hadn't slept much, and he'd resisted drinking water during the night, even though his throat was dry and parched.

He clicked on his flashlight, waking Harry, who also grunted and complained as he pushed himself upright. "Damn, forty-six is the new eighty, I guess. Sleeping on the ground isn't as comfortable as I hoped it would be."

Brian started the water boiling for another pot of coffee. "Are you as hungry as I am?" he asked as he split a protein bar, offering half to Harry, who declined and took out a bar of his own.

"I could stand to lose a few pounds, but this diet's not going to work for me. We have over a hundred of these bars. The water's going to run out long before the food does. I say we live on the edge. Let's each have two bars a day. Why not?"

Brian nodded, and they ate in silence. At last he said, "What's on the agenda for today?"

Harry laughed. "Not a lot, unfortunately. Rescue would be good, but I don't think it's scheduled yet. I was thinking we might check out the third tunnel that runs off this cavern. After we found the boxes yesterday, I got so excited I forgot about it. The room where the gold is also has two tunnels that branch off it, but I'm not sure how much farther we should go. We may run into critters without even a stick to defend ourselves, but maybe dying by snakebite would be preferable to the alternative."

Brian wanted to keep exploring for several reasons. First, they had nothing but time, and escape was the only thing that mattered. A way out might lie somewhere down a tunnel, or they might find a water source to sustain them longer. To be honest, adventure was in Brian's DNA. He'd survived seemingly hopeless situations, and he would try anything, no matter how risky or far-fetched, to escape their prison.

They went to the next room, Denton's body lay on the floor where they'd left it, but as they approached the cache of boxes, Brian noticed something unusual. "I don't remember putting the lid back on that box yesterday," he said.

It wasn't nailed down; it just wasn't where they'd left it. Harry lifted it and saw the gleaming coins. "How did this happen?" he asked. "I'm certain we didn't put it back like that."

"We've had nothing but a little coffee, some protein bars and a few sips of water since we got trapped in here," Brian said. "Maybe we did it but don't remember." They gave it some thought and agreed they hadn't replaced the lid. Then they considered the ramifications; was someone else in the cavern? Why would he go to the trouble of putting it back without making his presence known? How did he get into this lower cave without passing through the one where they'd made their camp and spent the night?

Brian suggested, "Before we explore the third tunnel leading off the main cavern, we should first look at the ones that branch off this one. I can't believe someone else is in here, but if it's true, he knows a way out that may save us."

Neither could know what to expect when they crawled into the dark passages, and they opted to take a few things along in case something went wrong. From the stash of supplies, they loaded their backpacks with water, protein bars, their phones and flashlights, and an extra light stick. Brian stuck the hammer in his belt, thinking it might help

226

fend off an animal or break up rocks blocking the way. And he took the emergency whistle in case they wanted to signal the mysterious person.

Harry wasn't keen on that last item, saying they might be better off keeping quiet. He could be friend or foe, although he agreed with Brian that if the person had meant them harm, he could have killed them while they slept.

Packed and ready, they examined the entrances to both tunnels. The smaller one would require crawling on hands and knees from the outset. Perhaps it would get roomier, but there was no assurance the passage would become larger. If they found no place to turn around, their only egress would be to back out. Harry admitted to being claustrophobic and thought this one would be a challenge. If it meant the difference between survival and death, then he'd tackle it, but for now he opted for the other, initially more spacious tunnel.

With a height of only four feet, this passage required them to bend at the waist, but it was more than six feet wide and gave them breathing room. They moved the backpacks to their chests and started duck-walking down the corridor. Brian led the way and held the light stick while Harry shuffled behind him. After around twenty feet, Brian said, "Do you feel air moving through here? This is exciting! It could mean another exit somewhere up ahead."

Huffing along, Harry snorted, "Just keep going. I told the girls earlier I wanted to be an adventurer like you, but I take it all back. The deeper we go, the darker and colder it's getting. Plus, the ceiling's getting lower and lower. I swear if I ever get out of here, I'll never be your friend again."

Brian laughed, and Harry was right—the roof and sides of the tunnel had constricted considerably. Now his elbows brushed the walls as he pushed ahead, and his back ached from constant bending. He mostly looked at his shoes, putting one in front of the other, but he noticed something ahead and stopped to look down the tunnel.

"Harry, look! There's light up ahead."

"Please tell me we're not approaching the gates of

Hell."

The tunnel made a slight right turn and suddenly expanded to twice its size. Now they could stand upright, and just in front of the place Brian stood, a small ray of light shone down onto the ground. He looked up, felt air flowing downward, and exclaimed, "I think there's a shaft up there."

Harry joined him and said if it was a shaft, it must be very narrow and have twists and turns. Regardless, light filtered in from somewhere, and that was a very good sign.

"Listen," Brian said. "Can you hear that noise? It's like a rushing sound from farther down the passageway."

With a sarcastic grin Harry said, "By all means, let's go even deeper and find out. Maybe it's the River Styx and Satan's waiting for us on the other side. Oh, and honest, my claustrophobia's no problem. I'm just scared out of my wits, that's all. Lead on, Indiana Jones. And watch out for the snakes."

Brian laughed and said he was more worried about not being rescued than about being trapped in this corridor. "One way or another, we're going to get out of here," he added. "Too many people are looking for us."

"We must be realistic, Brian. There was an earthquake; it's not so bad in here, except that the escape route is blocked, but we have no idea how things look on the outside. The entire face of the mountain may have changed. The iron door may be at the bottom of the ravine, and tons of rock may have obliterated the tunnel entrance we came through.

"You're right that there must be an enormous search and rescue effort going on, but even if the iron door's still in place, it has successfully eluded a hell of a lot of people for over a hundred years. We found it, and so did the person or persons who killed Denton Kopaddy. Whoever put that lid back on the crate last night knows about it too. But the rest are looking for a needle in a haystack. When they finally find us, it could be too late. Will somebody kill us before the searchers arrive, or will we die from natural causes? You have to admit our prospects aren't that promising."

"Keep that glass half full," Brian chided. "We may find a way out before they're able to get in here and rescue us. That's why we must keep exploring. Now let's go a little farther down this tunnel."

They moved along the steadily descending passage until it narrowed once again. Ahead they'd be crawling on their bellies, pushing their packs along in front. Another breeze wafted through, a sign that an opening might lay ahead, but Harry was done.

"You go check it out, and I'll sit here in the dark and wait for you. I have the extra light stick in case something goes wrong, and I can find my way back to the main cavern if I have to."

With that, Brian pushed his backpack into the snug hole and wriggled in behind it. Harry watched the soles of his boots slide farther and farther away until they were gone, and he struggled to keep himself from throwing up. The mere thought of going into that tight space made him light-headed, especially since it was impossible to know what lay ahead. If the way was blocked, Brian would have to shimmy backwards. If something else was there— something worse than a blockage—then who knew how he'd escape.

Harry pushed those thoughts from his mind. Being trapped in this maze of tunnels without Brian along was too much to handle right now. Instead, he prayed for his friend's safe return.

# CHAPTER FORTY-EIGHT

After only a few minutes sliding on his belly like a snake, Brian wondered if Harry had been right. If he couldn't find a way to turn around, it would take far longer—hours maybe—to slither out backwards in a prone position, pushing with his hands and hoping for traction with his feet.

All it would take was another small tremor...or a venomous creature...or a sudden end to the tunnel...and he would be trapped or dead. What an inglorious end to an adventure-filled career, he thought as he inched his way along, his belly on the floor and his back two inches from the top.

*Maybe I should quit taking so many risks. I have Nicole, and I'm not getting any younger. If I get out of this alive...*

He stopped himself, recalling other times in his life he'd thought the same thing. Like the man who promises to quit his vices if God will only save him, Brian was addicted to this kind of danger. Not at the time he was up to his eyeballs in it—like now—but later, once he was safe and retelling the story. When in peril, he felt the fear crowd into his psyche, telling him he might not make it back, and he thrived on just that type of situation. A place like this one—a tunnel becoming more constricted and stuffy and scary—was what drove Brian Sadler. Only this time he knew he'd gone too far. If he couldn't turn around, he doubted he could maneuver himself backwards.

Calling out to give Harry an update was futile; his

voice wouldn't have carried in the cramped space. He noticed the rushing sound they'd heard earlier had stopped. He pressed on, pushing his backpack ahead of him, but then it disappeared. He heard it fall and hit the ground. Holding the light stick between his teeth—the only place available—he slithered ahead a couple of inches and reached the rim of a dark hole—the one his backpack had disappeared into.

This could be good news or bad. If the hole was large enough to crawl down into, he might be able to turn around and go back headfirst. It also might lead to a way out. Or it could be twenty feet deep and ten across—effectively the end of the line that would mean hours of backtracking on his belly.

He inched his way forward until his head peeked out over the rim, maneuvered his arm, and took the light stick from his mouth. Aiming it down into what he hoped wouldn't be an abyss, he saw that the opening was indeed a shallow hole, and his backpack lay on the ground just four feet below. A single ray of light fell upon it. He crawled ahead, slipped down into the hole, and looked up. The light came from a shaft twenty feet above with enticing, wonderful daylight at its top. Across the hole, the shaft he'd been crawling through continued off into the darkness, as narrow and cramped as the one where he'd been.

Suddenly he heard the rushing noise again, coming from the tunnel on the other side and accompanied by a frenetic rush of creatures flying crazily past him up the shaft toward the light. Hundreds of bats, sufficiently disturbed by his presence to venture out in daytime, soared up through the passageway, proving there was another way out of this dark world.

It was a frustrating discovery—a chimney that led to freedom, large enough for a man to shimmy up, but with no way to scale it from where he stood. Recovery could only be initiated from above by lowering ropes, and he doubted anyone would recognize a hole in the ground as a link to the whereabouts of two missing men. Shouting would be of no use—the distance was too great—and he had no way to signal. The tantalizing daylight, so close and yet so far, was maddening, and he almost wished he hadn't found the shaft.

*Come on, man! It's not like you to give up. Glass half full, right? This shaft is going to be your and Harry's salvation. You just have to figure it out.*

He looked closely at the hole's dirt floor and saw shoe prints smaller than his own. The hairs on his arms tingled, the prints might be very old, but they meant only one thing to him—somebody on the surface had stood in this very spot. Maybe he was the person who put the lid back on the box filled with coins; regardless, if he knew he and Harry were missing, maybe he would lead the authorities to the chimney.

The bats had come through the tight passage that continued ahead, and he had no interest in going farther. He faced an equally harrowing journey back and had had enough for today. From his pack he took a piece of paper, wrote his and Harry's names, drew an arrow pointing to the shaft through which he'd come, and placed it on the floor of the hole. If someone found It, they'd know which way to go.

Before heading back, he looked up at the elusive daylight one last time, but something unexplainable happened. As if he were watching a solar eclipse, the faint light at the top of the chimney began to fade from one side to the other until the ray of daylight disappeared, and there was nothing but blackness above.

*Oh my God! Did I just see what I think I did?*

*Someone covered up the hole.*

*Please God, please let that person tell the searchers we're down here. Because he knows.*

# CHAPTER FORTY-NINE

Exhausted when he finally made it back to where Harry waited, Brian collapsed on the floor of the cave. Harry was ecstatic to see him and hear what he'd found. Once they were back in the main cavern, they ate their usual meal—a protein bar and some water—and Brian described the shaft that was lit from above one minute and dark the next. The person who covered it knew exactly what he was doing.

Harry said the man might not be friendly. "Maybe he's one of the men who killed Denton. Those guys know this cave is full of treasure, and I think helping rescuers find us is the last thing on their agenda."

Brian wasn't so sure. "They found the iron door and the gold, but I'll bet they never went as deep into the tunnels as I did today. Someone else did, and I'll bet the same guy covered the shaft."

"If you're right, who is this mysterious person? Why hasn't he made himself known? What if he's the one who killed Denton? Maybe he's in cahoots with the other two."

"Hell if I know. I guess only time will tell. Either he leaves us down here to die, or somehow he helps us escape. Meanwhile we survive on rations."

"Are we going to be rescued?" Harry wondered. "It's been forty-eight hours. How long until we give up?"

"Never. Not until our last breaths. Keep your glass half full, Harry," Brian said, stretching out on his pallet and putting his head on his jacket pillow. "I'm exhausted.

Maybe I can sleep better this time around." Within moments he was snoring lightly.

Hours later, Harry sat bolt upright on his mat and listened. Something had wakened him. A noise or maybe some movement in the cavern. The dying light stick emitted a weak glow, enough to see Brian sleeping. He lay back down, but quickly sat up again.

He had heard something, and this time he was awake. A rustling noise—a rat, perhaps, or even worse, a snake. He fumbled for his flashlight, brought it up, and switched it on.

Across the room he made out a shape—a person sitting on his haunches, watching them in silence. He gave a shout, causing Brian to leap from his pallet and knock the light away. "Grab it!" Harry yelled. "There's someone over there!"

As they directed the beam around the empty cave, Brian asked if Harry had been dreaming, but he adamantly declared what he saw. "He was no dream. It was a man crouching by those rocks, just waiting and watching."

Brian examined the ground across the cave. "Look at this," he said, pointing to shoe prints that led to and from the second tunnel. The prints, smaller than Brian's own, were the same as those Brian had earlier found in the shaft—smooth, not a bare foot, but not a sneaker either. More like a moccasin, Brian thought.

"You're right; you weren't dreaming. He was here, and he came from the same tunnel we took today. Let's go find him. Now we know that he has a way to come in and out of here. I want to know where it is!"

It took a few minutes to put on shoes and reload their packs, allowing the man a considerable head start, but Brian was intent on finding him. He could have killed them as they slept but didn't, but he also didn't make his presence known. What was he up to, and would he help them? They had to get answers.

They scurried down the tunnel to the smaller room where Harry had stopped earlier. "I have to go back in there," Brian said. "I'm certain he came from that shaft I found."

"I'm sorry I can't go too," Harry said. "I got physically ill just thinking about you being in there last time."

"No problem. It wouldn't work for both of us anyway. We'd have to crawl one behind another, and there's barely room in the bottom of that shaft for two people. It's better that I go alone. I'm going to leave the pack since I know how far it is and what's there. Wish me luck." He put a light stick in his mouth and crawled on his belly into the tunnel. Within moments the soles of his boots were once again out of sight.

Harry sat in the dark as he had done before, a light stick and his flashlight close at hand. The minutes ticked slowly by, and he was lost in thought when he heard something—a voice as soft as the breeze that wafted easily through the passageway.

"Your lives are in danger," it whispered.

Harry jerked his hand toward the flashlight, but the voice told him to leave it off.

"Who...who are you?"

"I am your protector. I want to keep you free from harm."

His words carried a light accent, as though English wasn't his primary language. They echoed throughout the small chamber as though coming from everywhere at once.

"How do we get out of here?"

"With patience, you will be shown a way. Your lives are in danger. Stay aware and alert at all times."

"Is someone else in these caves? Who's going to harm us?"

The disembodied voice was silent now. After a moment, Harry switched on the light and shone it about, finding one other living creature in the small cavern—a mouse that sat up, looked at him in surprise, and scampered away into the darkness. The man was gone. Who was he, and why had he decided to protect them? And from what? Other than being trapped below ground, how were their lives in danger?

He looked down the shaft Brian had taken, hoping to see a mysterious person slipping away down the tunnel, but it was empty. He called to Brian and tried to find another way the man could have escaped the room.

Harry knew he should tell Brian about his encounter with the disembodied voice. The man's warning was important, but Harry feared he might be losing his mind. What if he had been sitting in the dark all alone, and his mind created the scenario with the mysterious visitor? Harry never saw anyone, nor could he find the man's method of rapid ingress and egress. Maybe the whole thing hadn't happened at all.

*My greatest fear is claustrophobia, and here I am facing my nightmare, trapped underground, crawling through tunnels that might cave in at any moment. Is the stress taking its toll? Did I imagine that conversation? Was I hallucinating? Or is it something else—something I've only ever read about but never believed?*

At that moment Brian slid back into the cave and asked why Harry had called him. Harry told him everything, including his fear that the whole thing might be a fantasy from his imagination. He said, "I even wondered this—what if that voice was real, but he's a shape-shifter? What if he spoke to me before turning into a mouse?"

Brian had heard of shape-shifters, believed by some cultures to be humans who can transform into animals at will. He said it might explain how someone could come and go in the cave without detection, and he didn't consider Harry delusional, but he wasn't willing to go that far just yet. "We saw footprints. Let's follow the threads of plausible possibility before stepping into the world of fantasy," he said. "Unless you spoke to a talking mouse or you've been nipping the brandy while I was gone, I think we're looking for a man—a real man—who knows his way around this tunnel system."

"There's something else," Harry continued. "I'm worried sick about my mother. It was selfish of me to go off on an adventure when she's dying, and I can't imagine the anguish she's experiencing now that you and I are missing. I'll never forgive myself if something happens, and I'm not there."

Brian said, "Julia's one of the strongest women I've ever known. She's a fighter, and she believes in God and in you. I can't imagine the pain you all are going through, but I have faith that we're going to be rescued, and that faith will carry me through. We're in a dilemma not of our making, and all we can do is hope, pray, and work like hell to find a way out of here. God has a plan for both of us, and we're on that plan."

"You're right, and thanks for the positive words. I needed them right now." He followed Brian back through the tunnel into the room that had become their base camp. He ate his protein bar in silence, and Brian gave him space to consider things. Each person dealt with life and death in different ways, and they prayed for Julia and the family before they laid their heads on the pallets and slept.

# CHAPTER FIFTY

On a mesa a mile from the searchers' base, two men sat in lawn chairs under a tree, one holding a controller that maneuvered a powerful Inspire 2 drone while the other watched a live camera feed as the device flew back and forth in a grid sequence. The man controlling the drone, a seasoned veteran in aerial reconnaissance, had guided it for several hours as Frank Innocente kept his eye on the screen. All morning they had been looking for a sign—anything that might reveal another entrance to the caves where Brian and Harry were trapped. Frank couldn't have cared less about the men—all he wanted was the treasure he'd seen when Denton had led him there. But to get it, he had to find another entrance.

At last it appeared they could be onto something. Frank ordered the drone to remain stationary as they watched a shirtless man on horseback approach a grove of scrubby trees, dismount, and disappear into the thicket. The horse remained in sight, grazing idly as he waited for the man's return, but more than an hour had passed. Where did he go? Frank had an idea, and he told the operator to mark the coordinates and bring back the drone.

"Help me find the place you marked," he told the man as he packed up the drone. They drove two off-road SUVs about a mile across the mesa to the thicket of trees, and Frank slogged through waist-high weeds and brambles until he came upon the horse and a three-foot hole amid a pile of rocks that led down into the earth. This was it—it had to be! The man had used this entrance to get inside the vast cave system.

Certain of what he'd found, Frank sent the man on his way, donned a headlamp and backpack, and lowered himself into the hole. In case he came across the rider whose horse waited outside, he unholstered the pistol on his belt.

———

Brian and Harry were desperate to find an exit, but everywhere they went, there were more passages leading off the caves. Brian had already crawled through one of the two where they were now, and he'd found the shaft with daylight at its top. The other, a much tighter passage, remained unexplored. Brian believed the person who spoke to Harry had vanished through one of those, which meant they could possibly locate a way out. He must go, and he must go alone.

"Don't get stuck, and don't die in there," Harry admonished him. "There's nothing I can do to help you when you're shimmying through something smaller than a drainpipe. If you can't keep going forward, how the hell are you going to back out of that one? It's too tight."

"Wow, I feel a lot better," Brian said. "I hadn't thought about all those positives. Sure you don't want to join me?"

Harry regretted it, but he wouldn't last a minute pressed inside the narrow opening—it was a claustrophobe's worst nightmare. And it might get even tighter. The thought nauseated him.

"What do I do if you run into trouble?" he asked, and Brian said the man had gone somewhere. If he could squeeze through a cave, Brian could too. At least that was his hope. "If I get trapped, I'll inch my way backwards. It may take a while, but I can get back out."

Harry kept his worst fears to himself. In his opinion, if Brian got trapped, it would likely mean the end for both. Dying in a cramped hole far underground was the worst thing Harry could imagine, and as his friend crawled headfirst into the tunnel, he recalled Brian's comforting words when they talked about his mother and God's plan. He dropped to his knees and began to pray.

Brian was praying too, hoping to God there would be a space to turn around so he could return without having to backtrack. Moving forward required intense effort, working muscles he didn't often use. The air was stale and the way ahead pitch black as he snaked forward, his arms stretched out in front and his shoes inching him along. He'd tied the light stick around his neck, and he could see maybe two feet ahead, enough perhaps to see a snake but with no means to deal with it unless it remained still and allowed him to strangle it to death. As he sucked in stale air and dust, a wave of light-headedness swept over him, and he began to hyperventilate.

*If I allow myself to think about this, there's no way I can do it. Go ahead, Brian. Push yourself. God's going to give you an answer. You just have to trust.*

"I trust You," he said aloud, and a moment later he noticed the stagnant air dissipate as the walls widened and the ceiling rose. Another room lay ahead, just thirty feet or so from where he'd left Harry. It was a blessed, wonderful, dark and cool chamber, and not that far from where he started.

He shouted into the tunnel, "Harry! Harry, there's another room in here! It's not very far."

"Great! Check it out and let me know what you find!"

*Even if I find Shangri-la, he's not coming,* Brian thought with a smile. But if there was a way out, at least the claustrophobic maneuvering would only take Harry a few minutes. He removed the light stick and held it in front of him.

"Dammit!" he cried when he saw movement somewhere along the far wall. "How did you get in here?"

Sitting cross-legged on the floor was a tall, thin man, naked from the waist up and wearing ragged trousers and moccasins.

"Sit, Mr. Sadler. I have things to tell you. You and your friend are in grave danger."

243

"Can you help us? Do you know another way out of here?"

"The danger lies outside these walls, not within. The dead man in the other chamber gives testimony to my words. Now sit and listen."

Brian did so, asking, "How do you get around in here without light?"

"My people call me the Protector. I know every inch of these caves; they are far older than the white people imagine. I do not need light to traverse this place. Over time my eyes have acclimated so that I can see with almost no illumination, and I could crawl the tunnels blindfolded. For a thousand years, long before the Spanish arrived, my people have lived in these mountains. We have seen outlaws bring gold and silver, one of our chiefs showed the cave to your president, and we have observed many men on horseback who searched for the iron door. Now listen carefully, for your time is short."

The man was Native American—not a member of a specific tribe, he told Brian, because his ancestors predated named tribes by hundreds of years. They lived in North America long before Europeans discovered it—he spat the word "discover" as if it left a bad taste. Each tribe designated a Protector—one whose job it was to surveil, listen and warn leaders against dangers, internal or external. Most Native American tribes today had become "civilized," building casinos and schools and hospitals. They were so integrated into Anglo culture and society that the idea of a protector would be laughable.

Not all North American tribes followed the path of modernization. Some—mostly in the southwest—held to the old ways, keeping language, customs and rituals alive. Researchers called some of these "lost" tribes, but really they weren't lost at all. They merely kept to themselves, living in remote areas, avoiding social interaction outside their community, and going about their business unburdened by the shackles of the twenty-first century.

The Protector's tribe was one of those, living in remote cliff dwellings as had the Anasazi. He rode on horseback every day, watching the gorges and canyon rims, alert for anything that would affect his people. The cave of the iron door was particularly important because many people came looking for it. He'd observed Brian, Harry and their keepers from the time they arrived, and he knew the rockslide had trapped them inside.

"There is another way out," he revealed. "It is not as difficult as the tunnel you just came through. Your friend has less fortitude than you, but he can make it if he will have faith and heed my instructions. I have more to tell you, and then I must go. When I return, we will leave together."

# CHAPTER FIFTY-ONE

After fifteen minutes of anxious waiting with no word, Harry called out, "Brian! Are you okay?"

"I'm fine," came the faint response. "I'll be back there shortly."

"Did you find a way out?"

"No, but I have a lot to tell you when I get there."

Brian listened as the strange man finished. When he stood, Brian asked how he knew his name.

"The canyons are alive with activity. Your people are searching for you and President Harrison. Although I am the Protector, I am also a man living in your world. Mine is a simpler existence, but I am a member of your society as well as mine, and I am aware of what happens around me."

"What do we do next?"

"You must bring your friend here. He is afraid, he does not have the faith in himself that you have, but he believes in God as you do. Tell him what I have said, bring him to this room, and wait for me."

"How long will we have to wait? Should we bring food and water?"

"Have faith, my brother. Now go."

Fueled by adrenalin and optimistic after the enigmatic conversation, Brian shuffled back through the passage much faster than he'd come. He found Harry hopeful that there was good news, and he sat listening in fascination as Brian related what had happened on the other end of the tunnel.

"The man you saw is no shape-shifter," Brian said. "He's as real as we are. He calls himself the Protector."

"He told me the same thing."

"He's totally familiar with this cave system, and he's able to see in almost absolute darkness. He's been watching us, and he says there's a huge search effort outside."

"I would certainly hope so. That's encouraging news."

"Yeah, but the rescue effort won't be successful. They'll never find a way to get to us in time."

Harry shouted, "Now just wait a minute! He told you that? He said we're going to die in here?"

"No, he didn't say we're going to die. He didn't say we're going to live either. He said there's another way out, it will be difficult, but we can do it. He's willing to help us, but we must have faith."

"Doesn't sound very helpful to me. It's just a bunch of words. What's he talking about—faith in him? Or God? Or what?"

"For me, what he said was immensely helpful. He gave me hope. It's about faith, Harry. You're a believer, so you understand how easy it is to have faith."

He muttered, "I'm a believer in God, not some mumbo-jumbo 'protector.'"

"He's all we have. I'll tell you the rest of what he explained, and you can decide what you want to do."

When he finished, Harry said, "So this guy knew we were trapped but didn't tell the searchers?"

"Right, and it has nothing to do with us. It's simply that his people have no desire to involve themselves with our twenty-first-century problems."

"Can't say as I blame them. What a different world theirs must be, without politics or wars or mass shootings or inflation. In many ways, it would be a refreshing trade-off for ours."

Brian had learned the Protector was the one who covered the air shaft where Brian saw a ray of sunlight. It was for their safety; the men who brought Denton's body here planned to kill Brian and Harry too. He'd been inside while they were there, and he'd heard everything they said.

The man concluded by saying there was another exit, and if they had faith, they would live. Then he had sent Brian back into the tunnel to bring Harry through.

Harry pointed to the passageway. "You're saying I have to crawl on my belly through there?"

"Faith, Harry. Like I said, it's all we have."

# CHAPTER FIFTY-TWO

Harry dreaded what he had to do. "What if I pass out halfway through? It could happen," he said. Brian came up with a plan; he tied the rope around Harry's torso and kept a hand on it as he wriggled through first. If his friend couldn't make it, or if he passed out, Brian could theoretically pull him the rest of the way.

Harry's faith and Brian's encouragement saved the day. He emerged into the cavern and collapsed on the floor, gasping deep breaths of air. "I hope this guy's telling the truth," he wheezed. "I honestly couldn't go back. I'd have to die here."

When Brian encountered the Protector earlier, he hadn't checked out the small room. Now as he walked its circumference, he found several tunnels leading off in different directions. Some were tiny holes too small for a person, but two would require only a slight bend of the neck to enter. Whether they narrowed along the way remained to be seen.

Despite the Protector's suggestion that faith was all they needed, they'd brought backpacks with food, water, cell phones and light sticks. The makeshift beds they'd left behind, hoping the man didn't plan to keep them waiting day and night. Since they had time, Harry asked if Brian wanted to hear the last part of the treasure story—the part about how the gold they'd found got into the cave of the iron door.

"Let's hear it; I promise I won't fall asleep this time." He laughed. Harry took his printed sheets and began where he'd left off.

*The six outlaws on horseback drew alongside the payroll car, watching the smoke in the distance as the engine chugged away. Inside the car, Bill Anderson looked through the window at a man on horseback brandishing a Colt .45 and waited for instructions.*

*"Everything okay in there?" Jesse James asked the railroad man, who gave a thumbs-up. "Then let's open 'er up."*

*Bill removed the six padlocks that secured the door from the inside as the riders—five men and a woman— dismounted. She rode Western style and wore pants and chaps like the men. When Jesse swung himself up into the car, the Pinkerton's detective glared at him, shaking his head.*

*"Jesse James, you lowlife scum," the lawman said contemptuously. "Why am I not surprised to see you? You and the Younger brothers are too damn lazy to hold a real job, so instead you rob banks and hold up trains."*

*He was surprised to see a female enter the armored boxcar. "You using girls to do your dirty work now, Jesse?"*

*The woman sauntered over to the detective. "I'm no girl. I'm Belle Starr, Mr. Pinkerton's man. Put that name in your thinking cap, 'cause you'll be hearin' it a lot from now on."*

*He replied, "Belle, you're a pretty girl. Why the hell you want to hook up with a bunch of thieves is beyond me. But today you've chosen your path, and you can't turn back ever. You're going to hang. Before you even have a chance to grow up. Think about that every night before you go to sleep, and don't ever let your guard down. I'm coming after you, and when I find you, you'll hang."*

*She laughed and tossed her head as Jesse said, "Let's get the boxes unloaded so they're ready when Cole gets back with the wagons." They formed a line; Bill picked up the boxes one by one, stepped through the gate, and handed each one to Belle, who passed them through the door outside to Jesse, who stacked them on the ground. It*

252

was tiring work unloading fifty thirty-five-pound boxes, and
they had just finished when the other gang members rode
up, along with two wagons, each drawn by a pair of mules.

Cole ordered the muleskinners to pull the wagons
alongside the boxes while Jesse opened the large slatted
doors on the cattle cars, freeing the crowded animals. They
lumbered out, shook and stretched, and meandered off in
search of grass and water.

"I guess it's time to settle up with you and let you
get on your way, Bill," Cole said to the railroad man.

"Yessir. It's been a pleasure doin' business with
you all, it certainly has, Mr. Younger." He watched
expectantly as Younger retrieved a hammer and a cloth
sack from his saddlebag, walked to one of the boxes, and
broke open the wooden top. Bill rubbed his hands when he
saw the coins inside.

Anderson had sold his soul for ten thousand dollars,
and soon he was astride his horse, a burlap sack filled with
gold tied on either side of his saddle and his pack secured
behind him.

"Thanks again for your help," Jesse said. "Any
idea where you're going from here? You know there's a
price on your head now, just like ours."

"There's no tellin' how many of them Pinkerton's
men'll be after me, Mr. James. So I'll keep my eyes wide
open from now on. And yes, I know where I'm a-goin'. I
just ain't too interested in tellin' anyone else, no offense
intended. Good luck to you all." He pulled the reins and
turned his horse to the right, gave him a slight nudge with
his heel, and the horse cantered away.

"Jesse, that was money well spent." Cole took a
plug of tobacco from his pocket and put it in his cheek.
"His information made it all happen. We'd never have
gotten the engineer to stop the train out here in the
boondocks. Stashing our wagons nearby was a brilliant
plan, and you were right. After it happened, the engineer
just kept on going. He can't even telegraph for help, since
there's nothing between here and Denton."

The going was slow as the mule teams pulled the

*wagonloads of heavy boxes westward. When they came to the settlement called Cache, they turned northwest, heading directly into the Wichita Mountains. This area was rough and dangerous—there were countless twists and turns through ravines and gullies bounded by sheer rock faces reaching hundreds of feet into the sky. A man could easily get lost in these hills. It was the hideout's remoteness that made it ideal for the purposes of the James-Younger gang.*

*The muleskinners directed the animals right and left as they wound through the maze of gullies and washes that led them deeper and deeper into hostile, unfriendly terrain. Rattlesnakes, wild animals and hostile Indians were only some of the dangers around them. At last they arrived in a place called Shadow Gulch. "Here's our marker," Jesse said, pointing to a large oak tree with a spike protruding from it.*

*They dismounted; Cole pointed up to a cliff and said to Belle, "See the iron door?" She didn't, and he laughed. "Pretty well hidden, I'd say!" They climbed through the rocks up to a ledge, and she saw the old boxcar door hidden behind bushes. Cole removed some padlocks and slid the door open on its railings.*

*By sundown the gang had placed the boxes far back in a small cave. Everyone was exhausted except Belle, who prepared dinner over a campfire in the larger main cavern. The gang members, done with their grueling task, poured whisky and ate hearty meals, smoking hand-rolled cigarettes afterwards as they sat out on the ledge, watching the glorious starlit sky. Sleep came easily that night to the members of the outlaw gang.*

*When they left the next morning, none would have imagined they'd never see the iron door again. After close brushes with the law, they moved north, robbing banks from Missouri, where the Youngers and the James brothers lived, all the way to Minnesota. Pinkerton's Detective Agency made the capture of the outlaws a top priority but never succeeded in rounding them up.*

*For more than a hundred years, the door guarded its treasure. The sun occasionally gleamed off the surface, and a rider now and then noticed the door high above the canyon floor. When they heard the legend of Spaniards, Indians or maybe outlaws hiding vast treasure behind the door, many returned to search for the door they'd seen. But no one managed to find his way back through the twisting gullies and washes that run like sidewinders through the Wichitas. The iron door kept its secret into the age of iPhones, the internet and instant availability to all the information a person ever wanted to know about train robberies and loot hidden in a cliff. Everything was available online...except how and where to find it.*

"That's it," Harry said. "You stayed awake this time, probably because you'd have to use a rock for a pillow."

"It's a fascinating story, and you make a great narrator. I can see how much this means to you, and no matter what happens, I'm glad to have been part of the discovery. Whether we get out or not, somebody's bound to find all this now."

"Not if I have anything to say about it." They leapt to their feet, looking across the room at a figure standing there. Engrossed in the story, neither had seen or heard an intruder.

"Is this our Protector?" Harry asked, raising his light stick toward the man.

"Quite the opposite," Brian said. "I'll bet a hundred bucks this is Frank Innocente. How'd you get in here?"

What he really wondered was if Frank had encountered the Protector on his way in. There had been no sounds of a scuffle, although the dense tunnels muffled every noise, so they might not have heard.

Frank turned on his headlamp, illuminating the room a little. Waving his gun, he told them to move away from their packs and sit on the floor. Then he said, "I found another entrance, and I can't tell you how pleased I am that things worked out this way. No one knows I'm here, but I have a way out. No one knows exactly where you are, and it may be weeks before they find your bodies, if ever. You've managed to get quite far back into the cave system, and that's helpful to me, since I have to move all that gold to the back entrance."

"What's this all about, Frank?" Brian asked. "I'm sure you're the extortionist who threatened to release the video. You say they're going to find our bodies, and I guess that means you don't intend for us to leave here alive. At least tell us why."

"Instead of sending Meghan to our lunch appointment, you should have come yourself. It would have made all this a lot easier and maybe kept you and President Harrison from ending up here in this cave. There were things I wanted from you, and I had to get them other ways."

"What's your beef with me, Frank? I never met you until today. Is all of this—the extortion, killing Denton and bringing him here—is everything just about getting the gold?"

"No; the gold is just my reward. All of this goes way back, Brian, back to the very beginning of your career. Remember when you were a high-flying stockbroker and got in trouble with the SEC? That's when you met your lawyer, who became your wife, who became the president of the United States. Then you met Darius Nazir and got in bed with his old friend John Spedino, whose connections and money helped you jump-start your new career as an internationally acclaimed dealer in ancient relics and a host of television documentaries. Thanks to John Spedino, you became wealthy and famous."

"So that's what this is about? Johnny Speed, the mob boss who drugged Nicole and videotaped her? That worthless bastard's in Sing Sing for the rest of his life, and he should have been executed, as far as I'm concerned."

Even in the gloom they couldn't miss the change of expression. Frank's face turned red, and his jaw clenched. "It's John Spedino, you asshole, not Johnny Speed."

Brian sneered, "So you're one of Spedino's lackeys? I didn't know he still had loyal goons working for him. Did he set you up in the trucking business? Did he make sure you had plenty of business to get started? From the moment I looked you up on the internet, I wondered how a guy like you could be so successful. Turns out you weren't. You just got in bed with the right people."

Frank shook off his anger and composed himself. "Talk all you want, Brian. You and Harry Harrison are going to die here. I think it's only fair to let you know why. I'm not one of John Spedino's lackeys. I'm his son."

# CHAPTER FIFTY-THREE

"My father was one of the most influential men in New York politics," Frank said. "He never ran for office, never sat at the head table at a fund-raising dinner, never introduced a candidate at a rally and never appeared on a campaign donation report. But behind the scenes, he kept the New York machine running for decades. A person wanting to run for office came to my father, hat in hand, and asked for his blessing. If he or she got it, they were guaranteed to be elected, because primary challengers would be quietly told to back off, and the other party had no foothold in our state.

"He did the same thing in the City. Archie Perrin launched his career as mayor with my family's help. Every step along the way to the presidency was planned and abetted by my father. Every step."

"'Abetted' is an interesting choice of words," Harry commented. "Would your father's help include the fortuitous assassination of the president-elect?"

"Absolutely. My father promised Archie he'd be president, and he delivered on that promise. He's as powerful behind bars as he was on the outside."

Brian stared into the man's face. "I don't see the resemblance. Maybe you take after your mother."

Frank laughed heartily. "That's a fact. Here's another—to keep me and my sister, Claudia, from the negative publicity attached to our family's name, he changed ours to my mother's maiden name. Innocente—innocent in English. It fits, don't you think?" Another boisterous laugh.

Brian goaded him. "What a shame he wasn't proud enough of his name to let you wear it too."

"You asshole! No wonder he wanted you dead! By the way, he said your wife was a great lay. A little passive for his taste, but who'd have known he screwed the girl who would become president!"

"Since your father put drugs in her drink, was he surprised she was passive? What a role model, doping girls to get laid, then telling your kid about it. A real man, that John Spedino. Speaking of that, there is no copy of the video, is there? You only knew about it because your pervert daddy told you."

He grinned. "Big talk for a man who's going to die. You think you can rattle me, but you can't. I'm holding all the cards, Brian. And you're right about the video. I figured that would upset Madam President sufficiently to get page 87, and you both fell for it. By the way, after you're dead, I still plan to ruin her career. I'll threaten to release the video again unless she resigns. And she will, Brian. She'll obey me just like she did my father."

"Like father, like son. What a wonderful man to emulate—a slimy greaseball rapist murderer who's rotting in the penitentiary. Maybe someday you'll have a cell next to his."

"This little chat's getting tiresome," Frank said. "I think it's time for you both to go." He raised the pistol, and Harry drew back, but Brian remained calm. He'd been in tight situations before, and the longer they talked, the greater the chance something might happen to save them.

"Before we go, how about you tell us about Horace Wilmington Fleming. You blackmailed him too."

"How do you know about that?"

"The FBI has audio from your visit to Denton's office. You had a friend Oskar there too, and Fleming told me a man named Oskar threatened to expose his secrets. How did you learn he had secrets?"

"Horace's childhood home in Brooklyn was just down the street from ours. There was no father in the picture—just Horace and his mother. She cleaned house for my parents, and my father pulled strings to get her a job with the federal government. Horace had an interesting childhood, he was a precocious little pedophile, and he ended up in a lot of trouble.

"The mother turned to my father for help, and he made the problem go away. She kept a tight rein on her kid after that, and either he gave up his predilection for little boys or he managed to keep it under control. One thing led to another—she got a better job with the government and moved to DC, and Horace ended up as the keeper of the book."

"Your father always collected on his favors, didn't he?"

Frank nodded. "In that respect, he was no different than any American politician. I'll scratch your back, but someday you're going to repay the favor. Can't blame the man for that."

"Except when it involves blackmail and extortion. Murder too, don't forget. What a legacy dear old dad left you."

"This is for you, Pop!" he screamed as he stood and raised the pistol. Just then a voice from somewhere behind him whispered, "Don't do it!" Frank whirled around, dropped to a crouch, and aimed the gun at a figure standing in the shadows. "Get him!" Brian yelled; he and Harry flew across the chamber towards Frank, but before they reached him, he slumped and fell backward onto the dirt floor.

They knelt beside him. Harry felt for a pulse, but the man was dead. "Look at this," Brian said, pointing to a thin wooden shaft that protruded from Frank's throat. As he reached for it, the Protector stepped into the room.

"Don't touch that!" he cautioned. "The poison on its tip will kill you in seconds."

"Obviously." Brian examined the thin reed. "It's a dart from a blowgun, right? Bet nobody's died that way in a long time."

"My people have killed game and predator animals with this weapon for centuries. It still works today."

"Thank you for saving us, but how did you get behind him? You left before he arrived."

"I was still underground. As I said earlier, there are side tunnels everywhere. When I heard him approach, I stepped into one, watched him pass, and followed him down the corridor. I waited as he talked to you and acted only when his motive became clear. Killing isn't allowed in my culture, but we may act to protect good from evil. Come with me now. I will guide you to the surface."

"We owe you our lives," Brian said. "We'll never be able to thank you enough."

The Protector smiled. "You are fortunate. All I ask is that you let us live in peace."

# CHAPTER FIFTY-FOUR

From the base camp at the bottom of the canyon, Colonel O'Reilly's radio crackled. President Farber was on the line, and his aide-de-camp patched her through.

O'Reilly and Nicole had spoken every few hours since the search began, their last conversation had been only ninety minutes earlier, and he was surprised she called back so quickly. He stepped away from the others to talk.

"Colonel, I have good news." He heard the upbeat tone of her voice as she advised him that Brian and Harry were walking north on the eastern mesa at the top of the canyon about a mile away.

"Great, Madam President! I'll get right on it. But how on earth did you find that out?"

"Because he called me, Colonel. Now go get my husband!"

Ten minutes later, a Jeep pulled alongside the two men walking down a dusty trail. "May I offer you gentlemen a ride?" the corporal said with a salute. He drove them back to where it all began—the parking lot where they'd picked up their horses to go into the Wichita Mountains. At the far end of the lot, Colonel O'Reilly and the director of the Secret Service waited to greet them. A Black Hawk helicopter stood nearby.

Wearing a broad grin, O'Reilly saluted. "President Harrison, Mr. Sadler, welcome back! A hundred men were looking for you, and here you came, just walking along the rim of the canyon like you were out for a stroll. How'd you manage that?"

"No comment at this time," the Secret Service director snapped. "Debrief first, talk later. Let's get them back to the base." Suddenly aware of his gaffe, he turned to Brian and Harry. "Apologies, gentlemen. I didn't mean to order you around. If you wish to make a statement now, that's your prerogative. I'm just saying it would be protocol for us to interview you before you speak publicly about what happened."

Harry laughed. "Since I'm the one who appointed you director, and you swore to obey the rules, then by all means, let's follow protocol. Colonel, when we get to base, do you think you can rustle up a couple of burgers and fries? And a six-pack of cool ones? Those protein bars just didn't do the trick for me, and right now the biggest item of protocol is for the detainees to get food and hydration!"

As they climbed into the chopper, Brian asked why they were flying instead of driving, as they'd done every other time. O'Reilly said dozens of reporters were encamped just outside the entrance to Fort Sill. This way they'd avoid the hassle. There would be plenty of time for talking to the press later.

Everyone gathered in the conference room. Around the table sat Colonel O'Reilly, the directors of the FBI and Secret Service, and the head of the OSBI. Recording equipment was ready to roll, and there was a low buzz as people talked among themselves while Harry and Brian gobbled down the burgers, fries and a couple of Coors.

"Since President Farber told us where to find you, I presume you've both spoken to your wives," the director said. "Do you want to make a Zoom call before we begin the debriefing process?" Both declined, saying they would call afterwards.

"We're ready," they announced, and the director asked for mike and camera checks. "There's no need for each of us to tell our version of what happened," Harry said. "We rarely separated, so our stories won't vary much. One of us can talk and the other fill in where necessary." The man agreed, and Harry deferred to Brian; since he narrated adventure tales for a living, he was a natural to tell their story.

After debating revealing the existence of the Book of Secrets, they decided it must be done. The oath had been violated so many times already that one more couldn't hurt. They wouldn't have found the treasure if they hadn't had the clues, and the story wouldn't be complete without including Roosevelt's cryptic poem. They left nothing out about their time underground, and the only loose end seemed to be the whereabouts of Frank Innocente's man Oskar.

After forty-five minutes of discussion and a Q&A involving all the agency heads, the recording stopped, and the base commander made an interesting statement. "You all must realize we can never let this story become public."

The Secret Service director looked up from his notes. "What are you talking about?" The others wondered too—even Brian and Harry weren't sure where he was coming from.

"Think about it. Famous adventurer Brian Sadler finds boxes of stolen gold in a legendary cave—a fortune in treasure. Two bodies are still in there, and a mysterious Native American who calls himself the Protector roams the area. Think of the sensation this story is going to create. A former president and the husband of the current one follow the clues in a poem created by Teddy Roosevelt that he added to the President's Book of Secrets, which most people, including me, didn't believe existed.

"Everything in this story happens in the middle of a federally protected wildlife refuge. Right now the park rangers control entry by requiring permits for hikers and overnight campers. They limit the number of people so they can protect the environment and reduce the fire risk. But once you tell everybody what Mr. Sadler and President Harrison saw, it'll become a madhouse. With only a few rangers to patrol thousands of acres, it'll be impossible to stop people coming in from every direction on foot or horseback or ATV. There aren't enough resources to control amateur treasure hunters doing God knows what to find the gold. We can't allow that to happen."

"How do we stop it?" the Oklahoma State Bureau head asked.

"By swearing everyone to secrecy and ensuring the recording never goes public."

The FBI chief said, "I understand the reasoning completely, but what's done is done. We've all heard the story. So let's see a show of hands. Who agrees with what Colonel O'Reilly is suggesting?" Every hand went up. "Okay, then whose approval do we need to keep it under wraps?"

Brian came up with the answer before anyone else. With a smile he said, "I'm pretty close friends with the president. How about I run it by her? If she issues the gag order, would that suffice?"

A few minutes later the room emptied, and a technician set up a secure laptop for Brian's Zoom call to his wife in the White House. But instead of Nicole, her assistant, Fiona, appeared on the screen, telling him the president was aboard *Air Force One* en route to Fort Sill, with an ETA of thirty-seven minutes. Jennifer Harrison was on the way too, in a military helicopter that would land in less than ten minutes.

Shortly the two adventurers were reunited with their wives. Jennifer updated Harry on his mother's condition, which hadn't changed during the three days they were in the cave. Julia was understandably anxious, and Harry placed a Zoom call so they could all wish her well. He promised to tell her what he could the next time he saw her.

Nicole had brushed away a tear when she entered the room, and she admonished Brian for once more putting her through hell while he was off on an adventure. Watching her hands shake as she took a sip of water, he remembered what stress she'd been under.

"Do you want to talk privately?" he whispered while Harry was on the call, and she said it was fine to talk here.

"We've never gotten the copy of the video. The extortionist still has it, and I wonder when the next shoe will drop. I think I should resign."

"Not a chance." He said everything would come out when they watched the video of the interrogation Brian and Harry had finished earlier. "I should have told you this earlier, but here's a preview to ease your mind. Frank Innocente's the extortionist, and he's also dead. He learned about the video from his father, who happens to be John Spedino. And there's no copy. It was all a lie to get you to give him the page from the book. All's well."

After the viewing, Jennifer and Nicole asked questions of their own, and Brian laid out the base commander's theory that revealing this story would be a disaster for the federal wildlife refuge. Nicole asked more questions and finally agreed, saying, "I don't know how this sort of thing gets done, but I'll make sure it happens."

And with that proclamation, the saga of Brian Sadler and Harry Harrison became one more secret in the legend surrounding the cave of the iron door. The people present during the interrogation were sworn to secrecy, the audio and video recordings were turned over to President Farber, and the matter was closed. As much as reporters and the public demanded more information, all they'd get was a concocted story about two men getting lost in the wilderness, trapped in a cave during an earthquake, and making a miraculous escape. "It was all about faith," both would say time and again. "We just had to have faith."

# CHAPTER FIFTY-FIVE

*Seventy Days Later*

Flanked by Secret Service agents, Nicole and Brian walked up the front steps of the same church where they had mourned the fictional loss of Harry, Jennifer and their girls a few years earlier. That time the president had participated in an elaborate trap to catch a corrupt politician, and even Harry's parents were led to believe they all perished. On this bright morning in Nichols Hills, Oklahoma, the mourning was real. Julia Harrison, mother of a former president and matriarch of the family, was dead.

Nicole's bodyguards joined others along the walls who were there to guard Harry and the several cabinet members present. Brian and Nicole slipped into a pew just behind Harry, his family and his father, Henry. The church was filled with friends from across the country, and the brief service highlighted her life of behind-the-scenes service as wife of a United States senator. There were funny remembrances, poignant eulogies, and a brief, stirring message by the man who'd been Julia's pastor for fifty years. Her faith and courage were the family's strength after her diagnosis, the pastor said, and she would be remembered as a pillar of fortitude in the face of personal crisis.

After the service, Nicole and Brian were whisked back into the presidential limousine for the short trip to Wiley Post Airport. Although they wanted to join the family at Henry's home, the presidential security requirements would have created an issue for the many friends who stopped by to visit. Instead, they flew to the ranch and waited for Harry, Jennifer and the kids to join them in a few hours.

They fixed drinks, and out of curiosity, Brian placed a call to Innocente Freight Lines in Dallas. Since everything about their adventure remained secret, the public believed that Frank and Denton Kopaddy were missing persons. He wondered what the company's position would be. He asked for Frank by name and was switched to Shelly Villanova, who had been Frank's assistant. He recognized the name from her attempts to set up a lunch between her boss and Brian. He introduced himself and asked if anyone had heard from Frank.

"No, Mr. Sadler, and they say that every passing day makes it less likely they'll find him."

"What do you think happened?"

She hesitated a second. "This is only my opinion. The trucking business has some rough players. Some people have gotten hurt by doing business with the wrong people, if you know what I mean."

"You're not saying the Mafia's involved, are you?"

She backpedaled instantly. "Oh gosh, no! I didn't mean that at all. It's just a bunch of rough guys for the most part. There are fights sometimes—stuff like that."

"Who's running the place in Frank's absence?"

"The directors brought in a man from New York named John Rizzo. He's acting president of the company."

"Is there a man named Oskar with a 'k' working there?"

"Oskar Corso. He's in charge of dock operations. Do you want to talk to him?"

No, Brian said. He'd learned Oskar's whereabouts and hoped he'd hear nothing more now that Frank was gone. They talked a moment longer, and when the call ended, Brian googled the name John Rizzo. A onetime union organizer in the trucking industry, the FBI called him a capo, or trusted ally, in the Gambino crime family.

Brian read a final sentence aloud to Nicole. "He began his criminal career as a lieutenant in the Spedino family, whose boss John Spedino is serving a life sentence in Sing Sing prison."

"Well, well. They kept Innocente Freight Lines in

the family," Nicole said. "No surprise there."

The Harrison family arrived around six, and they reminisced over cocktails and dinner, then well into the evening. Since Brian and Harry had been college roommates, he'd known Julia for over twenty years. Stories were swapped, memories shared, and the discussion eventually turned to the future.

Harry reminded Brian that their adventure in the Wichita Mountains began with Brian's asking what Harry was going to do when he grew up. "If I'd been smart," he said, "I'd have gotten as far away from you as possible. Instead I let you get us lost in a cave."

"My, how quickly we forget the facts. I think you've been a politician so long that lying's in your blood. That was *your* adventure; I just came along for the ride."

Harry laughed. "I think that's stretching the truth a bit as well. However it happened, I think it was enough for me. You'll never get me into a cave again. The panic of claustrophobia almost suffocated me more than once."

Nicole asked, "So what's next?" Jennifer said she couldn't wait to hear the response, since she was wondering herself.

"I'm going to write that book I mentioned before. It'll be about trains, train robbers and outlaw gold in Oklahoma and Indian territories. There are plenty of stories like the one about the iron door, and I'm thinking about a compilation of all the legends and folklore. My main goal is keeping an eye on Dad in Oklahoma City, and I can write from here at the ranch. It'll be good for us to have a peaceful family life for once."

"How about you, Nicole?" Jennifer asked. "You've got a few years left in your term. Are you going to be our president all the way through?" This time it was Brian's turn to laugh and say he wondered the same thing.

"A year ago if you'd told me where I'd be today, I would have called you insane. One thing's certain—Archie isn't coming back, and I'm no longer the acting president. I haven't been on the job long, but parts of it grow on you. You understand, right, Harry?"

"I do. The perks are great, but so is the burden of being the nation's leader. You're still in the honeymoon stage. Pretty soon the other side will blame you for anything that goes wrong, the mainstream media will pick apart every word you utter, and a person or two you rely upon most may be revealed as traitors determined to undermine your success. That last part never happened to me, but I've seen it over and over. Oh, and there's the loneliness. I know Brian's not going to be a stay-at-home first gentleman, and there will be times—lots of them—when you feel absolutely alone."

Nicole smiled. "Well, after that encouraging picture of the next three years, I can hardly wait. To tell the truth, I don't know what's next for me. I'm only the second nonpolitician ever to occupy the Oval Office, and I think I'm a good deal more stable than the first one. I'm young, and my mind's sharp, and right now I'm enjoying the challenges that pop up every few hours of the day. When the newness wears off, and when the politicians and pundits start attacking, maybe I'll leave. I'd need to have a vice president by then. We don't want Madam Speaker running our country." She looked at Jennifer and said, "It's your turn. What's next for you?"

"I've been the stay-at-home wife because that's what I wanted. I'm raising two wonderful girls, I've been privileged to spend quality time with my parents and Harry's, and I did the Washington thing for years. Dinner after dinner after speech after speech. Blah, blah, blah until all I wanted was to be back at home, wherever home was. My new career will be in philanthropy. Along with his dad, Harry and I are putting a few million into a nonprofit that will provide educations for underprivileged children. We'll hire a professional to work in Oklahoma City, and I'll go in whenever I need to."

"Sounds like an excellent plan," Brian said. "Everybody's established their short-term goals."

"And you, my dear husband? When will you ever settle down and quit getting into scrapes? Talk about someone who needs to grow up!"

"Hey, hey, lighten up. Just because you're the president doesn't mean you can boss me around. Haven't you learned anything about diplomacy? Since you asked, here's my plan. I have four galleries, each with an excellent manager and staff and ever-increasing profits. Dallas, New Orleans, London, Jerusalem—just overseeing those will keep me occupied. I also have the documentaries, and sadly, there won't be one about the iron door, but *c'est la vie*. The man who saved us—the Protector—asked only one thing in return—that we let his people live in peace. If I told the story, that wouldn't have happened, so it's for the best.

"Maybe now and then if my famous wife loosens the leash a tiny bit, I can sneak off and do something more interesting than simply being a pretty face at state dinners." That brought a laugh from everyone and a finger-wagging from Nicole, who warned him not to irritate her or he might end up getting a comprehensive IRS audit.

Around eleven, Brian's phone dinged with a news alert. He read it aloud. "Massive 7.5 magnitude earthquake rattles remote Wichita Mountains in southwestern Oklahoma." Harry turned on CNN as the story was unfolding.

The newscaster said the massive tremor in the Wichita Mountains wouldn't have made the national news except it happened in a canyon called Shadow Gulch, the place where former president Harrison and President Nicole Farber's husband, Brian Sadler, had disappeared days earlier. The pair had returned unharmed after being lost for several days in a cave system.

This tremor, a massive aftershock from the earlier quake, caused no deaths or injuries. If it had occurred while President Harrison and Mr. Sadler were missing, the death toll could have been tragic, as more than a hundred Army troops and lawmen had worked from a base camp in Shadow Gulch, climbing the cliffs to search for the missing men. The camp had been at the epicenter of the earthquake, but now both it and the searchers were gone.

The news reporter continued, "So far, authorities

have not released any information about Sadler's and the former president's whereabouts during the three days searchers combed the area for them, and any hope of getting further clues ended with the second tremor, when a massive rockslide dramatically altered the cliff faces. On a side note, a railroad boxcar door from the nineteenth century was found in the rocky debris on the canyon floor. Local treasure enthusiasts claim it is a legendary iron door that once hid a vast treasure. One man told reporters now that the door no longer marks a cave entrance, the cache of Spanish gold, outlaw booty, or whatever, would never be found."

"Now they won't find the bodies inside either," Harry said to Brian after the newscast ended. The next morning they learned from Colonel O'Reilly at Fort Sill that the hole in the grove of trees through which they escaped—the back entrance to the caverns—was gone as well, having disappeared as the ground shifted during the earthquake. Both it and the cave of the iron door were erased, leaving Denton Kopaddy, Frank Innocente and millions in stolen loot entombed forever.

*Thank you!*

Thanks for reading *The Iron Door*. If you enjoyed it, I'd appreciate a review on Amazon or Goodreads.

Reviews are what allow other readers to find books they enjoy, so thanks in advance for your help.

Please join me on:
**Facebook**
http://on.fb.me/187NRRP
**Twitter**
@BThompsonBooks

## MAY WE OFFER YOU A FREE BOOK?

**Bill Thompson's award-winning first novel,
*The Bethlehem Scroll*, can be yours free.
Just go to billthompsonbooks.com
and click "Subscribe."**

**Once you're on the list, you'll receive advance
notice of future book releases and other
information.**

Made in the USA
Columbia, SC
20 November 2023

26844730R00154